AN INAUSPICIOUS BEGINNING

Charity had long dreamed of finding herself alone with the man of her dreams, the Marquess of Kenrick. Now she was alone with him, in the greenhouse of his country estate.

The setting was perfect for romance. Unfortunately, Kenrick was unconscious. Charity had smashed a flowerpot over his handsome head. She could only hope that he was still alive.

"My lord—Lord Kenrick," she said, since she did not even know his given name, for it was never used at the great house. "My lord, please wake up! Please."

Clearly Charity had gotten off on the wrong foot with the marquess—and heaven only knew how she could make it right. . . .

EMILY HENDRICKSON lives in Lake Tahoe, Nevada, with her retired airline pilot husband. Of all the many places she has traveled around the world, England is her favorite and a natural choice for a setting for her novels. Although writing claims most of her time, she enjoys gardening, watercolors, and sewing for her granddaughters, as well as the occasional trip with her husband.

A Country Miss

Emily Hendrickson

A SIGNET BOOK

NEW AMERICAN LIBRARY

SIGNET, SIGNET CLASSIC, MENTOR, ONYX, PLUME,
MERIDIAN and NAL BOOKS are published by
NAL PENGUIN INC., 1633 Broadway,
New York, New York 10019

First Printing, November, 1988

1 2 3 4 5 6 7 8 9

PRINTED IN THE UNITED STATES OF AMERICA

1

A PALE-GRAY PIGEON fluttered from the peak of the hothouse, parting the delicately swirling mist in its agitation. It dropped on the ground with a ruffled flourish, strutting past a lop-eared rabbit who looked rather woebegone in the crystalline dampness. The rabbit twitched its nose and waited patiently by the wooden door of the hothouse.

The door opened and the rabbit left the mizzle for the fragrant warmth of the hothouse. Light filtered down through the whitewashed panes, bestowing a strange delicate green cast to the two people beneath the rows of exquisite orchids. The rabbit hopped across the worn slats of water-stained wood and settled at the feet of his mistress. Safely hidden beneath the old wooden potting bench, it seemed to listen, one ear carefully alert while the other hung crazily over its left eye.

Charity was grateful for the diversion. Roscoe was always to be depended upon when needed. While it might be unusual to have a pet rabbit, there was little conformity in Charity Lonsbury.

Although the eerie glow from the windows did not enhance her chestnut curls or her peach-tinted skin, it gave her stead gray eyes intriguing depths, hinted of secrets concealed beneath the demure exterior. Her slender figure was well-balanced, though her gardening apron hid the sweet curve of her bosom from the approaching squire's gaze. Her chin tilted defiantly as she considered the words most likely to reach her ears.

She stiffened at the familiar and very irritating sound of Squire Hamilton Bigglesby clearing his throat. It was a raspy staccato, guaranteed to vex ears less sensitive than hers. She cautioned herself not to allow her mind to wander during his effusive prose. If she murmured agreement at the wrong moment, she would find herself betrothed to the wretched man. The mere thought of his cold, pudgy hands on her body was enough to make her toss her tea.

She thumped a small clay pot on the bench and began to fill it with her special blend of moss and shredded bark. This was for potting the last of four sections of a sympodial orchid that she had divided earlier. If she must hear the squire out, she could at least get something accomplished. He was too persistent to leave her in peace. As she gently transferred the plant, she nodded her head. "Proceed, Squire." What else could she say? He would speak regardless. His prose would spout like water from an ice-cold spring, sharp and unrelenting.

Squire Bigglesby was disconcerted by his intended's lack of maidenly flutterings or suitably receptive posture. However, he wouldn't allow this to deter him from making her his bride. After they were wed he would end this nonsense of orchids and rabbits.

"Ought to take that demmed rabbit and make a fine stew out of him instead of cosseting him like this," he muttered. Then, realizing these intentions were better silenced for the moment, he again cleared his throat, seemingly unaware of the resistance in the rigid figure near him. "My dear Miss Lonsbury . . ." He paused and drew nearer, taking care to keep a distance from the dirt-stained bench. "Charity, dear lady, for we are surely past all such formalities, are we not? You must know I am the most patient of men. 'Tis clear I hold you in the highest esteem." He cleared his throat once again, unmindful of her wince, and continued. "I would that you allow me to announce the date of our marriage. Surely you will accept my offer. You will find none better . . . or higher." His eyes narrowed, nearly disappearing into the folds of fat that rounded his face. The chit would accept him this time, he was certain. There was little income to sustain her, and she must long for the pretties his purse could buy.

"I can afford to keep you in a handsome manner," he reminded her in an unctuous voice. It put Charity in mind of the grease that dripped from a roasting pig: thick, oily and slightly malodorous when left to stand.

Charity squared her shoulders and inhaled a precious breath of free air. If she agreed to marry the squire, it would be the last she took. "Sir, you do me great honor, I'm sure. I cannot agree to wed you, however."

He bristled with indignation. "You are over the year of mourning for your father. There is naught to stand in our way. You are twenty, are you not?"

"That is true, sir." She raised her eyes to look at the figure awaiting her answer with such overweening confidence. Such a figure he thought he cut. His cravat was an economy of linen and the bottle-green coat hung neatly over his wide shoulders. If his primrose pantaloons strained against the bulk of his thighs and his puce waistcoat threatened to burst its buttons, it was a compliment to his cook, her roast beef and trifle. The coarse redness of his nose attested to his fondness for port, and his rough skin reflected his love for a bruising ride to the hounds, none of which was reprehensible . . . to most. Charity reflected that if his face was a road map of his life's journey, the trip had indeed been a rough one.

For a moment Charity's thoughts skimmed to another man, one tall and slim, dark-haired, with eyes of the most intense blue she'd ever seen. She had often watched as he called on her father, the late reverend. She would linger near the top of the stairs or hover in the garden to catch a glimpse of him, then listen for the deep richness of his voice. A sigh escaped from her lips as she contemplated the impossible, her *preux chevalier*, the knight in shining armor who would never come to her rescue. The Marquess of Kenrick was far beyond her in every way, and she was well aware of the complete futility of her dreams. She was destined to love him without any hope, for she had no dowry, no chance to meet him face to face. Still, that did not make acceptance of the tedious Squire Bigglesby inevitable.

She would fight against that horror in every way she could.

"Nevertheless, I must decline your most gracious offer." That ought to mollify the pompous prig, she decided. His conceit was just short of second to none.

He drew up in offended dignity and deepening anger. "I have been patient beyond all reckoning. I have made my decision! I think your father would be most gratified to know his daughter is married to a man of my stature. We *will* marry, my dear. If you do not choose the date, I will set it for us." His eyes gleamed with the knowledge Charity would be forced to agree with his logic.

"That cannot be. You cannot force me against my will, and I will not marry you. There is no one to ask for my hand, for there is no one I am answerable to in this world. My word and mine alone is what counts here. And I say no." The time for ladylike politeness fled. She must stand her ground against this man. Marriage to him was unthinkable! It was a blessing he was not privy to Mrs. Woods' repeated urgings to seek help from the Earl of Nevile, Charity's uncle. Charity had no doubt the squire would attempt to seek a means of demanding that gentelman compel Charity to accept the squire as a worthy husband.

Bigglesby paced the narrow wooden slats of the hothouse floor in pensive, ponderous steps. One plump hand stroked his chin while he mulled over the problem he faced. He no doubt deemed her a recalcitrant miss. Her refusal angered him greatly, she could see that. Then he stopped short, as if an idea had struck him all a heap.

Charity stared at the figure who stood so completely out of place among the orchids. Delicate blooms of lavender and green, pink and white, cascaded over narrow ribbons of leaves all about him, their beauty totally ignored. She doubted very much that his nose was sensitive enough to catch their elusive scent.

The clearing of his throat drew the expected wince as well as a tremor of fear. There really was no reason for the latter, as the squire had always deported himself in a seemly fashion. Yet he was known to get his way in all things, and she was sadly lacking in support to withstand any threat. Alone at the cottage with only Mrs. Woods, the former housekeeper at the rectory, she had little protection. Josiah Bent would defend her, but what could an old man like him do, other than wield his gardening hoe? She met the pale-blue eyes, now beaming with satisfaction, with rising trepidation.

"I am going up to the great house to pay my respects to Lord Kenrick. You knew he had arrived? Perhaps I will mention the use of the hothouse to him. Yes." The squire looked about with a smug air of victory. "I'm certain he would wish to be appraised of the way you use, or should I say abuse, his gracious generosity to your esteemed father, our late Reverend Lonsbury. Your cottage is part of his lordship's domain as well, isn't it? You rent from him? Quite dependent upon his generosity, I daresay. I wonder how he will view all you have done, Miss Lonsbury." With a jab at her composure more perceptive than he realized, he added, "I sense more goes on here than he knows." He made a futile attempt to draw in his girth before making a sketchy bow to a worried Charity. Turning to exit the hothouse, he stumbled over the soft furry body in his path. Though Charity couldn't understand his muttered words, she guessed their meaning from his angry tone.

She scooped up Roscoe and scolded him with a hint of frantic laughter in her voice. Burying her face against his plushlike fur, she gently berated him. "Oh, that was naughty, dear Roscoe. He'll hate you even more, and the danger of your ending up in his stew pot will be all the greater."

Roscoe wrinkled his nose and settled in her arms.

Charity leaned agaisnt the potting bench, ignoring the possibility of dirt smudges on her soft gray cambric work gown or the wrinkled apron Mrs. Woods insisted she wear. Brows furrowed in anxious apprehension, she considered the problem.

Would the squire actually inform on her? What would he say? That she was growing the orchids in the hothouse? The same as her father had done? The squire couldn't possibly know Charity was actually selling the plants. At times she sold the blooms as well for special occasions, during those seasons when the market supply was short. It wasn't seemly for her to be in trade! Selling plants? And flowers! It was a good thing he knew nothing of her impulsive entry in the Horticultural Society contest to find an orchid worthy of presentation to the Prince Regent!

Charity shrugged and wondered how she was to cope without her earnings from the orchids. She had no desire to yield to the blandishments of the tediously worthy squire. The sum left to her after her father's death was sufficient to rent the cottage from Lord Kenrick's estate manager, and provide a scant amount for food and other essentials. Only the careful management of Mrs. Woods kept them from deep straits. She refused to join her sister Hope and her young captain in America, nor would she intrude on her sister Faith and her vicar on that chilly island off Scotland's west coast. Her father's sister, Lady Tavington, was somewhere off in Asia. A letter might reach her if one knew where to write, which Charity did not. Truth was, Charity stubbornly clung to her independence and her beloved orchids. She would not leave them nor part with her freedom willingly.

Over the past months since her father's death Mrs. Woods had pleaded with Charity to abandon her obstinate refusal to contact the Earl of Nevile, elder brother of her father. "Ye can't eat your pride, miss," Mary Woods would storm. "It won't put meat on your bones."

Charity's heated reply gave Mrs. Woods no ease. "Do they even know we exist? Or care that my dear papa died? Nary a word have I heard this past year or more, other than that stiff letter of condolence. I won't cast myself at their feet for a scrap of pity. Food, neither. We'll make out with the chickens and the rabbits."

Mrs. Woods would sniff, then mutter. "Never heard the like of it. Raising rabbits when the world knows you let them run free. And what would his lordship say to ye capturing a few of his rabbits to breed for food? Borders on poaching, that's what!"

Charity shrugged. "He never comes here anymore. His mother does on rare occasions, and she would not bother with our cottage. What they don't know cannot hurt them or us."

"Oh? And what about the orchids, miss? What's to become of ye if his lordship discovers ye have been using his hothouse to raise orchids to sell? Answer that, if ye can!"

"I have presumed on my father's arrangements." It was a good things Mrs. Woods didn't know Charity used his lordship's initials when she wrote to the gentlemen orchid fanciers her father had corresponded with these past years. She reasoned that since she was using the Kenrick hothouses for her operation, what better thing than to adopt his initials? It was undoubtedly the closest she would get to his cherished presence. She had achieved a modest success with her work, and she wasn't about to allow the squire to bring ruin down upon her head.

Then the full meaning of his words penetrated. His lordship, the Marquess of Kenrick, was here! At Greenoaks! Her heart began a fluttery beat beneath the firm rounded bosom. Her *preux chevalier*! Rather than save her he was likely to toss her out on her ear if he came down here and discovered what she was about. She sent a fervent prayer soaring heavenward that his lordship would be otherwise occupied for the duration of his stay. There was no reason why he should inspect the hothouses. It wasn't customary. She made no demands that would reach the ears of his bailiff, and she tried not to interfere with the duties of the head gardener, Josiah Bent. She helped him as often as he helped her, in fact of the matter.

"There is no manner in which Lord Kenrick can discover I've used his initials, Roscoe," she assured the pink inner ear of the rabbit. The dark eyes blinked with a knowing glint, as though reminding her there were other things his lordship might find objectionable.

"Though, if I am discovered, it will be my undoing. I'll be disgraced, my reputation in tatters. I must not allow that to happen, Roscoe." All of a sudden it became vital to save her good name. But what could she do about it? If Lord Kenrick chose to visit his own hothouse, there was naught she could do to prevent it.

Absently she stroked the silken fur, deep in convoluted plans. She would bar the door. No, that would make it difficult to work. She could post Roscoe by the door to warn her, but all he could do was sniff. "Why don't you meow, Roscoe? Then you could help. Though you did try with the squire, didn't you? I don't think you ought to trip Lord Kenrick though, Roscoe. He might get hurt."

The very idea of the elegant lord tumbling amid the dirty environs of the hothouse set her to sweeping up the wooden strips that composed the floor. Usually she was too occupied to tidy the place, only forcing herself once a week to clean and straighten the interior of the hothouse. The possibility he might see it as it was now was unthinkable. Roscoe observed her unusual activity with placid eyes from his perch atop the potting bench.

Charity scurried out for a pail of water and the stump of a mop she used to finish her cleanup. It was a comedown for the cherished daughter of the Reverend Lonsbury to be on her own and working in the dirt, she supposed. But she loved her freedom, and the dirt didn't bother her in the least . . . usually.

"Ye will never get those hands soft and lovely if ye persist in keeping them in the dirt, Miss Charity," Mrs. Woods would moan at the sight of Charity scrubbing her hands at the end of the day.

"It's more to the point that we eat, Mrs. Woods. I refuse to starve with satin hands in my lap." Charity's voice was gentle, but there was no doubting her firm resolve.

She rose early each morning to put in an hour on their neat little kitchen garden. She adored her flowers, the orchids in particular, but you couldn't eat them. Fortunately her gift with plants extended to vegetables. It gave her great pleasure to see the abundance she produced from their tiny plot of ground.

Mrs. Woods had a way with a pot and the hearth that the squire would fancy, had he occasion to sample her cooking. What she did with herbs and fresh vegetables in a good rabbits stew made one long for supper. Being of practical mind, it didn't bother Charity to serve up the small gray rabbits from the little hutch where she raised them. They were a world apart from dear Roscoe.

Charity put away the mop and surveyed the greenhouse, wondering how she was to manage to avoid the one man in the world she longed to see. "He won't be coming here, silly. We have nothing to fear." Somehow her words rang hollowly in her ears. Roscoe wasn't reassuring either.

By now the squire was likely on his way back here. His threat hovered in her mind. He insisted she was to give him an answer, the answer he desired and none other. She couldn't. She would run away before doing that. She'd even go to the despised Earl of Nevile before she would marry the squire.

She knew better than to hide. The squire would seek her out wherever she might be, and she didn't especially relish Mrs. Woods being privy to either the proposal or the threats that might issue from the squire. It would put her in a rare taking, and Charity had enough to cope with at the moment. She fingered an empty clay pot of moderate size, moving to stack it with the others. What could be her defense for not formally requesting permission from his lordship to remain on the premises, caring for the orchids? She received no payments from him for her work, for the orchids were her own. The permission her father had obtained from Lord Kenrick did not extend to her, however. She was, in fact, trespassing. Even though she rented the cottage, it did not give her leave to make free with the hothouses. What was she to do?

Her fingers rubbed the smooth, hard surface of the pot as she mulled over her predicament. She held the pot in her hand, hefting it as her thoughts chased one another in furious circles. How she would love to toss this pot at the head of the idiotic squire, if only to discover whether there be anything within! He was pompous, true, but today she perceived a thing she had heretofore not seen: he could be dangerous when thwarted.

He had threatened her! He intended to inform the marquess of her activities. And he didn't know the half of what went on here.

Perhaps the marquess would simply ignore the ramblings of the squire. When that stout gentleman talked with his betters, he waxed even more prosy than usual. The poor marquess was to be pitied, to be forced to bend his ear to the squire. No doubt his bailiff would be instructed to see to the matter, and Charity felt certain she could handle that particular man.

Her newly discovered confidence sagged as she heard steps on the slate outside the hothouse. Behind her the door creaked open, wheezing with age.

Charity's eyes remained fastened on the clay pot she held firmly in her trembling hand. What would the squire report of his visit with his lordship? She could envision the conversation that must have occurred in the cream-and-gold room she once glimpsed while on an errand to the great house for her father. Or would they have met in the bookroom, where the housekeeper said his lordship went over the accounts with his bailiff on the rare occasions he visited Greenoaks? Wherever it took place, she longed yet feared to know the words exchanged.

Anger boiled within her slender form. It was the outside of enough that she must contend with the squire's unwanted, persistent attentions. A red haze of fury suddenly blinded her, fogging her thinking process. If she displayed a temper, it might give the squire a strong distaste of her. All to the better!

A tall, lean gentleman halted inside the ancient wood door that had allowed entry to the hothouse since his great-grandfather's day. So the squire spoke the truth. The young woman he mentioned in his vague ramblings was indeed here in the midst of the orchids. Orchids not mentioned in any report!

The marquess was curious and thought to select a bloom for the lady he had decided would make an excellent choice for the next marchioness, Lady Sylvia Wilde. When she arrived, the most perfect of flowers could be delivered to her room and, it was hoped, would make a suitable impression on that most lovely of creatures. The pristine beauty of an orchid would match the cool elegance of that worthy lady. How pleased his mother would be that at long last he was going to marry, set up a nursery as he had promised her.

The clouds that had glowered all day parted to allow a shaft of sunlight to pierce the panes of glass. It came to rest on the bent head, illuminating the chestnut curls so they seemed threaded with fire. He couldn't refrain from an intake of breath at the charming sight.

Charity, hearing the slight sound behind her, could wait no longer. Nerves strung as taut as the line from a fishing pole that had hooked its prey, she reacted with uncommon violence. Her simmering anger bursting forth, she raised the clay pot in her hand and whirled to let it fly across the hothouse toward its victim.

As it sailed through the humid, fragrant air, she saw that it was not the stolid figure of the squire who would receive the blow, but the figure of her *preux chevalier*, the marquess. She screamed a warning too late.

She watched in horror as the pot sailed through the air in seeming snaillike pace and hit its target with deadly accuracy. The astounded figure of the marquess crumpled to the slatted wood floor amid the pots of young orchids and ferns.

Roscoe peered over the edge of the potting bench to

observe this most unusual occurrence as Charity rushed to the side of the fallen man, moaning as she ran.

"Dear, merciful heavens, what have I done? Speak to me, my lord. Please, speak to me. Say something! Anything! Toss me out on my ear if you must, but speak." She knelt to examine his wound. Blood was oozing from his temple just below his hairline where the thick, dark hair was wont to flop over his noble brow. The blue eyes were closed and Charity felt as though her heart would pound itself right from her bosom, so hard did it beat.

The bleeding was increasing. Charity pulled her skirt up and ripped a strip from her petticoat, checking to make certain it was not soiled before she folded the worn linen into a pad to press against the wound.

He was so still. If only he would move, even a finger. "Roscoe, what am I to do?" She heard a sound outside and called. "Josiah! Josiah! Come!"

The shock on the old gardener's face might have been comical at any other moment. Charity didn't notice. "Get someone to help. His lordship, er, had an accident. Quickly, please!"

The door wheezed partly shut and she wasn't aware it remained that way so engrossed she was with her victim. The implications of her act were swept to another part of her brain to be dealt with later. For now all she could do was try to revive the poor man.

"Your lordship, Lord Kenrick." She didn't know his given name; it was never used by anyone at the great house. "My lord, please wake up! Please!"

An anxious tear slid down one pale cheek, followed by another. Her arms crept about him, fearing the damp might penetrate his fine jacket. Anyone knew the damp was bad for one. His face was ashen, his lips nearly devoid of any color.

Her eyes remained on his lips, willing them to open, murmur a word. Even if he heaped scorn on her poor head, it would be welcome. A guilty flush stained her cheeks as she thought of what she had done, her deception. Now he had double reason to desire her gone.

No! She couldn't bear to leave here. She stared at his mouth. It was so close to her. She could see every vein, the smooth texture of his skin, the faint shadow of his beard. Timidly she raised one trembling finger to touch the rasp of it, then smoothed her finger across his brow.

Never had she expected to be so close to him in all her life. It certainly would not happen again. Her heart urged her to dare. Could she? Who would ever know?

Slowly, making sure the pad was firmly in place on his brow, she bent and placed her lips against his. A sweetness flowed through her she had never known before. If this was half of what a kiss might be, she was glad she had waited. It stirred a strange emotion deep witin her, somewhere below her heart. She had not known that sort of thing before either and found it strangely exciting. She was loathe to end the kiss, however innocent.

A swirl of damp air touched her cheek and she lifted her head, staring down at the beloved face with desperate pleading. "Oh, please wake up, my *chevalier*," she whispered.

The slim, white-haired, travel-weary figure at the door started at the sight that met her eyes. There on the floor was Charity with a man in her arms, the marquess, if what she had heard was correct. And they had been kissing!

Charity heard a distinct gasp and her head shot around. It couldn't be, could it? "Aunt Tavington?"

2

CHARITY WAS DOUBLY CONFUSED at the sight of her aunt. "Where? How? When?" The words flew from her mouth in rapid succession. How had her aunt appeared so suddenly? From where? Then, recalling the emergency at hand, she pleaded, "You must help me, Aunt Tavington. The marquess Lord Kenrick is injured. His head is bleeding and he *must* get care. The floor is so damp here, I know it must be bad for him."

Charity nodded toward the wood slat floor, still damp from her earlier cleaning efforts. She shifted, trying to ease her cramped body without disturbing his lordship.

Lady Alice Tavington entered the hothouse with a brisk step, glancing around. Before she allowed any accusations, she would ascertain precisely what had occurred. "That man you sent is getting someone to help. I can see his lordship would be too much of a burden for a slip of a girl and an old man. What happened?"

Fortunately for Charity, Josiah came in the door at that moment with two sturdy under-gardeners behind him. "Here we are, lads. Tom, you at his shoulders. Ben, you at th' other leg. We'll go for the cottage, as 'tis nearest." Josiah took a firm hold of one leg encased in a highly polished boot. He and Ben lifted, as Tom eased the upper body until they could slowly make their way from the hothouse. Although his lordship was no featherweight, the carriers managed not to jar him unduly.

Outside, the misty rain had ceased. Damp air swirled about the unconscious figure, causing his thick dark hair to form loose curls above the linen pad still firmly pressed against his forehead by an anxious Charity.

She stumbled along the path, more concerned about the man being carried than her own progress. "Mind now, be careful of his head. I believe that is his only injury . . . but he is so still." To Lady Tavington she added, "He hasn't moved so much as a finger since he fell." There was a hint of a sob in her voice.

The path to the cottage was narrow and winding yet smooth from much use. At last the party left the rough path and entered the yard to the cottage. Mrs. Woods stood before the open front door, her ever-present apron clasped in worried hands, her anxious words flowing nonstop.

"I've prepared her bed for his lordship at Josiah's word. What's to be done? Oh dear, oh dear. I warned ye, Miss Charity. Trouble. That's what ye'll get. Trouble. Naught but trouble do I see for ye now."

The men ignored her lamentations and squeezed their way past the wooden gate and up the walk bordered with primroses and pansies. It was a bit of a trick getting the tall, well-constructed body of his lordship through both the doorways, but at last the inert form was placed gently on the large four-poster in the best bedchamber. It was the room Charity used. Mrs. Woods occupied the small back bedroom, next to the kitchen.

Fading light revealed the shadowed, spotless interior, so neat yet devoid of the usual frivolities a young woman cared to have around her. Mrs. Woods lit a branch of candles and moved it to the cherry-wood stand by the bed. The pad on Lord Kenrick's forehead was a sodden mess of linen stained a dark red.

Lady Tavington brushed Charity aside and examined the wound. Over her shoulder she instructed Mrs. Woods. "Bring me a bowl of warm water and a clean cloth. I must see how serious this cut is. Quickly, woman!"

"I sent Ben for the doctor. We best not touch a thing

until he comes." Mrs. Woods reluctantly moved toward the door.

"Doctor? And what will he do? Bleed him, I suppose? Do as I ask. Please!" It was a firmly ordered request that allowed for no denial. Mrs. Woods hurried from the room to return moments later with the required items.

Lady Tavington set about cleaning the wound after handing Charity the blood-saturated pad, then quietly spoke. "It is not as bad as I feared. I suspect he is more concussed than anything else. I have seen the like before." She raised her voice to Mrs. Woods. "Get me my small portmanteau, the one by the door, if you please." Again the order was sweetly given, with no thought it might be ignored.

Mrs. Woods dumped the black leather bag on the bedroom floor. Lady Tavington instructed Charity, "Remove the roll of linen tied with a blue ribbon. It should be near the top. Good. Open it. Hold this pad on his forehead while I mix up something for that wound." She noted Charity's anxious frown and added, "While on our travels, my late husband was tended by a Chinese physician. I was much taken with his remedies and brought home as many as I could. He cured Lord Tavington of a fever in no time at all."

If the Chinese physician cured Lord Tavington, what had happened to her aunt's husband? Charity watched as a reddish-brown powder was poured from an envelope onto a small dish, then blended with a dab of unguent from a jar. This awful-looking mess was then carried to the bedside and smeared over the wound. It was thick, tinged with red, a sight guaranteed to unsettle a stomach.

Charity felt the awful burden of responsibility for the health and life of Lord Kenrick drape over her slim shoulders. He was unmarried, with a cousin as heir, a cousin not much admired at the great house. If Lord Kenrick died, it would be Charity's fault. Why, oh, why, had she allowed her anger to take control of her emotions? "Are you certain this will help the marquess?"

"As certain as I can be of anything, dear child." Lady Tavington bound up the wound, winding the srip of linen around the head, allowing the dark curls to flop over the neat bandage. "The powder is from dried red flowers. I have seen it work wonders." She gestured to Mrs. Woods. "Now, call back one of those men to remove his lordship's boots. We must get him tucked beneath the covers. Has word been sent to the great house? Someone there must be notified." She glanced at the white-faced young woman at her side. "Charity, perhaps you can heat a kettle of water for a restoring cup of tea? We'll tend to this."

Suddenly realizing they meant to undress his lordship, Charity blushed a deep rose and scurried toward the kitchen. Calling to Tom to lend a hand in the other room, she set about putting a kettle over the fire in the kitchen grate.

While waiting for the water to heat, she paced up and down in the confines of the kitchen. It was a cheerful place, neat white muslin curtains at the windows allowing the sun to brighten every corner of the tidy room. Herbs hung from the rafters; a string of onions dangled from the smoke-darkened beam next to the brick fireplace. She ran her hands over the high back of the maple rocker that invited a tired body to rest near the warmth of the fire. By the bow window a table large enough to seat four reflected the waning light on its polished deal surface.

Never had she been so confused, nor so upset. This day was becoming more than she could handle, what with Lord Kenrick occupying her bed and Aunt Tavington arriving in such dramatic fashion. What next?

She took her hand from the rocker and it swayed gently back and forth, as though occupied by a ghost. Stuffing her small, capable hands into the pockets of her gray cambric apron, she again turned her musings to her aunt. Where had she come from? How had she arrived? It had been many years since Charity had seen her father's sister, but she had a face and bearing one never forgot. But . . . where was her husband?

The last Charity recalled, Aunt Alice had been in India following her husband about as he did inspections of some sort for the government, collecting plants along the way. They had sent a packet of orchid seeds for her father as well as a box of plant cuttings. It had been the last project he undertook before he died, starting those seeds, watching them sprout and begin to grow. The cuttings had done well, nearly every one of them coming to flower. How fortunate her father had overcome his earlier problems with growing orchids. It had taken some time to learn that not all orchids required potting. Now many of the glorious blooms peeped from high in the hothouse, lashed to pieces of plum wood, requiring little more than air to survive.

A slight noise from the other room drew her attention. She went to the doorway and discovered a tiny brown animal sitting on the floor. It was a frail little thing with an extremely long tail that curled about him. Large sable-brown eyes gazed soberly up at her. A rounded button nose sat strangely above a sad line of a mouth. The white of his chin looked like an old man's beard. He appeared not a little afraid of her.

The bedroom door opened and Lady Tavington came out, followed by Tom. "You've found my pet monkey! Chico, bow to the lady." The monkey executed a jerky bow, then sat on the floor looking pleased with himself as he picked at the rug. "He's a good little thing. I rescued him from a hungry-eyed native when I was in Venezuela. I couldn't bear to think of him as someone's dinner. Come along, now." She motioned to Chico and scooped him up in her arms to set him on her shoulders. There he sat, surveying the room with bright, inquisitive eyes.

Tom exited hastily, unsure of the heathen-looking animal who didn't look like any he'd ever seen before.

He blurted something about going to the great house, and disappeared from view.

Charity hurried to brew the tea in her best china pot and quickly set a tray with her mother's fine china cups. She had wondered what might happen next, but she definitely had not expected a monkey.

"A cup of tea, I think. Then talk." Her aunt went to a basin to pour water and scrub her hands with lavender-scented soap. As she dried them on a neatly mended linen towel, she looked about with careful scrutiny. The house was small but respectable.

In recent years Lady Tavington had been exposed to a life and conditons far from those in which she had been reared. To be housed in a clean environment was not bad. Still, this was not the way she had expected to find her favorite niece living.

Lady Tavington turned to study the pale, shaken young woman who now stood by the window, pleating the gray apron she wore with an air of barely suppressed panic. "I will pour. We can sit in the other room, close to where his lordship is so if there is any change we can be at his side in a trice. I am quite certain Mrs. Woods will take the greatest care of him," Lady Tavington said calmly as Chico peered down from her shoulder.

"I feel I ought to be at his side. I'm very worried about him." Charity moved forward reluctantly.

"I have a few questions first. His lordship is not, I think, seriously wounded." She motioned to Charity to carry the tea tray into the sitting room to chairs close by the bedroom door. Seating herself with a graceful flourish, she poured out a cup of tea, extending it to Charity.

Charity, accepting the cup of tea, bravely met the curious eyes of her aunt. "How did you get here? We have had no word of you in such a long time. Where have you been? What has happened?" More to the point, where was her uncle? She perched on a small, uncomfortable chair opposite her aunt, waiting expectantly, hoping to stave off a quizzing for even a brief time.

"I've written, but the mail is not to be depended upon. I am persuaded more messages sink to the bottom of the sea than ever find their way to England. My dearest Edmund was killed while we were in China. I was told Mongols were responsible for cutting him down as he helped defend our group during some local skirmish." She paused for a moment, sipping her tea as a sudden spasm of pain swept over her. Her hand reached up to stroke Chico as though she drew comfort from his presence.

"I made my way home as best I could, but it took me some time. I was forced to travel by way of Australia, then around the southern tip of South America, where I was certain we would perish in the extreme waves that swamped our poor ship. I stopped off for a rest in Venezuela. There were rumors that ships might have difficulty crossing the Atlantic. I sought to be sure it would be as safe as possible nowadays. That was where I found my little pet, my Chico. Once home, I stopped in London to bring my wardrobe up to date. That was when I found out about your father, dear child. I was devastated. So tragic, to have lost him and know nothing of it."

She sighed and petted Chico absently as she continued. "My abigail, Parton, ought to arrive tomorrow or the next day with the things I ordered in London. I was impatient to see you, dearest Charity, and could not wait until all was ready. Parton will bring everything else I require. I have a surprise I had hoped to present to your father, some orchid plants I picked up along the way."

Lady Tavington glanced around again as she sipped her tea. "We shall have difficulty managing so many people in such a small cottage. How is it you are here, child? Surely you should be with one of the family? I cannot believe they would leave you alone and unprotected."

Charity sipped her tea before answering. Lady Tavington had the look of a managing female about her. Charity had had enough of people trying to order her life. She liked her freedom and quiet days. If the nights were lonely, it could not be helped. She would not willingly alter her plans. "Papa left me some money and I receive a small portion from Mama's estate." She briefly recounted what had occurred in the past year or more since Lady Tavington had the last communication. "I have Papa's orchids. I could not *bear* to leave them." The accompanying thought of the man in the other room who made leaving the area insupportable she ignored. "I was able to rent this house through the grace of Lord Kenrick's bailiff. Mrs. Woods had been with our family for many years, and is now my cook-housekeeper and looks after me well. I am content with my life."

"It will never do, my dearest. The thing for you is to marry. You must know a woman cannot be alone in the world. *That* is what I shall do for you." A firm nod of her head confirmed the idea. "Although I have been gone from society for some years, there must be some way we can contrive to find you a good husband." She tapped her finger against her chin in thought.

"But tell me about our wounded guest. What happened in the hothouse? Did he accost you in some manner? Was there an impropriety? I cannot think it is right for you to work in that place all alone, with naught but plants around you."

Charity paused before answering, fascinated with the long tail that curled over her aunt's shoulder. Chico cocked his head and grimaced before leaping to the floor, then to a chair some distance away. Charity had been obliged to refuse Roscoe the house, Mrs. Woods taking exception to him. Charity decided to change all that.

She said faintly, "Josiah is usually not far away, and to tell the truth, I am rarely disturbed by anyone. Today was an exception."

"Explain, please."

The command was gentle, yet the kind instantly obeyed. Charity complied, and soon the events in the hothouse stumbled forth from trembling lips.

"I see." Lady Tavington studied her pale, worried niece, then rose from her chair. "We must check on Lord Kenrick. Did Mrs. Woods send a message to the great house? I'll warrant his lordship's valet will attend him shortly after he is apprised of the situation. Mrs. Woods indicated there is no party in residence at Greenoaks."

"I heard his lordship had just arrived. I know nothing about any guests." The scene of the great house was far removed from Charity's world. She rarely paid any attention to the comings and goings up there, what few there might be.

The great house sat on a south-facing slope, surveying the lake that Lancelot "Capability" Brown had set out some years before. The land rolled away smoothly from the house across the lake to the horizons of hill crests and unfolding forestry. The cottage Charity rented was on the edge of this parklike scene. She was convenient to the hothouses, the principal reason she had sought out this cottage once she heard it was vacant.

Charity set down the cup and hurried to the bedroom door. Mrs. Woods looked up and shook her head.

"He hasn't moved, my lady. I'd best see to making some restoring broth. He'll need something if he comes to."

Charity directed a black look at the housekeeper. "When, Mrs. Woods. When. Don't even think 'if.' "

"I am persuaded Charity is right, Mrs. Woods. It was the believe of my Chinese physician, Wang Fu, that one ought never to speak anything but positive words before an unconscious patient lest the mind absorb bad emanations from what is said."

Charity watched her housekeeper slant a disbelieving look at Lady Tavington and sweep out the doorway. With an anxious frown, Charity drew the small, straight chair closer to the bedside and perched on the edge of it. "My lord, please open your eyes. Move. Say something." She reached out to touch the firm, white hand. It was a strong, warm hand. There was no sign of the coldness that had come over her father as he lay dying.

"I believe he will come 'round soon. Give him time, my dearest child." Alice observed her niece's face closely for any clue to her feelings regarding the gentleman on the four-poster bed.

Charity was oblivious to her aunt's searching look. Clasping that strong hand in her own, she whispered a prayer for the recovery of his lordship. As much as she feared detection, she wished above all things for her *preux chevalier* to be conscious and well. Her eyes strayed from the hand that lay so still on the counterpane to the face that rested on her pillow. She longed to smooth the tumbled curls away from his brow, to caress his cheek. She dare not think of the touch of his lips. That was forbidden . . . but lovely, she sighed.

There was a rustle at the door and a thin gentleman with graying hair and an air of consequence entered the room. Charity was shaken from her admiration of his lordship to wonder at the intrusion.

The gentleman bowed to Lady Tavington, then to Charity. "I'm Moffat, his lordship's valet. Your housekeeper informed me his lordship has been injured."

Moffat hurried to the opposite side of the bed from where Charity sat and examined the man who lay so still. "Has the doctor been here so soon? I have heard the quack who takes care of the village is often slow to attend his patients, if he ever arrives at all."

"My aunt, Lady Tavington, has tended Lord Kenrick. She dressed his wound quite well, I think. I doubt if the good doctor could do any better."

Lady Tavington moved forward to the bedside. "I've had some experience at caring for the wounded and ill. It has been necessary for me to learn many things on my travels."

Moffat studied the calm face at his side. The lady was a pleasant woman of middle years, chestnut hair liberally laced with gray escaping from the lace cap on her head. Steady gray eyes much like her niece's met his in a reassuring manner. Here was a lady of undoubted quality and more, a lady of compassion and capability.

"I'm sure your care is of the best, my lady." He made a slight bow of acknowledgment to her skills.

"His lordship's clothes and boots are on this chest by the door. Perhaps you wish to take charge of them? My niece will not easily relinquish her place by the wounded. Her concern will not let her leave his side."

Moffat observed the troubled countenance across the bed from where he stood, and nodded. The young lady appeared to be firmly situated by the bed. She did not look to have any missish airs about her, seeming of a calm disposition and even temper. The gentle clasp of her hand over his master's was not missed. Not knowing the full of the situation, he could only go by what he saw. He was inclined to let Lady Tavington establish the rules. Here was one woman who was capable of assuming control with no effort at all.

Once Moffat removed the soiled clothing from the room, murmuring his distress at the scratched surface of the previously highly polished boots, Charity settled closer to observe her patient.

"I believe I'll settle in my room. I'll have to make arrangements for Parton before she arrives." Lady Tavington suppressed a smile at the concentration bestowed on the man in the bed. She doubted if Charity had heard a word she said.

Mrs. Woods explained that Moffat had returned to the great house to fetch some things for his lordship. Lady Tavington nodded and proceeded up the circular stairs to inspect the bedrooms on the upper floor. She gazed around at a scrupulously clean and cheerfully decorated bedroom. The furniture consisted of pieces she recognized from her brother's household. Next to it was another small, low-ceilinged room quite sparsely furnished. Both had dormer windows overlooking the front garden. Somehow they would contrive well enough in these rooms.

Lady Tavington patted her hair in place, then joined Mrs. Woods in the sitting room as a carriage drew up before the cottage.

" 'Tis the doctor, my lady. I'll let him in.'' The eagerness with which Mrs. Woods went to attend to the doctor attested to her doubts regarding the mixture Lady Tavington had smeared on the wound. Between the monkey and that heathen medicine, her doubts about Lady Tavington were growing by the moment.

Lady Tavington drew her slim self erect, all five feet and three inches. While not tall, she was aware she cut an imposing figure if she so chose. Dignity plus assurance had worked well for her in the past. It had helped in no small part when she was forced to make her way to the Chinese coast to seek passage to England. When she thought of the stinking, rotting vessel she had sailed forth on, she knew she could face anything. This country doctor was nothing.

He was a stout man of at least fifty years, with a sad coat of unpleasant brown over a stained waistcoat of a horrid mustard. His buff breeches were soiled as well, a thoroughly unprepossessing picture.

"The injured gentleman is in this bedroom." She ignored his gesture of dismissal and escorted him to the bedside. She patted Charity on the shoulder. "You had better go in the other room for the moment, dear child. The doctor will examine his lordship now."

"You may go as well, my lady." The voice was rough, thick, his hands unsteady. From the redness of his nose she considered he might well have a fondness for port.

"I think not. I wish to observe your methods."

There was no denying her, so he set about his inspection of the patient. "He appears unhurt but for this gash on his forehead." He made to wipe off the unguent Lady Tavington had placed there earlier, and she stayed his hand.

"Leave it be. It is a special mixture I made for him

myself. While in the Orient I picked up a certain knowledge of medications. It won't harm him and may indeed cure him."

Dr. Wadley reluctantly nodded as though sensing the lady was not to be persuaded otherwise. He turned to his case and brought out his jar of leeches.

"You will not leech him, Doctor." Her tone made it clear she would not allow any interference with her wishes. "Nor do I want to see his head shaved for any ointment. It will not be necessary, I am sure."

This was obviously too much for the good doctor. He protested in vain, finally departing in a great huff. Why had they sent for him if they didn't intend to allow him to practice his calling? he demanded of the housekeeper.

Charity returned to the bedside, again testing the hand that lay so still. "I cannot believe that noise did not waken him."

"He will wake in his own time." Lady Tavington hoped she was right. Lord Kenrick had fair color in his face. If only he would open his eyes . . . "I think it is time we had a little talk, my dear."

Charity glanced fearfully at his lordship.

"Don't worry, he won't hear us. I sense a regard in your manner toward his lordship that concerns me greatly. Tell, me dearest child, have you formed a *tendre* for this man?"

Charity rose from the bedside and slowly walked the few steps to the window, keeping her face away from the too-sharp eyes watching her. "What a foolish thing to say. I have never met the man before. I'm quite certain he has never seen me. He visited Papa on rare occasions in the past. I saw him then, but only from a distance."

"Yet there is a something in your attitude that tells me otherwise, I think."

"He is a handsome man . . . I'll grant you. But he is a touch above me. If you think to find me a husband, look elsewhere, as long as you do not look to the squire. Never will I marry that man."

Charity's utter loathing for the squire rang in her words. She looked to her aunt to verify that dear lady understood nothing would alter her stand. As she turned her head, she noticed that the hand which had lain so still now moved. Charity rushed to the bedside and stared anxiously at the beloved face on her pillow. Her hand unconsciously sought his. His eyes fluttered, and she released the breath she had pent up.

Lady Tavington also moved to his side. "Lord Kenrick? I fear you have had a bit of trouble."

3

THE MOST HONORABLE DAVID Edward Brandon, Marquess of Kenrick winced at the light from the branch of candles. His head pained him and he felt disoriented. Who were these women, and how had he come to be in this four-poster bed? The warmth of the small hand that had covered his was missed when it was abruptly withdrawn.

He looked first at the younger woman at his side. She was very pretty. Her mouth was softly tender, cheeks gently rounded. Her gray eyes were anxious. She had an exceedingly guilty look on her countenance, which made him wonder a little. The candlelight caught in her hair, and a rush of memory told him where he had seen that particular hair before.

"You were in the hothouse. What happened?"

He thought she wasn't going to answer him at first. A dainty tongue teased her upper lip in a rather enticing manner. The worried glance she shot at the other woman told him something was amiss, more than his injury. Too much guilt was in those crystal-clear gray eyes.

"I was getting ready to leave the hothouse for the day. I . . . thought you were someone else, my lord. I never would have injured you on purpose. I am terribly sorry." She closed her eyes as though awaiting her doom.

"Do you usually greet people entering the hothouse in this manner?" His voice was cold, the hardness stemming from the pain that pounded in his head when he was so rash as to move it.

"No, my lord. I had been sorely tried, and I am

afraid I did not consider it might be other than the one I anticipated.'' She bent her head, but not before he observed a pink flush stain her cheeks. Intriguing, if only he felt like bothering his aching head over it.

"His lordship must rest, Charity. Tell Mrs. Woods to bring a bowl of that restoring broth she prepared. You can answer more questions once his lordship is feeling more the thing.''

The young woman named Charity hastily popped up from the chair beside the bed and hurried from the room as though an ogre were chasing her.

The older woman drew closer to his side. "I'm Lady Tavington, Charity's aunt. You doubtless recall her father, the Reverend Peter Lonsbury? She said you visited him a number of times before his death a year ago.''

"I did visit him some years ago. I wasn't aware of his death.'' Had his bailiff mentioned the death of Reverend Lonsbury? He dimly recalled his bailiff requesting him to appoint a new clergyman to the post. He hadf been busy at the time with other matters at his favorite estate north of London and had paid scant attention to the matter.

"I'm sorry to learn of his death.''

Lady Tavington straightened the bedcovers and checked the bandage on his forehead before replying. "It left my niece alone. I did not learn of his passing until I arrived in London. I've been away for some time, you see.'' She stood back and surveyed his face, nodding decisively. "You'll do, I'm sure, given time.''

"And the damage?'' He raised his hand to his forehead to explore. There was a neat bandage across the upper part of his brow. Her words were not at all the kind he usually received, those being more in the line of flattery.

"You were hit with a flower pot, empty, fortunately. It bruised the skin.'' She sighed. "I'm afraid it also gave you the concussion. We were most thankful when you regained consciousness, my lord.''

"She threw the pot, didn't she? Quite a formidable aim." He closed his eyes for a moment, then reopened them when he heard a gentle rustle accompanied by a delicious aroma that teased his nose.

"I pray you will take this good broth, my lord. Mrs. Woods particularly excels in such." Charity placed the steaming broth on the cherry-wood table before looking to her aunt.

"We had best ease you up . . . unless you would prefer one of us to feed you." Lady Tavington's gaze was measuring and he returned in kind.

He was suddenly possessed of a desire to study the little Charity. "The young woman can feed me. I fear my hands would be none too steady, and I am not certain I dare sit up."

Lady Tavington frowned. It was obvious she did not want Charity to be feeding him. There was no reason for Lady Tavington to remain in the room, either. He could hardly attack the young woman's virtue when he was loathe to move himself one inch, much less a foot. Reluctantly, she nodded, sending another shrewd gaze in his direction before she made her unwilling departure.

Charity spread out a neatly mended linen napkin, no doubt a remnant of earlier days at the rectory. Kenrick tried to ease himself up, thus becoming aware for the first time that he was beneath the down comforter with little clothing to cover him. He had been so preoccupied with the identities of his nurses and the circumstances of his injury he had overlooked this small matter.

"You have tended me since I was injured?"

"A good deal of the time. I feel so terrible about your injury, my lord." She appeared on the verge of tears. He admired her resolution to resist any missish airs. Relaxing against the lavender-scented pillow, he watched her face closely. He was quite fatigued, and not just from the blow. He had been overdoing as of late. It was a change to be cosseted in bed . . . and not by his mistress.

Charity's hand trembled just slightly as she leaned forward to place the first spoon of broth in his lordship's mouth. It was as delicious as it smelled.

"Tell me what occured following my injury."

There was a gentle command in his voice that was not disobeyed. "After I saw the clay pot hit you, I hurried to your side. I tried to stem the bleeding while Josiah— he's your head gardener, you know—went for help. Tom and Ben assisted Josiah in carrying you to our cottage. You see, you were much closer to this cottage than to the great house."

Her earnest words were meant to explain, possibly reassure. He found himself studying her eyes as she slipped another spoon of broth into his mouth. She had been right in one thing: Mrs. Woods, whoever she might be, did particularly well with preparing broths.

Those eyes captivated him. They were a cool, shining gray, almost luminous, with dark, thick lashes outlining them and delicately arched brows above. He met her inquiring look. "And then?"

"They brought you to my, er, this room. You were treated by my aunt before the doctor could get there. He does not always come when summoned, you see," she added gravely. "We watched over you until now. Dr. Wadley did come later, but he merely checked you. Aunt Tavington would not let him apply the leeches. Nor would she allow him to shave your head to apply an ointment."

He could not prevent a slight shudder. "It seems I have to be grateful to your aunt. Where came she by this fount of information?"

"She said it was in China, my lord. She traveled with her husband across India and China before his death. She met a Chinese physician from whom she learned much in the art of healing." It was evident Charity did not share her aunt's confidence in the good Chinese doctor. "The name Wang Fu falls strangely on our English ears, does it not?"

He began to nod before he remembered how it would

pain his head, and abruptly stopped. Even then, the pain was enough to make him shut his eyes. He shifted, easing himself up a bit. He was very tired and wondered if he was more in need of sleep or sustenance. His humor asserted itself. "And did you put me to bed as well? I gather this is your bedroom?" He shifted again and the bedcovers slid down his bare chest.

The sight of the masculine chest, with the mat of dark hair peeping above the edge of the sheet, brought delicate color to her cheeks as he hoped it would. She shook her head vigorously in denial. "No, my lord. Tom helped Lady Tavington prepare you for bed. She said she had experience nursing the ill. However, this is my bedroom." Her cheeks turned a delicious rose, and the long, dark fringes of her lashes swept down in delightful confusion.

Lord Kenrick was not in the habit of paying attention to a miss out of the schoolroom, nor any of the raft of young women making their bows to society. However, this was a different case entirely. For one thing, Charity was not making her entrance to society. For another, he perceived she was long out of the schoolroom. She was entrancingly different, he had to admit. Still, her ways were a bit open and undoubtedly countrified, though it would be unavoidable, living in the backwaters as she did. He glanced with a certain disdain on the plainness of the room. It would not be kind of him to flirt with her. She might take him seriously with those enormous gray eyes of hers so full of mystery and guilt. Guilt?

"You are greatly concerned over my injury." He tried to keep his voice neutral. His dear friend Charles warned him he had a tendency to sound cold and aloof at times. Intimidating, he supposed, to lesser persons.

Her start answered his question, if he had needed to ask it in the first place. "Oh, yes, my lord. I feel dreadful about hitting you on the head. I will never forgive myself. You cannot know how thankful I am Lady Tavington has assured me you will be fine in no time."

Lord Kenrick watched her as she fed him more broth. For someone who confessed and knew her salvation around the corner, she still looked remarkably guilty of something.

"You said you anticipated someone else? Who?"

Her hand trembled, and she stilled it with an effort. "I believe Squire Bigglesby was the one to inform you I was in the hothouses, was he not? I had expected him to return with news of your conversation. He had been, er, ah, well, there was a question he asked earlier that I answered not to his satisfaction. He had given me time to alter my reply." Her voice quivered a trifle, as though she fought control over it.

"And you were not happy with the question?" His soft words demanded a truthful reply.

"No." The blunt denial was not the soft answer a lady would have given, reinforcing his impression of her country manners. "I have no desire to wed the squire. I should above all things find it detestable. He does not admire my orchids, you see. And he wants to put Roscoe in a stew pot."

The horror in her voice was almost amusing to a tired, slightly jaded member of the *ton* who rarely worried about putting anything in a stew pot, unless it affected the display that reached his own table. He left the menus of his table to the decidedly superior skill of his French chef, Antoine.

"Roscoe?"

He must have placed an inflection in his voice that revealed his feelings, for she flushed in that enchanting way she had once again, ruefully shaking her head as she did.

"I *am* sorry, my lord. What a rag-mannered idiot I am to be rattling on like this. It is nothing to you that Roscoe is my pet rabbit. Pray swallow the last of this broth. I can then leave you to rest in peace." She deftly spooned the last of the broth into his mouth with the practice of one who has done a great deal of that sort of thing. He wondered if she had nursed her father before his death.

"Was your father ill for some time before he . . . passed on?"

Her eyes darkened into stormy seas with suppressed emotion. "You mean, did I nurse him? I did. There was little Mrs. Woods or I did not have to do for him." She paused, taking a peep at the glimpse of manly chest exposed above the sheet. "It is just that you . . . appear much younger." That highly obvious and obscure remark was left dangling in the air as she gathered the tray and swept from the room before he could quiz her further.

Moffat surprised him by entering the room to deal with the preparations for the night. Moffat was full of admiration for the estimable Lady Tavington, and to Lord Kenrick's surprise, encomiums for the young Miss Charity. Moffat usually had little to say on behalf of most young ladies, and then, few words that were kind. Like most valets, he was a very high stickler for all that was proper. It was a source of wonderment to consider his approval for a country miss with few manners to recommend her and no substance at all.

David was awakened during the night by first his valet and then Lady Tavington. When he irritably queried the reason for these rude awakenings, he was informed Wang Fu decreed that following a blow to the head, one ought to ascertain the continuing alertness of the patient. Lord Kenrick's pithy comment regarding the need for alertness while in deep sleep was prudently ignored.

Next morning Charity hesitantly knocked before entering the bedroom through the open door. "Breakfast, my lord." She was obviously wary of him, probably wondering what to expect.

He had been shaved and made as presentable as possible under the circumstances. Confound the girl. Why must she look at him with the guilty expression in her eyes? He decided to set her mind further at ease.

"I don't believe I made it quite plain that I forgive you the head wound. I understand better than you realize . . . after visiting with the worthy squire yesterday.''

Her smile was tremulous. "Thank you. It's more kindness than I deserve. You will continue to allow me to live here, then? And I may keep on with my work in the hothouses? I know I ought to have obtained your permission to work there with the orchids, but you are so seldom here. I didn't like to bother your bailiff with such unimportant details. The plants are all mine, you see. And I see to the tending of the fires to maintain the heat. Actually, it's far better for the buildings to be in use than allowed to rot unoccupied. The damp would be harmful, I am sure." She nodded in a quaint, confiding manner, very engaging and quite enchanting. He couldn't help but wish his friend Charles could see her. Charles would appreciate the fresh charm before him. Country charm, to be sure.

He turned to the light meal of toast and perfectly coddled eggs. It was hardly the hearty breakfast he usually ate. He supposed Lady Tavington and the eminent Wang Fu were responsible for this, too.

It was difficult to keep his eyes off Charty's slender figure. With that abominable gray apron gone, her gentle curves were much to his taste, if he were inclined toward country misses. Which he wasn't, he reminded himself. It was only the boredom of being flat on his back and the pain that at times cut through his head that was making him pay attention to a young woman he would ordinarily ignore.

Her fair skin could be made to blush so easily, though he would swear she was usually quite steady a person. Her parson father was probably responsible for that quality. He observed her capable, well-shaped hands as they folded the towel used for his shaving. She stowed an article of clothing away in one of the drawers of the cedar chest, then turned to survey him.

"Aunt Tavington is resting now. She and Moffat took turns sitting up with you last night. Are you feeling tired? Is there perhaps something I might fetch you?''

In spite of his handsome forgiveness she still had a quality of guilt lurking in her eyes.

"Nothing. Sit down here and talk to me. I find it boring to be alone."

"Yes, I suppose you are accustomed to more lively company than you find here."

The possibilities of that subject neatly escaped her. He was sorry to miss the blush he supposed might flush her cheeks if she but considered what her words implied. There was none of the coquette about her. Totally lacking in sophistication, she was still charming in her own peculiar way.

"Tell me about your orchids," he said. It was his experience that a person revealed far more of himself when conversing on a favorite topic.

She wavered. "I hardly know what to say, my lord. My father raised orchids as a diversion. His collection is quite excellent, I believe. Your father showed an interest. They used to discuss the various theories on proper cultivation with much heated argument between them." She smiled shyly. "I think they rather enjoyed their debates."

"You took over his collection?"

"Papa taught me everything he knew about the cultivation of orchids. I helped him while he was alive, kept up with his correspondence, all that. I endeavor to increase the collection as best I can. I was potting a division I had made of one of the orchids that was a sort of bulblike root when the squire came yesterday. That is how I happened to have a clay pot handy."

"You enjoy working with the plants? Digging in the dirt?" His voice assumed the coolness he was noted for among his friends. "It does not seem at all the thing for a young woman to do."

She flushed slightly, then tilted her chin. "The orchids are cultivated in many ways, my lord. Some are potted in moss and shredded bark. Others are grown in wicker baskets lined with mold over which the rootstock is placed, then covered with moss. Still others are wrapped in moss and tied to the stems of a tree. I cut notches, the plant is inserted like a graft, and moss is stuffed around it until the roots of the orchid can establish themselves. I do not use dirt.'' Her chin raised again in defiance.

He said idly, ''What do you do with them?''

She compressed her lips. and her hands fluttered before clasping each other in frantic distress. ''I believe I heard my aunt in the other room. She told me she wished to speak privately with you when she arose. I will doubtless see you later, my lord.'' She whirled out of her chair and scurried from the room before he could question her unusual behavior.

He wasn't sure if Lady Tavington came to see him, for he fell asleep while awaiting the lady. The remainder of the day was spent with Moffat bustling in and out, Mrs. Woods hovering near the door, and not a moment for private conversation of any kind. The following morning he made it plain to Moffat that he wished an interview with Lady Tavington as soon as the dear lady could arrange it.

As he waited for her arrival, he passed the time inspecting the room. It was neat, spotlessly clean, and totally devoid of the frills and furbelows he believed dear to the hearts of young women. Above the cedar chest hung an exquisite watercolor of a pale-lavender and deep-purple orchid. Another beautifully done watercolor of a remarkable deep-violet orchid hung on the other side of the room. Moffat told him there was another watercolor hung above the headboard.

Other than these touches of beauty, there was little to tell a young woman lived here. Odd. She exhibited no sign of flirting or coy teasing. Strange. Must be the country miss. Or could there be something else, some other reason for her mysterious behavior?

While pondering over this enigma, Lady Tavington bustled into the room, directly proceeding to remove the bandage on his forehead. She nodded in a very pleased manner. ''It is healing very well, my lord. Very well, indeed. By tomorrow you can dispense with this bandage, I'm sure. I doubt if there will even be much of a scar as a memento of this occasion." She proceeded to apply the paste she brought with her, then bandage the wound again.

"Miss Lonsbury said you wished to speak with me."

Lady Tavington did a peculiar thing then. She walked to the door the inspect the outer room. Satisfied at something she did or did not see, she scooped a small animal up in her arms, then returned to his side.

"Pray, do not mind my Chico. I find great comfort in him. I made sure to see if Charity had gone up to the hothouses, and she has. I wanted to speak to you about her, my lord."

Lord Kenrick raised his brows in question. His thick, dark hair still persisted in wanting to flop over the white bandage. The distinctive carriage of his head pronounced him a man likely to catch the eye and make hearts sigh as well, or so he had been told. Those brilliant, intensely blue eyes pierced the composure Lady Tavington wore with such aplomb.

"I entered the hothouse shortly after the gardener left. The door was ajar, and I could see my niece on the floor with you cradled in her arms. You were very close, my lord. And, I might add, you were kissing." This was all announced in a very matter-of-fact tone, as though she was imparting news of the weather.

"Now, I doubt you would dangle after a miss such as Charity. Moffat informed me he suspects you to offer for a young lady quite soon. A Lady Sylvia Wilde, I believe. Since you and I know the circumstances were perfectly innocent, there can be no question of foolish demands for a marriage or some such silliness. However . . ."

He marveled at the regained composure, the adeptness with which she was sailing through waters others would not dare hazard. What charm she must have exerted to wrest that information from a taciturn Moffat. Whatever else Lady Tavington might be, she was not timid. "Go on. I can scarcely wait."

She ignored his dry tone and proceeded. "The gardener saw you. Who else may have peered in that door I cannot say. I do not want any scandal attached to the name of my favorite niece."

"What do you propose?" He discovered, in spite of a rising anger, he wanted to find out what this audacious woman had in mind. She reminded him of his mother with her determination. Her utter disregard for what might have been a means of compelling him into a forced marriage was to be commended. He had observed such a ruse more than once, and it could be damned effective for springing the parson's mousetrap.

"I have no great desire to settle in England again. I have traveled the world for too long to be content with teas and parties. You might say I have become a bit of an adventuress in my own way. I long to go to Egypt before the place is decimated of all its antiquities." Her sigh was filled with sincere longing. She gave him an assessing look. "However, I will not leave Charity here to fend for herself. She needs a husband. I believe you ought to help me find her one."

Sharp and to the point! He cleared his throat, frowning at her in a totally perplexed manner. "I don't see how I can help find a husband for her."

"I am aware her clothes, her open ways are not those of a London miss. I do not know what my brother was thinking of, allowing her to molder in that hothouse all the time instead of acquiring the necessary graces for a young lady of her position. He was, after all, the younger son of the Earl of Nevile. Her mama was a Cloverly, a fine family who need make no apology for their ancestors."

Lady Tavington shook her head, lost in thought for a moment. "I shall make her my heiress, for I have no children, and a large part of Edmund's fortune is not entailed. His younger brother has sufficient. With her family background and the promise of a modest fortune, she could do well. I would have her meet someone worthy of her, my lord. I fear I have been gone too long from society to be of use there. That is where you come in, you see.''

He simply gazed in silence at this masterful explanation. A pity Lady Tavington was lost to the theater. If he didn't miss his guess, she would have done well there.

"If you could have a house party or some such so that Charity might meet some eligible young men you deemed fitting for her, it would be quite the answer to the problem, I am persuaded.''

"That is all?'' His reply was mild, but the lady didn't miss the touch of irony in his voice.

"I'll see to it Josiah understands what he thinks he saw as well as discover if anyone else was in the area at the time. There will be no problems there.''

"I will admit I am surprised you are not attempting to compel a wedding between your niece and me.'' The irony in his voice had deepened.

"It would never do, my lord. Although Charity is of acceptable birth, she lacks the, er, polish I am sure you require. Am I not right? As well, I wish above all things for Charity to be happy with her choice.''

"She is a taking thing, I must confess.'' Why did it annoy him that Miss Lonsbury would not be happy with him as a choice? "However, her clothing is quite outmoded and her behavior is that of a country miss. A diamond of the first water she is not. Do you feel you can instill a bit of sophistication in her in time for a house party? Of course I intend to have one. I am certain I can think of a few men who would make an eligible *parti*.'' One for snap decisions, he decided a house party would suit his own plans quite admirably. He gave Lady Tavington a shrewd look, wondering how she might bring that country miss up to snuff in time. "I can see you will need help. I am pleased to know I may be of assistance in my own small way. But what about her clothes? There can't be a modiste locally who will be acceptable?''

"I've looked in her closet and it is in a sad state of

affairs." Lady Tavington shook her head. "I will record her measurements and send to London for all that is required. Money can often accomplish wonders, can it not?"

"Money might accomplish wonders, but what about her behavior? As you said, she needs polishing." He regretted he had not been aware of that kiss. What prompted it? Intriguing thought. He would enjoy the touch of that petal-soft mouth on his.

"Leave that to me, my lord."

Outside the bedroom door a slender figure trembled beneath her chestnut cap of tumbled curls. Anger and hurt such as she never experienced before cut through her. This was her *preux chevalier*? This man who dismissed her with such hard assessment? She admitted to being a country miss, but lacking in manners? Her father would be most distressed to hear such accusation after his attempts to instill an education in her. She could not help her clothes, there had been no money for a fancy wardrobe. Swallowing bitter tears, she firmed a resolve. He would see! She would be as refined as any society lady!

4

EMOTIONS STILL SEETHING WITHIN her slender frame,
Charity sought the pale sunshine outside the cottage for
a few moments to compose herself, plan her actions and
words. Roscoe hopped up to her, begging attention.
Bending to scoop it up in her arms, she comforted
herself with the softness of its fur, its eagerness for her
company. She snuggled the warm, furry body close to
her, resting her chin against its head. It would take all
the resolution she could summon to deal with the anger
that churned inside her. What audacity his lordship had
to state she was such a . . . a . . . nothing! That Aunt
Tavington appeared to concur was overlooked for the
moment.

"Plague take it! Roscoe, I'm not all that beyond
hope, am I?" An impish grin crept across her face. She
would develop a manner so elegantly refined, a disposition so amiable, be such exhilarating company that all
his friends would seek her out. As for clothes? She
tugged at one of Roscoe's long ears in frustration. That
was a problem. Perhaps Aunt Tavington could contrive
something. She seemed to have a fund of money. If
Charity sold more blooms or plants, perhaps then. . .?
She shook her head in dismay. With more optimism
than reality, she hugged Roscoe close to her and
returned to the sitting room, careful to allow the door to
shut quite noisily behind her.

"Charity, dearest girl, come here." Lady Tavington
beamed at Charity from the doorway, beckoning with
an imperious motion of her hand.

Charity walked slowly to the door. As confident as
she might be, this was by far the most difficult thing she

had ever attempted to do. Could she actually pretend that she had not heard those awful words? He had cut her dreadflly with his cruel assessment. Yet she meant to show him what manner of woman she really was. It would take courage. She raised her chin in a way her father would have recognized boded no good for the one who angered her.

"What is it, Aunt Tavington?" Hervoice was soft and dulcet, just begging to give satisfaction. Roscoe wiggled as her hand tightened in its fur. A puzzled glance from her aunt drew no response.

"I have the most pleasant news, dearest child. Lord Kenrick is planning a house party. He insists we attend. You'll be able to meet some lovely new people."

Charity struggled with her expression, willing her eyes not to betray her inner feelings toward her erstwhile *preux chevalier*. Her shining knight in armor had developed a fatal case of rust. He was a stuffy, top-lofty snob. She was no fairy princess, for certain, but she was not a total antidote either. She hated him with all her tender being. What narrowness of heart, what littleness of mind he displayed. He was not worthy of her love!

Her face revealed a sweet mien. She gave a charming, proper reply. "What a lovley prospect, Aunt . . . my lord." She bestowed on him a smile that failed to reach her lovely eyes, eyes now frosted with her dislike. Her little curtsy was all that was right and suitable for the occasion. "It is very good of you to include me in your group. However, I fear I must decline. The clothes my papa deemed fitting for a village miss are hardly the thing with which to greet those newly come from London." The guileless look would have deceived anyone but her papa, and he was no longer there to caution her to guard her ways.

"That is easily dealt with, dearest girl. I have but to take your measurements and send them to my modiste in London. You shall have a wardrobe fitting for a young woman of your position." Lady Tavington gave a pleased nod, indicating she knew precisely what was to be required in spite of her being out of the country for so long.

Charity didn't doubt that in the least. A day or two in London with a modiste of the first stare would correct any outmoded ideas, to be sure.

"You are more than kind, dear Aunt. I can't believe it right for you to spend large sums on me. I fear it would take a great deal to turn this country miss into a society lady. I have not desired new clothes, and the orchids do not mind what I wear as long as they receive their attention."

She strolled to the window, then turned to face the others so her back was to the light. She couldn't depend on her slim acting ability to see her through this scene. Perhaps later she might be able to dissimulate with greater ease. It was one grace she hadn't anticipated cultivating.

Could she permit her dear aunt to purchase the clothes necessary to make her splash in the middle of Lord Kenrick's pond? It must be borne. It appeared to give the lady great pleasure, and Papa taught her to be gracious in receiving charity from others. This was one grace she had practiced a great deal.

Lord Kenrick's face wore a serious look. She caught a flare in his eyes, whether in anger or puzzlement, she couldn't tell.

"Pish tush. You will get all my estate once I'm gone. Why not use some of it now?" Aunt's question was artless, almost whimsical.

"You need the clothes. Surely you wish to attract a suitable husband?" Lord Kenrick said with an impatient wave of his hand, as though to brush aside her paltry objections.

"Naturally, that is every woman's desire, I'm sure." Charity quelled the urge to do something violent to his lordship. "However, I have enjoyed my solitude here, ma'am. Perhaps I am more given to the spinster state?" She stroked the soft fur, glad her trembling hands were concealed from view, while presenting an artfully woeful countenance to them. "What guarantee do I have I will find a man to care for me *and* my orchids? I wish for a kind, obliging, good-natured husband, a true gentleman. I would have the happy marriage my dear parents knew. Nothing could persuade me to marry without a deep feeling for my husband." Her eyes flashed in defiance as she glared at his lordship, so cosily ensconced in her own bed.

"You may change your mind, child, once you have an opportunity to meet eligible young men." Aunt Tavington clasped her hands in apparent dismay. The interview did not appear to be going as she wished.

Charity smiled to herself, concealing her amusement at the look of disdain on his lordship's face. She plunged forth into her next sentence after a fortifying breath. "Since his lordship appears to be so much improved, I took the liberty of suggesting his carriage come for him. Moffat agreed and has made all the arrangements. Surely his lordship will be more the thing in his own home? Lord Kenrick has recovered all his faculties, and you said his wound was healing nicely. He will no doubt improve even more rapidly in the comfort of his own bed with his own chef to prepare delicacies to tempt his palate." Charity glided over to the door, then paused. "Moffat should be here any moment with fresh clothes for you, Lord Kenrick."

She repressed a satisfied smile at the frown that settled on his lordship's forehead. It was evident he was not accustomed to anyone eagerly desiring his departure. It might be well to make clear just how little she wanted his company.

Lady Tavington gave Charity a vexed look, said nothing, then bustled over to the bedside. "Allow me to examine your head just one more time before you leave us, my lord. I will make another application of Wang Fu's most efficacious ointment to ensure the healing. I am persuaded it has done far more good than the local quack's nostrums might have."

Briskly setting about her task, she carefully checked

the wound, obviously pleased at the progress her treat-
ment brought about. Nodding, she bound the nearly
healed wound again, then gathered her small case in her
hands. "I trust we shall see you before too many days
elapse, my lord. Between us, we shall solve my small
dilemma, I'm certain."

"I appreciate the care you've expended on me, Lady
Tavington. Wang Fu and his medicine, plus your
attention, have made me a new man." He had needed
the rest as well, but could have managed without
Charity's assistance in that direction.

"Will your mother be in residence, Lord Kenrick? We
were bosom bows in our come-out days. I vow it will
give me great pleasure to visit with her once more."
Lady Tavington held her neat medicine kit in her hands
as she stood in graceful repose by the door, waiting for
Moffat to return with the carriage and Lord Kenrick's
clothes.

"As you know, I have need of a hostess for the house
party. Moffat has already sent my plea to her to assist
me. No doubt you will have ample opportunity to have
a comfortable coze with the lady. Perhaps we may
impose upon you to regale some of the highlights of
your travels for us? My mother has led a quiet life, for
the most part. She will enjoy a hearing of your more
daring exploits." Kenrick believed Lady Tavington
experienced far more than her share of unusual
episodes. The Mongol skirmish might be a bit too hair-
raising for a gently nurtured lady like his mother,
though. "Suitably edited, or course."

Lady Tavington made a rueful moue, giving a slight
nod of her head. "I understand far better than you
think. I doubt if my dear friends would believe my tales
were I to relate the whole cloth of it all. Why, just the
trip home, stopping along the South American coast,
seeing the amazing things people do with themselves is
almost beyond my belief . . . and I was there."

"Life here must seem dreadfully tame by
comparison." He found he had a liking for this
energetic and delightful lady.

"Every dinner has some bland foods to balance the spicy, my lord." She shook off the melancholy feeling that settled on her when she thought of the past year, and addressed the problem facing her at the present. "But Moffat comes to help you dress for your trip home. It is fortunate you live so close by here. You'll be under your own roof shortly. One always sleeps better in one's own bed." Then recalling young men and their romantic wanderings, she added, "Or so I've heard."

Lord Kenrick suppressed a smile and nodded with suitable gravity. "Quite so."

Moffat bustled into the room with a change of clothes for the impatient gentleman in the four-poster. In no time his lordship had left the room, bestowed a pat on the soft head of little Chico, said all that was proper to Lady Tavington, praised Mrs. Woods, and bowed over a subdued Charity's hand. He was the very image of a polished London gentleman. It shook Charity's resolve to remain firm in her dislike.

She strolled along at his side toward the handsome carriage awaiting him, commanding herself to be unswerving in her determination. She played idly with the delicate softness of Roscoe's ear. "I must thank you again for your kind invitation to your coming house party. I look forward to making the acquaintance of your friends . . . especially the gentlemen. I cannot impose on my dear Aunt Tavington indefinitely. You were right to suggest I find myself a husband."

His very touch had sent small thrills through her. Now, his eyes seemed to glow with a tender regard. Would that it was sincere! "If I may, I'll look upon you as the elder brother I never had." She bestowed a winsome smile on the tall man at her side. Trying to pretend his lordship was a freckled-faced lad who might lend support was stretching her abilities to the ultimate. "I have long envied my friends with older brothers to guide them through the labyrinths of society. Do say you'll not mind." Her plea was ingenious, the hands clasped below her chin pure inspiration.

Lord Kenrick's composure was ruffled at the sight of

the undoubtedly charming young woman begging him
to consider her as a sister. It was an experience he'd
never had in all his lifetime. It rankled; it didn't sit well
in the least. For all her country ways, she was a very
captivating minx. There was nothing he could say to it,
however, so he nodded politely. "I will be pleased to
assist in any way I can, Miss Lonsbury." To Lady
Tavington he added, "Don't hesitate to call upon me if
the need arises. I can sympathize with the enormity of
your problem. Thank you again for all your kindness."

Lady Tavington darted a shrewd look at Charity.
Custard wouldn't melt in her mouth at the moment.
"Let us not forget the unfortunate accident that
brought you to this cottage." She made a suitably
expressive face as she glanced at Charity. "I consider
this as a challenge, my lord. I find it comforting to
know I can depend on you for help." Lady Tavington
stood back to watch as Lord Kenrick entered his
carriage, then signaled his driver to proceed.

Charity remained before the cottage as the elegant
equipage disappeared from sight around the curve of
the road. He was gone. Hateful, odious man, so sure of
himself, so condescending! Pleased to assist her! She
knew what those thinly veiled remarks between the
marquess and her aunt meant. She was a challenge.
How lowering to have her inadequacies revealed in such
a way! Oh, the injustice of it all, to have her manners
and her looks cast into a shade by such a man. At last
she slowly sauntered back to the cottage, reluctant to
face her aunt after the performance she'd just given.

Mrs. Woods fluttered in verbose delight at his
lordship's kind words on her cooking abilities. Lady
Tavington directed those energies into changing the
linen on the bed and dusting the spotless room. She
ignored Charity for the moment, something for which
Charity was profoundly grateful. Charity wandered list-
lessly back out the door and into the garden, the sparkle
gone from the day, the sunshine dull, uninviting, even
though good weather was surely drawing to a close for
the season.

September promised to be a glorious month if the
delicate cerulean sky with wisps of clouds was anything
to go by. The temperature was warmer than normal,
leaves clinging to the trees with colorful abandon, their
golds and crimsons splashing a riot of autumn display.
Deep forest greens accented the completely unnoticed
variegated exhibit.

"He is gone, Roscoe," she announced to the rabbit
she placed on the garden path. "Now I have to perfect
all those graces with which I intend to impress his
friends. Aunt can surely help me; she met a great variety
of people on her travels, I'm sure. Customs can't have
altered all that much since she made her bow to society.
Perhaps the ladies of the Chinese court. . . ?" She
giggled at the mere thought, cheered at her silliness.

Lord Kenrick had looked more elegant than all of her
memories rolled into one. He was taller than she
recalled, with that commanding air of his even greater
than before. His rich voice, that thick black hair she still
longed to thread her fingers through, those penetrating
eyes, made him an altogether daunting prospect. She
had discovered a dimple beside his mouth when he
laughed at Chico's antics. Teeth that were straight and
white had flashed an engaging grin, and those eyes, so
blue, so intense, had looked deeply into hers until she
was certain he could see every thought, every secret in
her heart. She had so gently touched his hand, and liked
the firm, smooth skin. None of which assisted her determination to remain aloof from the man. And then he
had crashed her pretensions to the ground with his cruel
assessment of her. It was too, too much, she whispered
to Roscoe.

Her meditations were interrupted by the sound of an
approaching coach. Although acknowledging the
unlikelihood of his lordship returning to pay her
fulsome compliments, her heart leapt up at the thought,
and she rushed to the gate.

A coach covered with the dust of a long trip pulled up
in front of the cottage. Undoubtedly it was Parton,
belatedly arriving with Lady Tavington's effects.

The promise of being measured for new clothes and the lure of pretty parasols, new shoes, and other dainty things to go with the dresses brought a reconciled smile to her face. It was the first thing Parton saw when she scrambled from the hired coach.

"La, if I had to ride another mile I'm certain I'd have expired for sure." The tall, sturdy woman could not have been more unlike the slim, dainty Lady Tavington. Parton brandished her parasol about as she directed the coachman and his man to set down the trunks, ordered this and that with the greatest of aplomb. She was almost masculine in her voice, which was a deep contralto. But she was efficient, seemed kindly in her manner, and didn't shriek when she observed Roscoe snuggled in Charity's arms. With this last item she won Charity's everlasting devotion.

Once the boxes and trunks were deposited in the cottage, Parton looked around with an assessing gaze. "I have all your things, my lady. Where shall I place your clothes and all?"

Charity motioned to the bedchamber his lordship had recently vacated. "I would have my aunt use this room. I'll help you, Parton. You rest in the garden, dear Aunt. We won't be long in arranging your things."

Mrs. Woods sniffed. "As if I'd let ye do that when I've two perfectly good hands. Away with ye, miss. Let those who know how to cope with trunks and parcels at their work." She was bursting with curiosity and could scarcely conceal her anxiousness to converse with this abigail. Parton was not condescending in the least, a fact Mrs. Woods mightly appreciated.

Charity slowly trailed behind her aunt into the somnolent quiet of the garden. Afternoon sun anointed the flower with touches of gold. She watched Chico's antics with a brooding smile on her mouth.

"Well, miss? And what do you have to say?" Lady Tavington strolled over to a wooden bench and seated herself in the shade of a beech tree.

Charity took a basket and began to snip off the heads

of damask roses to dry for potpourri. While the flowers were better plucked in the morning, she needed something to occupy her hands. Together with white jasmine, cloves, and allspice, the potpourri would provide a delightful scent all through the cottage during the long winter months. She would sew little muslin bags to place potpourri in all the drawers and set bowls of the aromatic petal mixture in every room.

"Tell me why you chose to instruct Moffat to call for his lordship's carriage without consulting either Lord Kenrick or myself. It was very forward of you, miss."

"You said he was much better and Parton was to arrive. The cottage is not large, dear Aunt. We would have been crowded. Yet I did not want his lordship to feel I was complaining or anything of that kind." Charity raised her shoulders in a sort of indifferent shrug.

Lady Tavington watched this display with a touch of disbelief on her charming countenance. "What you say is true. Yet I get the impression there was else behind it." Sensing Charity would not confide in her at the moment, she changed the subject. "As soon as Parton and Mrs. Woods have finished settling our things, I intend to begin taking your measurements and compiling the list to go to London. Do you ride, Charity?"

The young woman raised her head with amusement clearly written on her face. "And how would I learn with a papa who detested the animals? I haven't had the pleasure, Aunt. Though I *am* familiar with all the country dances, reels, and the like. I've not learned the waltz, however. Papa felt it was far too wicked for an unmarried girl."

"Fiddle! I vow that brother of mine was not as saintly as all that when he was a lad. I will engage someone to instruct you. Doubtless the waltz will be performed at Lord Kenrick's ball. What *did* my brother allow?"

Charity sank down in a graceful heap near the wooden bench, her basket of blooms a colorful contrast against the demure white gown she wore. "I helped him with his book on Christian names. He was ever fascinated with the beginning of things, names in particular." She slanted a mischievous look at Lady Tavington. "For instance, Alice is from the Greek, meaning 'truth.' "

"Lord Kenrick's given name is David."

"David means 'beloved,' or so Papa said." A disbelieving sniff accompanied this revelation. "Not all names are appropriate. Now Miss Euphremia Spencer's name means 'fair speech.' The original Euphremia was a virgin-martyr of Bithnia. You will most likely meet our Euphremia, as she comes to visit often." Charity grinned at the thought of Euphremia face to face with Lady Tavington.

"And is she of fair speech?" Lady Tavington was enjoying this side of her dear niece very much.

"I cannot say about fair, but she certainly is full of speech." Euphremia was full of airs, too, being the daughter of a baron. Charity wished the squire would look in her direction for a lady to wed.

Parton briskly strode from the cottage. "All is in readiness, my lady. We can begin now if you wish."

Lady Tavington rose from the bench and followed the large frame of her abigail into the cottage. Charity drifted along, reluctant to reveal her anxious desire to have the measurements made and the order sent off to London.

"Parton is quite capable at measuring, Charity. Come now, remove that sweet dress and allow her to proceed."

Charity blushed at the idea of standing in the sitting room in her shift and petticoat, but complied all the same. It was a fascinating, though tiring procedure. Once completed, she donned her dress again and seated herself at the deal table next to Aunt Tavington, with the estimable Parton on the other side.

"What do you think, Parton? Ivory, peach and cream, russet and gold. I think these are the colors that will set off the lovely complexion and those charming gray eyes."

The deep contralto boomed forth, "Periwinkle as well, my lady. It would do nicely for a warm pelisse. Coral might be good on her, with her coloring. Deep brown, too."

"The warm colors . . . to reflect her warm nature, to be sure. I know the rage is for white and delicate pastels, but we seek to make you an original, child. Insipid colors would wash you out, I vow. Though a dress of mignonette green might be all the thing for you."

Charity listened in a growing daze as ball dresses, walking dresses, pelisses, afternoon and evening dresses, and even the new pantalettes—ordered with rows and rows of lace—were placed on the list. There was to be a gold crape over white satin, a dress of net over a slip of delicate periwinkle sarcenet. Other specifications included mameluke sleeves on one garment, a ruff at the neck of a day dress. Suggestions for embroideries around the hems were elaborate. Charity felt her head begin to swim when Lady Tavington wrote down the order for an ivory satin ball gown with the design of oak leaves executed in gold around the hem, to emphasize the idea of living at Greenoaks.

"Dear Aunt Tavington, all this will cost a fortune. I fear I cannot allow you to such excesses."

"Pish tush, child. I haven't had such fun in an age. Now for the hats. I have a few instructions regarding this subject as well. Is there anyone in the village who might have the bonnets to trim?"

Charity gasped weakly. "There is a shop near the center of the village where the latest in bonnets, so I'm told, are to be found."

"Perhaps. I'll order feathers to match the dresses . . . and I may as well list a few bonnets. My modiste has exquisite taste and I trust her implicitly. She is sure to think of anything we may have forgotten. I declare, I do like all the feathers in vogue at the present. So feminine." She added to Parton, "Do you recall the ladies at the Chinese court? Their headdresses and embroidered silk gowns? It is good to be home again. At least for a while."

The two ladies welcomed the steaming pot of tea and delicate cakes Mrs. Woods set upon the table.

Charity rose from her chair on trembling limbs. The efforts of the past hour had driven all thoughts of the elegant Lord Kenrick from her head, for the moment. "I don't know how to thank you, dear Aunt. It is too much."

She acknowledged a feeling of guilt for the anger she harbored in a niche somewhere in the recesses of her mind. It was clear Lady Tavington was an essential part of the scheme to make Charity over into a lady of the *ton* and suitable marriage material.

"Little enough for my favorite niece. Mind you, when you go out, put a bonnet over that lovely hair. We must eliminate that sprinkling of freckles from that little nose."

"I know just the thing," Parton intoned.

Charity picked up the bonnet, frowning at the unadorned brim. She had been happy to have any kind of a bonnet to place on her head in the past. Slipping past the two women engrossed in the writing of the order, she fled to the garden.

Roscoe hopped up to her, a pleading look in its eyes. She scooped the rabbit in her arms and wandered over to the wooden bench beneath the beech tree. She stroked its satiny fur, murmuring into a suitably receptive ear, "Won't there be one freckle left to call my own?"

5

"CHARITY, DEAREST GIRL, YOU are drooping like a new planted cabbage. I can't think this is all too much for you." Lady Tavington surveyed the lovely figure submitting to the proddings and pinnings of the modiste while emitting faint sighs and wistful looks out of the window.

Charity gave a startled glance at her aunt. "Indeed not, Aunt." The image of Lord Kenrick before he entered his equipage to return to the great house persisted in haunting her. All that seemed to stay in her mind was that delightful look of tender regard that had briefly warmed his eyes. Her cheeks pinkened even as she thought of it. She straightened her spine and lifted her head to challenge the memory. Best to think of him as a brother, not the lover she dreamed of all these years. Somehow Lord Kenrick refused to fit her perception of a brother. She simply wasn't trying hard enough, that was all. As she had never had a brother, the problem was not simplified for her.

Lady Tavington repressed a smile at the valiant figure swathed in peach silk. Actually her posture was exemplary, but no woman could forget herself and permit a droop of the spine to creep over her. "Your mama did well by you, child. You carry yourself quite nicely. But then, you and your sisters had a loving home, did you not?"

"We were fortunate, indeed, Aunt. I was very grateful to Mama that we did not have to suffer a backboard to perfect our posture as did poor Miss Spencer. It may have been her example that made us all determined to stand straight so we would not require such a thing." As a child Charity had pitied Euphremia for being forced to wear a heart-shaped backboard strapped to her back. Thankfully, Charity's mama had leaned toward the philosophy of Maria Edgeworth when it came to discipline. Mama had accepted that affection could accomplish more than beatings. Her girls could acquire a dignified and gentle bearing without such aids.

Charity jumped as a pin penetrated her cambric undergarments and her skin. She made no complaint, remembering that ladies should not allow such things to upset them.

"Enough on this one, I think. Since you sent the measurements along with the list of garments you require, my work is that much easier, madam." The modiste bobbed a small curtsy in Lady Tavington's direction before easing the peach silk evening dress over Charity's head.

Lady Tavington poured a cup of tea from the fresh pot Mrs. Woods had just brought to the table, and offered it to a weary Charity. "It was so thoughtful of Lord Kenrick to send one of his grooms to London with the order for your clothes. And then to have him wait until Madame Clotilde was prepared to come was beyond anything! However, I am glad you have the sense not to form a *tendre* for his lordship. Not that you are ineligible for his attention. Never forget you are the granddaughter of an earl. But," she gave an attractive sigh, "his lordship is quite high in the instep, I'm sure. Moffat informed me that his lordship's intended, Lady Sylvia Wilde, is all that is proper. If Moffat is to be believed, she never puts a foot wrong."

"How deadly dull," muttered Charity to her teacup. She smiled at the modiste who was shaking out a periwinkle pelisse such as Lady Tavington had specified. The pelisse had a lining of soft gray fur that caught Charity's eye. What luxury! "Aunt. . . ?" Her anxious look was correctly interpreted by her dear aunt, who shook her head in a cautionary admonition.

"It will not be long until the chill of autumn is upon

us. You can scarcely find a suitable husband while in bed with a fever." She checked over the lengthy list in her hand once again, glancing at the clothes heaped on chairs about the room as she ticked off each item on the list.

"All that remains is the ball gown with the embroidery of oak leaves entwined around the skirt. It ought to be in gold on ivory satin, I think." She murmured something to Madame Clotilde, and the two women bent their heads over a sketch the modiste drew from a thin folio where she kept the drawing of the gowns she created.

Charity peeked over her aunt's shoulder and smiled with delight at the design on the paper. The elaborate interweaving of oak leaves and acorns was extremely pleasing. She turned to dress, then made a retreat to the hothouses. Her orchids were in danger of being neglected, and no man was worth that.

Her aunt put out a staying hand. "Charity, I would that you put on one of the dresses Madame Clotilde brought with her. You never know when the guests will arrive or when you may confront someone."

Nodding, Charity donned a pale-apricot muslin, wondering just how she was supposed to keep it spotless while she worked around the orchids. The gray apron was surreptitiously tugged from its nail and smuggled from the room. Fortunately, Aunt Tavington was so occupied with Madame Clotilde she did not notice.

Roscoe hopped along the path as Charity wound her way to the hothouses. "You won't know me by the time they finish, Roscoe. I'm to have my hair coiffed and there is a box of bonnets that simply overwhelms me every time I look at them. Aunt Tavington says I must learn the waltz. To my knowledge there is no dancing master near by. I wonder how she intends to locate one for me?"

Charity sighed, then scooped up her rabbit, disregarding any smudges it might make on her gown. Fortunately the apron prevented little furry feet from making contact with the delicate muslin. "I perceive this entire exercise is going to be more than I anticipated, dear Roscoe."

The days that followed were full of fittings and the promised coiffure. While on a visit to the marchioness, Lady Tavington discovered a dancing master was teaching in the next town. Summoned to the cottage, he deigned to instill the steps of the waltz to a graceful Charity, who proved an adept pupil.

Later, following her somewhat exhausting schedule, Lady Tavington compelled a reluctant Charity along with her to tea in the great house. Charity was of the opinion it was better not to know what she must forgo with Lord Kenrick now off her list of eligible men. However, she could not explain to Aunt Tavington why she felt as she did.

The meeting with the marchioness was a distinct surprise. First of all, she was a plump woman of average height, hardly what one might expect of the mother of so tall and impressive a figure as Lord Kenrick. Second, she was as charming and sweet a woman as anyone could hope to meet. *His* charm was dubious and he wasn't sweet.

"My dear Alice, how long it has been since we shared secrets during our come-out days. David tells me you have traveled all over the world since then. How brave of you, my dear. I shudder at the trip from London down here."

Lady Tavington smiled, promising to share a few stories later. She glanced at Charity. "You have met my niece, Charity Lonsbury? My brother Peter's girl. She lives on the estate in one of the cottages while she tends her father's collection of orchids. Alas, he has been gone this past year or more. Such a shock, returning to England to discover he was no longer among us. I cannot allow her to remain alone, however. The naughty girl has refused to turn to my brother, the Earl of Nevile, for assistance. Instead, she persists in living here with only the cook-housekeeper for company. I intend to change that, I can tell you."

Charity rose and wandered off to gaze out the window. It was simply too embarrassing to sit quietly while the two ladies discussed her future as though she was a piece of property. But then, wasn't that what a woman was? First she was her parent's property, then her husband's. Never could a woman call her life her own—unless a widow.

A stir at the door brought her head around. A peach blush tinted her cheeks as she saw Lord Kenrick enter the room to cross to his mother's side. Charity bowed her head to study her hands. Where had the bold miss who had stolen a kiss from this handsome man gone?

"David, you know my guests, do you not? Lady Tavington and I have been friends this age and I knew Charity's mama slightly." They had met but once, yet that hardly mattered at this point. Lady Kenrick beamed fondly at her son.

His eyes were caught in Charity's demure gaze. Her blush deepened as she recalled the touch of her lips against his. As though he read her mind, his expression softened, a tenderness rarely seen entered his eyes for a brief moment.

At the rustle of skirts behind Lord Kenrick, Charity turned her head to behold an exquisite blonde with pale-blue eyes who was dressed in the first stare of fashion. Her traveling dress of soft brown was accented with black braid *à la militaire*. A black plume curled over one cheek from the hat perched arrogantly atop her carefully arranged curls. She carried a sable muff, which Charity thought a bit overdone, seeing the weather was still pleasant. She greeted the marchioness and Lady Tavington with the aplomb of a seasoned society lady in a voice Charity could only describe as chilling. It reminded Charity of a mountaintop, cold and remote.

Charity acknowledged Lady Sylvia's civil greeting with a murmur, recognizing the Red Rose scent wafting her way from a visit she paid to the Floris perfume shop while in London. It was an unforgettable, expensive fragrance.

If she had any thought to engage his lordship's

attention or affections, they were well and truly sunk now. Lady Sylvia looked elegant, dressed like an illustration from *La Belle Assemblée*, and spoke with the soft, high-pitched accents of a well-bred woman—sophisticated, charming, all Charity felt she lacked. She endured the remainder of the tea with stoic calm, entering into the conversation when pressed, retiring when possible. Lady Sylvia was more than a bit overwhelming.

Then she recalled her vow: to captivate his friends, be scintillating, sparkle so all would be at her side. Ha! What a foolish notion that was. Another stir at the doorway and a gentleman entered at the heels of the stiffly reserved butler, Jameson. Lord Kenrick turned to greet the newcomer.

"Geoff, old man. Good to see you could post down here to join our little party."

"As if anyone would refuse an invitation from you. Doing it a bit brown, old friend."

"Ladies, allow me to present Lord Geoffrey Powell."

Charity observed the others as they greeted Lord Powell. He was incredibly dressed, to her eyes. His high starched shirt points vied with his neckcloth in exquisite detail. Several seals and fobs hung at his waist. His coat of bottle-green superfine fitted him with elegant care and the primrose breeches clung to surprisingly well-formed legs . . . for a man one might consider a dandy and not given to sporting interests. He was top-of-the-trees, for certain.

Lord Powell said all that was proper to the older ladies, greeted Lady Sylvia with the air of an old friend, then turned to Charity. Inspecting her mignonette-green dress of delicate muslin in the very latest mode, the chestnut curls peeping from beneath the brim of her elaborate cottage bonnet, he smiled and bowed over Charity's hand with a polished address. "Miss Lonsbury. It is indeed a pleasure to make your acquaintance."

Charity glanced at Lord Kenrick to note he appeared

displeased. Heavens, was she doing something wrong? She set out to captivate Lord Powell, as she had planned what seemed like so long ago. "Lord Powell, I'm delighted." She admitted a genuine pleasure at meeting Lord Powell. Any woman would be happy to have so admiring a gallant at her side. He was suave, with a delicately languid air, but there lurked a faintly amused gleam in his eyes.

Charity was glad that her mameluke sleeves hid her arms, which must be trembling. She hadn't participated in company quite this elevated before. Glancing down at the flounced skirt, wider than any she had owned in the past, she wondered what on earth she could say to the gentleman.

She was spared the effort as the proper time to depart arrived. Silently thanking the conventions that made it mandatory she and her aunt leave, she curtsied gracefully to the marchioness, the assembled party, and edged toward the door, for some reason avoiding the gaze from Lord Kenrick she sensed was upon her.

"Allow me." She found Lord Kenrick at her side, escorting her past Jameson to the front door, which now stood open, revealing the carriage that awaited Lady Tavington and her on the curved drive. There was no avoiding the touch of his hand as he assisted her into the carriage. Cream ribbons fluttered on her dress as her heart performed the most alarming palpitations within her breast.

"Thank you, my lord." She raised brave eyes to meet the intense blue of his. That displeasure had disappeared, replaced by a searching gaze that seemed to penetrate to her very bones. A rueful smile crossed his lips as his hand held hers just a bit longer than proper. He shook his head in a chagrined manner.

"You have begun well. It seems a female does not require much time or practice to learn to flirt." His mouth straightened into a thin line, his grip tightened on the dainty hand he retained.

"I am not a flirt, my lord. Unless that is what you call

mere politeness.'' Her expressive eyes were veiled by long, thick laches for a moment, then raised in a beguiling smile, her mouth curving with an ironic twist. ''I was under the impression you invited Lord Powell here as a potential husband for me. Surely I must put forth my best efforts at friendliness? How glad I am I have learned the waltz. I perceive it would be enchanting to be Lord Powell's partner. I am greatly in your debt, Lord Kenrick.'' She settled against the plush squabs with a pleased air.

Her hand was abruptly released.

''Good day, Lord Kenrick. It was nice to see you again. We will meet soon, I trust?'' Lady Tavington raised her brows in a significant manner, then signaled to the driver to depart.

Lord Kenrick remained for a moment before returning to the house. Only his mother noticed the faint abstraction that appeared to cling to him.

Confident of her powers of attraction, Lady Sylvia smiled at the assembled group with the satisfaction of a *femme du monde*. Never would one suspect that underneath the fine clothes and plumes, Lady Sylvia was in a state of near desperation. Just before leaving her home, word had come that her father had lost nearly all their money on a turn of the cards. Her generous dowry was gone. Her only hope was to bring Lord Kenrick up to scratch. Once the *ton* got word of her situation, she would be hard-pressed to find a husband.

In the carriage rumbling down the perfectly maintained, graveled drive, Charity chanced to peek at her aunt. The other woman was absently smoothing out her Limerick gloves while studying Charity.

''Perhaps it *is* instinctive. I know of no other reason. You *were* flirting, dearest child. Very nicely, too, I might add. I cannot understand why Lord Kenrick didn't applaud your efforts. Such sweet, genteel manners can only bring approval, I am sure.'' Lady Tavington beamed a satisfied smile and leaned back against the well-cushioned squabs with a sigh.

''Lord Kenrick would seem to have his hands full,

Aunt. Lady Sylvia does not appear to be the kind of woman who will let her intended look astray for a moment.'' Charity snapped the words testily as she thought of the cool blond beauty languishing in the great house now behind them. Not that Charity cared, mind you. It simply seemed to her that his lordship deserved a nicer woman that Lady Sylvia.

"And do you want him . . . to stray?" The soft question caught Charity up short.

"Never! I detest the man!" Her vehemence was a bit overdone, the words too dramatic.

Her aunt looked at the becoming blush, which revealed more than words how her niece felt toward Kenrick. So why the refusal to admit a *tendre*, no matter how small, toward the man? Pride? It would bear consideration.

Charity managed to elude the probing looks from her aunt by the simple expedient of retreating to the hothouse. Certain no one would disturb her at her work among the fragrant blooms, she watered, snipped faded flowers, and thought. Examining a plant that had produced an unusual, enormous, deep red-violet bloom, she paused. What was she to do? As much as she detested Lord Kenrick, she couldn't deny the powerful attraction she felt toward him. Was it possible to hate and love at the same time? She couldn't ask Aunt Tavington about these bewildering emotions. That dear lady might be shocked to hear such words from a supposedly pure-minded minister's daughter. Charity ignored the memory of the kiss that she was quite sure Aunt Tavington witnessed.

Roscoe stirred at her feet, and Charity looked toward the door. Mrs. Woods entered in a pother.

"Miss Spencer has come to call, Miss Charity. Yer aunt says to get there right now, if you please, miss." The order was given with the familiarity of a family retainer of long standing.

"Euphremia? What can she want, I wonder?" Miss Spencer came to call when she had a juicy tidbit of news or was wanting to learn something. The lady pretended to be the embodiment of rectitude, but underneath that proper exterior lay, Charity was sure, the heart of a true gossip. Thankful her dress was unsoiled from her time in the hothouse, Charity hurried down the path to the cottage.

The door was caught by Mrs. Woods as Charity sailed across the floor to greet her long-time friend and, she suspected, foe. "Dear Miss Spencer. How kind of you to call. Aunt Tavington, Miss Spencer is the daughter of Baron Peregrine Spencer. We have known each other since we were in leading strings. Tea, of course, dear Euphremia?" Charity led the tall, thin woman to the closest chair, seating her with solicitous care. "We haven't see you in an age."

Euphremia's unusually large hazel eyes fastened upon Charity first, then shifted to Lady Tavington. In her longish face, they were in proportion, but Lady Tavington later swore she had never seen such eyes in her life. If Euphremia was an accomplished equestrian, it would be very appropriate, for her face bore an unfortunate resemblance to that animal. Mouse-brown hair added to the illusion.

"La, dear Charity, I perceive you have been busy, what with the modiste from London and the dancing master as well. I do like your coiffure, truly most becoming." Her thin, high voice held a coy note that did not become her. Charity always had the impression that Euphremia would dearly love to see her at the ends of the earth. Euphremia's feeings were probably due to an attachment she formed for the squire. What a pity Charity couldn't simply hand the squire to a lady who would appreciate him. Charity draped her paisley shawl about her shoulders, absently enjoying the scent of patchouli that wafted up from it.

Mrs. Woods bustled into the parlor bearing a tray laden with a fat pot of tea and a selection of her special cakes and buns. Setting it before Lady Tavington, she retreated to the kitchen, there to eavesdrop quite shamelessly.

"I gather you know all about the party at Greenoaks. Quite the most excitement we have had around here in ages." There was more than curiosity in her voice and Charity wondered at it. "I suppose you will be joining them?" Miss Spencer was aware of the envious position Charity was in, what with her being the granddaughter of an earl and entertaining Lady Tavington just now.

The knowledge came suddenly to Charity. "I am certain his lordship intends to invite you to the little amusements he is arranging for his group. I suspect the squire will be in attendance as well. It is probably naught but a light alfresco refreshment, perhaps a ride to view the ruins at Lullingstone, and of course the ball."

"The ruins are a day's ride. Do you think his lordship really intends to go so far afield?" Euphremia asked.

The sound of a horse clattering up to the gate of the cottage brought all the ladies' attention to the door. Mrs. Woods scurried to the door even before the knocker was lifted.

Charity rose with a marked lack of enthusiasm. "Lord Kenrick! How . . . how nice to see you again." She glanced at the awed face of her guest and made the introductions. "We were just discussing the flurry of activity in the neighborhood."

Euphremia was determined to wangle an invitation if the squire was to attend. She managed it with no effort, for Lord Kenrick turned to her with flattering grace, requesting her attendance. Euphremia giggled—unfortunately.

Charity decided that with Euphremia's giggle and the squire's irritating throat, the two were meant for each other, though she was aware that squire detested Euphremia. She attended Euphremia as the tall young woman hurried to take her leave. If there was to be a picnic, a ride, and a ball, the dressmaker would have to be pressed to work with all possible speed. Her thanks were prettily said and she left in maidenly confusion.

Lord Kenrick didn't remain long, drawing Charity

with him to the gate as he left. "I, ah, thought perhaps you might enjoy this little trifle, Miss Lonsbury, knowing how much you enjoy the scent of flowers and all." He drew from his pocket a small package and handed it to Charity. "It is in the interest of bringing you up to snuff, of course."

Her hands touched his as she accepted the gift. A warm glow suffused her body as their fingers seemed to cling a moment as though reluctant to part. Then his last words penetrated and she drew away.

The "trifle" turned out to be a delicately beautiful Waterford scent bottle. Charity scraped off the wax of the seal, then lifted the stopper to inhale the fragrance of lavender. "How lovely . . . most kind." She slanted him a mischievous look. "Although this is more, I think, than a brother usually gives to his sister."

He ignored the annoying reference to his being like a brother, a depressing thought. "The man at Yardley's poured and sealed the scent at my request." He made an offhand gesture. "It gave my groom something to do while in the city." He didn't know why he was making so light a thing of his efforts. He had sent a written express to London, requesting the finest Waterford scent bottle to be found, insisting the lavender water be only from Yardley's. It gave him an inordinate amount of pleasure to see her delight. He had guessed she had had little enough of such fripperies.

"Indeed, Lord Kenrick, I am honored with your gift. I shall enjoy the fragrance." And think of him every time she applied it. Was that what he intended? She wished she knew. There was no lurking tenderness such as she glimpsed before, and she was sorry to see him become the stiffly proper gentleman again.

She wasn't certain she should accept such an expensive gift from him, but then his words returned, those words that had cut and pained her so much. She moved toward the gate in gentle dismissal, allowing the sun to rest on her head, pleased with the warmth on a cool day.

Lord Kenrick watched the graceful, poised young

woman before him. How had she bloomed so quickly? Lady Tavington must indeed be a magician. The sun shone on Charity's hair, making it appear as if she wore a halo of fire. He wondered if her temper had improved any. Fingering the thin scar near his hairline, he added, "Perhaps this will ensure I remain in your good graces?"

She understood his reference as she observed his hand leave his forehead. Her frown was sincere. "I hope you have suffered no further ill effects, my lord."

"None at all. Two more gentlemen are due tomorrow or the next day to complete the party. Perhaps the lavender scent will aid in catching one of them." He tossed the words off in a casual manner, putting her in her place.

If the scent bottle hadn't been Waterford and full of her favorite perfume, Charity would have thrown it straight at his top-lofty head. Instead, she watched silently as he effortlessly mounted his Arabian horse, fuming, but not betraying by a muscle how angry she was with him. Just why his words should put her in such a pother, she didn't pause to think.

She smiled with false sweetness. "I shall do my utmost, my lord. I do not wish to be a burden upon anyone, especially my dear aunt. I can only hope that one of your friends will be my solution." She took note of the quick frown that flashed across his face before he rode toward the great house.

Good. She had annoyed him. He annoyed her, too. She stamped back to the thatched-roof cottage, slammed the door behind her, then placed the scent bottle on the table with an ostentatious flourish.

"He gave me a present . . . to help me ca-catch a husband." Then she burst into tears and ran up the circular staircase to the comfort of her bed.

Lady Tavington picked up the costly scent bottle, a considering smile on her face as she watched her niece flee the room.

6

CHARITY GAZED LONGINGLY AT the elegant russet riding habit. Displayed on her figure as revealed in the mirror of the bedroom Lady Tavington now occupied, it was beautiful. "Aunt, I believe I *did* inform you that I do not ride? This is very lovely, the essence of everything I might wish for in a riding habit, but what good is it to me?" She made a graceful swirl around as she wondered where Aunt Tavington thought she might come by a horse even if she did overcome her reluctance to mount one of them.

"Did I forget to tell you? Lord Kenrick most thoughtfully offered to provide a sweet-going little mare from his own stable for you. Was that not kind of the dear man?" With a coy tilt of her head, Lady Tavington added, "I believe Lord Powell would delight in giving you instruction, dearest. He is noted to be a most accomplished rider, or so I have been informed."

A wisp of a smile fluttered across Charity's lips. Her cheeks warmed at the thought of that most polished and fashionable gentleman giving a lowly country miss her first riding lesson. "I imagine a groom as a teacher would be far more practical. It may turn out that I have no aptitude for the sport."

"Pish tush. You must have inherited the talent along with your beautiful hair. Your mama had an excellent seat before my dear brother decided horses were beyond him. He couldn't afford to keep a stable, so horses became a nasty threat to you all. I'm sure you'll do just fine, my love."

Charity's heart sank as she heard the unmistakable

sound of hooves clattering down the lane. "You didn't, he wouldn't," she stammered.

Parton handed her the tasteful hat that matched the habit, its russet plume smartly accenting the black beaver felt, then a pair of York tan gloves. Charity walked to the door, her black half-boots making mournful little clicks as she went. She had a sinking feeling this was not to be her best moment.

Near the cottage gate waited Lady Sylvia, Lord Kenrick, and Lord Powell, plus the little mare intended, Charity presumed, for her to ride. His face schooled to stoicism, a groom patiently held the reins of the mare. For a "little" mare, the horse seemed huge. Charity gave a wavering smile to Lord Powell as he gallantly opened the gate, then made her acquaintance with the docile animal.

"Why don't we ride on, Lord Kenrick? I am persuaded Miss Lonsbury will not thank us for witnessing her first go at riding." Lady Sylvia's cool tones rang clearly through the morning air.

Charity could only applaud the suggestion, though she suspected it came more from a desire to be alone with Lord Kenrick than an effort to spare her own blushes. The attendant groom who followed barely counted as a chaperone, but then, those two were almost betrothed, were they not?

The gleam in Lord Powell's eyes disconcerted her for only a moment. Wasn't this what she sought? "Thank you for your thoughtfulness. I could only wish I might spare Lord Powell the anguish of trying to teach me." She looked at Lord Kenrick and found him smiling enigmatically. The intense blue of his eyes blinded her to all else for a moment.

Wrapping her poise about her, she turned to Powell. "We may as well get this over, my lord. I confess I wonder if Lady Tavington has made a mistake in her efforts." She didn't explain the remark, hoping he might take it as referring to the riding. She glanced at the discreet groom, then to Lord Powell.

Lord Powell explained the basics she must master before giving Charity an assist into the saddle. It seemed alarmingly high in the air. She decided it was better to look ahead than down at the ground, less frightening that way, she was sure. Gradually she loosened the death grip she had on the reins and began not only to relax, but to enjoy the casual walk through the estate. So many times she had wandered this path by herself on foot. The view appeared entirely different from this perspective.

Smiling shyly at Lord Powell, Charity ventured her opinion of the morning effort. "I must confess I am agreeably surprised, my lord." She leaned forward to place a tentative pat on the mare's neck. "This little lady seems quite reconciled to my company."

"You surprise me, Miss Lonsbury. Are you certain you have not ridden before? You appear to have a natural seat on the horse. Let us try a faster gait." He signaled his roan, and before Charity knew it, her horse had responded to the increased speed, following behind Lord Powell.

She was almost sorry when Lord Powell called an end to the morning's outing. "You will find a certain amount of discomfort after performing an unaccustomed exercise. Might I suggest a warm soak in a scented tub?"

Detesting the heat she could feel stealing into her cheeks, she accepted his help in dismounting and felt foolish as she stumbled forward into his arms. "I am sorry, my lord," she gasped. "My legs seem strangely reluctant to cooperate."

Geoffrey Powell gazed down into the silvery eyes that beseeched him. "Actually, it is not so surprising. You will get accustomed to it in time, you know. Allow me to help you to the cottage."

Charity glanced to the side in time to see Lord Kenrick and Lady Sylvia approaching. Lord Kenrick gave her a solemn look before turning to smile at Lady Sylvia. Taking refuge in the kind attentions from Lord

Powell, she beamed her warmest smile at him, allowing him to help her into the house. The door closed behind her with a complacent click.

Mrs. Woods clucked at Charity as she nudged her toward her temporary room upstairs. "Lady Tavington insisted ye are to 'ave a bath. Aching muscles, I expect. Come along, miss. I've put a drop of my lavender essence in the water."

Chico decided to join in the bath time, swinging along from stair to stair, until it scampered into Charity's room and perched on her bed, watching with bright, anxious eyes. Unable to shoo it away, Charity fondled its head, then walked to the window as she began to unbutton her habit. She gazed down at the scene beyond the gate.

Charity noted the three figures meeting in the lane outside the house, then cantering off toward the great house. It had been an interesting morning as far as she was concerned. It remained to be seen what resulted, if anything, from this mornings efforts. Had his lordship proposed to Lady Sylvia? Or was he biding his time, making certain they would suit each other for such a permanent arrangement as marriage? Charity hoped he would not rush into his coming betrothal. A man so noble, thoughtful, and utterly maddening should not be precipitate.

After her long soak in the scented water, followed by a light luncheon with Lady Tavington, Charity walked to the hothouse to check her plants.

The duplicate of the plant she had submitted to the Horticultural Society was going to bloom, its bud forming beautifully. The society was soon to announce the orchid chosen to be presented to the Prince Regent. Her mind traveled to her last trip to London and visit to the society's hothouses, when she had encountered the Duke of Devonshire on one of his solitary walks through the gardens adjoining his property at Cheswick. His story of how the Horticultural Society had conceived the idea of a presentation to the Regent when so much had gone wrong in the poor prince's life captured Charity's sympathy. She decided to enter the unusual orchid she had brought up to London for the society's examination in the event. She had left the duke and hurried to the society's office to fill out the papers. Only later had she realized the foolishness of her actions. If her submission was to be chosen for the presentation, she might have to be present. She had been careful in her submission, using only those initials, handing the papers to the young secretary as though performing a task for someone else. Still, it was a stupid, dangerous thing to do. Everything could be lost if she was revealed. She did not want anything to dampen the pleasure her aunt seemed to find in assisting Charity in her quest for a husband. Never mind Charity might prefer to remain single. Though, to be honest, Charity acknowledged it was far better for her to be protected by a marriage than left on her own. The world was not kind to a woman alone and defenseless, vulnerable to the likes of Squire Bigglesby. Thought of forced marriage to a man of his ilk was quite enough to bring Charity into meek compliance with her aunt's schemes.

Roscoe hopped beneath the potting bench. Since the rabbit only hid when it sensed a stranger approaching, Charity turned to see who was entering. The door wheezed open and the elegantly dressed figure of Lord Powell entered, looking about with an undisguised disdain. His claret coat was an exquisite fit across his shoulders, and those biscuit pantaloons tucked into polished Hessians bespoke his fashionable status.

"This is actually where you spend so many hours? I could scarcely credit Lady Tavington's words when she said you had assumed care for your father's orchids."

"I believe many people will soon come to enjoy the culture of these beautiful plants, now that we better understand how to cultivate them. I spoke with the Duke of Devonshire about orchids when last in London, and he seemed most disposed to the idea."

Charity was not above tossing the name of the most famous of London society gentlemen into the conversation. The Sixth Duke of Devonshire was celebrated for his parties, though Charity found it hard to believe that he at times exceeded his great income in hosting such affairs. She had seen him as a lonely man, although she was well aware the "Bachelor Duke" did not lack feminine companionship. His increasing deafness was undoubtedly responsible for his seeking the solitary gardens and the company of the exotic plants grown at the neighboring Horticultural Society. If she had helped to pique his curiosity in the growing of orchids, all to the good. His would be a powerful influence. Perhaps someday he might be persuaded to assist in the expansion of the study of orchids.

"Devonshire actually showed an interest?" Clearly Lord Powell was intrigued that someone of such elevated rank and prestige would be associated with the mere cultivation of flowers. Lord Powell looked about him at the gorgeous blossoms hanging from overhead, the shelves of plants with long narrow green leaves, nodding blooms. He inspected with great care the fat buds, noting the dust and soil on the table where Charity leaned with no regard for her buttercup-yellow muslin.

Roscoe hopped forward, sniffing at Lord Powell much as a puppy might. Charity was amused to see the elegant lord back away, then raise his quizzing glass to peer at the rabbit beside his impeccably shod feet. "What is this?"

Suppressing a giggle at the expression on Lord Powell's face, Charity explained, "Roscoe is my pet rabbit. I have become quite fond of it."

"As your aunt is fond of that pesky monkey, I'll wager. Naturally you intend to dispose of your pet once you marry. These orchids as well, I daresay. Actually, I doubt you would find a man, other than perhaps the duke, who might be willing to take on such a project as this." He touched the potting bench with one finger,

wrinkling his nose with distaste when he observed the
soil that clung. His voice held a tinge of sarcasm, a thing
Charity found displeasing. Any man she married would
welcome her work with the orchids as well as her pet . . .
or she would remain single, Squire Bigglesby notwith-
standing!

"You do not approve of my interest in orchids, Lord
Powell?" Her eyes flashed with the gray glitter of sun
on a winter pond. "How unfortunate. I quite enjoy the
pleasure of working with beautiful things. And my dear
Roscoe is agreeable company." She bent over to scoop
up the rabbit, nestling it against her apron-protected
bosom. Stroking the soft fur, she peeked at the large
brown eyes, or at the one she could see, considering one
ear was dangling over the other eye. "It is a comfort to
me, and very much the guardian." Or at least he tried to
be, she amended.

Charity reluctantly left the warmth of the hothouse
and her furry friend to return to the cottage, Lord
Powell at her side. His relief at leaving the confines of
the hothouse disturbed her. It appeared he would
protest vigorously if she married him and continued her
interest in orchids, not to mention poor little Roscoe.
He would undoubtedly join the squire in consigning
Roscoe to the stew pot! It would seem her list of
prospects was shortened by one man.

Mrs. Woods let them into the cottage, where they
found Lady Tavington waving a large cream letter in her
hand. "My dear, this arrived for you today. Lord
Kenrick graciously sent it down for you while you were
over at the hothouse. Will you join us in a cup of tea,
Lord Powell?"

Though obviously curious to know what was in
Charity's letter, Lord Powell reluctantly permitted his
excellent manners to take precedence and declined,
leaving immediately.

Charity had suffered a spasm of anxiety when she
noted the return on the outside of the letter. The
Horticultural Society should have no reason to corre-

spond with her . . . unless it involved the preséntation of the orchid chosen for the Prince Regent!

She turned aside from her inquisitive aunt to unfold the letter, perusing the contents with growing trepidation. Her orchid had been selected. Horrors! Never had she really believed her offering would be chosen. One plant was to remain with the Horticultural Society, the larger, blooming plant was to be given to his royal highness. And they wanted Charity's presence. Double horror! The society expressed pleasure at the exquisite bloom and trusted Miss Lonsbury would convey to the grower the importance of personal attendance. There was a hint of curiosity as to the identity concealed by the use of initials. Could anyone at the society have made a connection to the Marquess of Kenrick? She fervently hoped that was not the case.

Sinking to a chair by the table, Charity absently poured a cup of tea, then dumped an unaccustomed spoon of sugar in the cup. She needed something, and she wasn't given to sherry in the afternoon.

"Well? Surely you are not going to keep me in suspense?" Lady Tavington raised one elegant eyebrow. She accepted the crisp cream page from Charity's limp hand with evident relish. Lady Tavington had never been one to shy away from satisfying her investigative zeal. She read the missive with growing consternation. "Explain, if you will." She eased her diminutive self onto the opposite chair and gazed at Charity expectantly.

"It is very simple, actually." Being around Lord Powell was affecting her. "I happened to enter one of my most unusual orchids in a modest competition held by the Horticultural Society to present an orchid to his royal highness the Prince Regent. I suspect the head of the society is attempting to interest the royal personage in supporting the desire for a new building, although the society claims the presentation is to cheer his royal highness. At any rate, they believe me to be a kind of secretary for the actual grower. As you know, *I* am the grower! I have been using mere initials for my sales and all the correspondence to date.'' Charity waited with dread for her aunt to react to her words.

"What initials?'' The words were calm, reflective.

Charity took heart from the lack of agitation on her aunt's face. "Actually''—there was that word again—"I used Lord Kenrick's initials, as I have been using the Kenrick hothouses to grow the plants.'' Charity began to stir the cooling tea with the spoon, watching the liquid swirling around and around in the cup with apparent fascination.

"You didn't! Dear me! That does present a problem. What do you intend to do?'' Lady Tavington leaned forward to consider the intriguing situation, her fingers drumming lightly on the table.

"I could always tell the society it isn't possible for the grower to be present. Though, I must confess it would be lovely to see the expression on the Regent's face as he receives my orchid. Truly, it is a beautiful bloom, Aunt.''

The drumming ceased as Lady Tavington rose to stroll about the room. "I don't doubt that in the least. From what I have seen, you have an exceptional collection of flowers, and I am certain your entry in this modest little contest, as you term it, deserves a reward. I do not see how you can accomplish this, Charity. What will you do? If anyone uncovers your use of his lordship's initials, your secret may be revealed. What then? All our hopes will have flown away.'' She clasped her hands before her in obvious distress, her usual confidence for once deserting her.

Charity wished she had never heard of the contest, though she owned it was rather nice to have won it with her entry. "It would be ruinous if the information is made known, I agree. So far, only Mrs. Woods, you, and I are aware of the situation. Let us pray it remains that way.'' It was a pity her *preux chevalier* couldn't ride to her rescue as in the tales of yore. As it stood, he undoubtedly would be angry at her use of his initials. To say the least! She and her plants would be told to

depart. Charity wondered if she might persuade the
Duke of Devonshire to house her orchids.

"Well, all we can do at the moment is to continue on
as though nothing was amiss. Keep on with your riding
lessons from Lord Powell, for one thing."

"Aunt, Lord Powell does not approve of my raising
orchids, nor, I fear, does he approve of our pets. He
made somewhat derogatory remarks about both of
them."

Lady Tavington glanced to where Chico perched atop
a chair and frowned. She had little regard for those who
did not accept her pets. Just because the current one
happened to be a monkey instead of a King Charles
spaniel was no reason to turn up a nose. "There is a
Chinese proverb that says it is easier to rule a kingdom
than regulate a family. I perceive a great deal of wisdom
in those words. We shall simply proceed one day at a
time. I am confident you have the *nous* to cope with the
situation."

Aunt Tavington had a great deal more confidence
than Charity at the moment.

The next riding lesson went extremely well,
considering how abstracted Charity was apt to be. Not
that she didn't appreciate his attentions. Memory of the
disdainful expression on his face as Lord Powell
surveyed the hothouse before leaving seemed to haunt
her. She firmed her belief it would be impossible to
encourage Lord Powell, and that seemed a shame, for
he appeared to be attracted to her, judging from his
lingering looks. She parted from him with a feeling of
relief.

As soon as she could, Charity escaped from Aunt
Tavington, leaving her to Parton's administrations
prior to a visit with Lady Kenrick. Slipping away to the
hothouses, Charity examined the bud of the prize-
winning flower, wishing she might share her moment of
glory with someone special, other than her aunt. Secrecy
was of the essence, however. Josiah might have to be
informed, though.

Setting up her watercolor pad and arranging all her

paints and brushes on the bench, she proceeded to
sketch the other prize flower already in bloom. It was
comforting to know she had two back-up plants in case
disaster struck. Any good gardener believed in being
prepared that way. It was simply common sense.

Minutes sped by quickly as she immersed herself in
transferring the delicate lines of the magnificent flower
to the watercolor paper. She didn't notice when Roscoe
raised its head to wiggle its nose in a delicate, inquisitive
manner, then retreat beneath the potting bench. Only
when the door wheezed open was she aware of an
intruder.

"So this is where you hide!" Lord Kenrick closed the
door behind him and strolled over to peer down at the
drawing upon the pad of paper.

Charity wished she could cover the drawing, conceal
it from prying eyes. He had seen the paintings in her
room and never uttered one word about them, so he
must have been politely ignoring their lack of quality.
"Good day, my lord." His smile sent tiny tremors
shooting through her. She couldn't control the surge of
pleasure at the sight of his elegant figure. "What brings
you to my domain?" It wasn't precisely hers, and she
hoped he might ignore that slight falsehood.

The arrogant lift of a brow told her he had noticed
her small slip. Then he bent over the drawing she had
just begun to paint and studied it in silence.

Charity held her breath. Though why she should care
what this man thought when he cared only to see her
married to another was not considered. She picked up
her brush and returned to her work. Glancing up, she
was startled to see a warm smile reaching into those
remarkable eyes with incredible results. She felt as
though as the breath had been sucked from her bosom,
leaving her like a gasping fish on the bank of a stream.

"Oh!" That was a most intelligent reaction, you
looby, she scolded herself. He will certainly think you a
chowder-head after that.

"Those paintings in your bedroom *were* done by you.

I intended to ask, but things got in the way. Most remarkable talent. Most remarkable. I have never seen flowers depicted with such a living quality about them, as though you might pluck them from the page to breathe in their scent or feel the texture of the petals beneath your fingers.''

His hand rested lightly on her shoulder. Charity was so aware of the warmth radiating from him, she could scarcely think. She glowed with pleasure, her gray eyes shining as though lit from within. "What a lovely thing to say, my lord. Thank you for the compliment. I do enjoy my painting, almost as much as growing the orchids.''

"Is this a particularly special orchid? I see it is different from the others. The royal-purple hue on the lower part is distinctive.''

Charity avoided his eyes as she sought the drawing below her fingers. Taking a brushful of paint, she returned to her task. "I believe it is, but then I am like a mother hen with my blooms. They are all very special to me.''

His chuckle warmed her, and she felt she had never painted so well as today. Everything was flowing just right, the colors achieved so perfect. The painting seemed to have a particular glow about it. Or perhaps she was looking at it with eyes that were not quite dispassionate.

To make conversation she pointed to a slender orchid to her left. "That is the *Phaius tankervilliae*, an orchid brought to England from China by Dr. John Fothergill in 1778. It was one of the first Asiatic orchids at Kew.''

"You have seen the display at Kew?''

Charity nodded as she carefully colored in the labia, or lip, of the orchid in her drawing. "I hope that someday that garden may be open to the public so that anyone can see the collection housed there. The Dowager Princess of Wales was a most inspiring patroness.''

Feeling his interest deserved some encouragement,

she pointed out, "That feathery-looking orchid over to
your left is an odontoglossom from the tropical
highlands of South America. The cymbidium over to
your right, the pink one with the spiked blooms, is
native to Asia. Aunt Tavington sent the plant to Father
a few years ago, some time before he died. The orchid I
am painting now is a *Cattleya labiata*, and my favorite.
I feel they are all more than simply curiosities, as so
many of our botanists seem to feel. Such fascinating
flowers must compel a greater study. Sir Joseph Banks
has made progress in this line. Perhaps the Duke of
Devonshire might be persuaded to take them up and
they will become all the rage." She smiled at such an
amusing idea, then bent over the painting again.

Lord Kenrick leaned over to watch the flow of the
brush as it touched the drawing, making it seem to come
alive. "I hope you don't mind my watching. I have
never observed a true artist before. So many young
women dabble at painting, but produce nothing of real
value such as comes from your brush."

Charity was finding it hard to concentrate, and as a
result, her work went slower than normal. Still, it would
never do to make a mistake. "Not at all, my lord." She
glanced up at him, the happy radiance of her smile
meeting the amiable regard in his eyes. His rich voice
thrilled her, his kind words soothed all her worries—for
a moment.

From the door of the hothouse, the two figures bent
over the bench appeared very close indeed. The
admiring look Lord Kenrick bestowed on the chestnut
head was unmistakable. The compliments were
generous and warm enough to bring hope to any
female's bosom. They hadn't noticed the carefully
opening door. It had been inched away from the frame
little by little.

Lady Sylvia swallowed the ire that threatened to
choke her and sailed up to the bench with a fluttery,
feminine step. She slanted a look at the delicate
drawing. Her expression indicated she deemed the

delicate watercolor to be of no value or importance, and with great care she casually brushed against the water pot holding now dirty water in it. The pot tipped over, and the colored water ran across the nearly dry painting, ruining it completely.

7

"HOW CLUMSY OF ME! Pray do forgive me, Miss Lonsbury. I hope I have not quite destroyed your little watercolor. That *is* what you were doing, was it not?"

Charity sat in stunned silence, trying to determine if it might be possible to save her painting. Further examination proved her first thought was correct: the painting was ruined beyond all redemption.

Lady Sylvia clasped her hands in true distress, at last perceiving that she had accomplished more than she intended. The look on Lord Kenrick's face was thunderous before it was masked with a polite yet concerned expression. That brief flash from his eyes had been quite quelling, however. Lady Sylvia wondered if she had sunk beyond all hope.

"I had no idea, I scarcely expected *important* paintings to be done in a place like this. I can see you are an accomplished artist, Miss Lonsbury. I am more upset than I can say to have caused such damage." Her histrionics were developing at a nice pace, her vinaigrette in hand, a handkerchief cleverly touching her eyes. "Please, please forgive me." The one lone tear was a fitting affectation.

Charity shook her head slowly, her anger retreating under such a prettily said apology. How could she give voice to her suspicions? "I forgive you, Lady Sylvia. I can understand your position. You could not expect to find me painting in a hothouse." Charity almost asked Lady Sylvia what she had come searching for in the hothouse, when the obvious answer was right before her. Lord Kenrick.

The ugly notion that Lady Sylvia had deliberately

knocked the pot of water over the painting was considered, then reluctantly dismissed as unworthy. Why would such an elegant lady, a diamond of the first water as Lady Sylvia, attack someone like Charity Lonsbury? There was nothing about the lady that indicated she might be the venomous type of woman, given to malicious deeds. She had so far seemed to be all that was gracious, an elegant, patrician lady in every manner.

Lady Sylvia continued to flutter vague words of apology until Charity was in great danger of exploding. It was becoming more and more difficult to contain her agitation. While Lady Sylvia might apologize, it did not remove the stain from the painting, nor did it replace the nearly completed work, one which so pleased Charity, with another painting as well executed.

Noting Charity's distress, Lord Kenrick touched Lady Sylvia's elbow, discreetly guiding her from the warmth of the hothouse to the bracing air outside. Studying the suitably contrite face of the woman he had thought to ask to be his bride, he wondered just how she could have managed to knock the water pot over. It would take more than a nudge against the table. Her shawl? Another searching look revealed that it might be possible for that enormous shawl she draped about her shoulders to have somehow swept the pot on its side as she moved around the bench where Charity labored.

The suspicion was lodged, however. There it took root, quietly coloring his view of the estimable lady who appeared less desirable now, though her innocence was probably true.

In the hothouse Charity sighed over the ruined painting. It had been such a good representation of the orchid. She had hoped it to be her best work, suitable for presentation along with the plant. She didn't feel much like painting anymore. At least not today. Unable to destroy the painting—for, after all, most of it was all right—she tore it from the pad, then rolled it up to tuck in a corner to refer to again when and if she attempted to repeat her painting attempt. She was certain no future effort could match this one. Lord Kenrick had somehow strangely stimulated her ability, compelling her to strive for her best, reach beyond what she had done in the past.

Roscoe hopped along with her to the door and out. Charity espied Josiah trimming a tree not far away. "Josiah, I have some news for you."

"What be it, miss?" He leaned against the tree for a moment's rest as he watched the young woman come across the grass. Looking sad, she was.

"I have had news from London, Josiah. One of my orchids is to be presented to the Regent. Please keep the news to yourself. I would as soon not have it known for many reasons. The hothouses *must* be kept at even temperature now. I would not have anything happen to the plant before it is to go. The nights are getting chilly. I will try to check the fires if I can, but with all the entertainments going on and the people around, I may not have the opportunity to do that. Would you be willing to take a look before you go home at the end of the day?"

Josiah nodded with solemn dignity. "Aye, that I can. 'Twon't do no harm to walk back and look onest more afore I get mesel' to bed, neither. Don't you worrit your pretty head about a thing." He moved from the tree and returned to his work. With his lordship in residence, a man had to look sharp.

Charity felt she could trust him to keep silent, though she hadn't impressed upon him just why there was a need for secrecy. She had tried to keep her orchid-selling as shrouded as possible, going to great lengths to conceal her shipments to London. None of those in whose cart she caged a ride cared a jot about her doings.

She continued toward the lane instead of returning to the path. She was in no hurry to return to the cottage. Dressing for dinner at the great house awaited her.

Lost in thought, she didn't at first perceive the sound of the phaeton clipping up the drive. It was very close when she collected herself, retreating to the grass once more. A rather handsome, very elegantly dressed man peered down from the equipage. She wondered if he was one of the men Lord Kenrick invited as a possible match for her.

"I say, I had no idea such lovely visions could be found in the country. I should have come down long ago." He handed the reins to the servant riding with him and jumped down before Charity. She didn't back away, holding her groud against this dandy of a man, with his high shirt collar, many shining fobs, the fancy waistcoat peeping from the casually open many-caped greatcoat. He swept a low bow, both elegant and charming. "Sir Oswald Edgeworth at your service, my lady. I trust you are a part of Kenrick's little party? I cannot believe how I have missed seeing you in London. Kenrick was always clever at finding new faces."

Charity found him amusing, all his pretensions concealing a puppylike friendliness. "I believe we are to meet at dinner, sir. Perhaps we ought to wait until then for a more formal introduction?"

"Not on your life. Harwood is due this minute. I mean to cut him out for once."

Laughter bubbled up within Charity. Really, the man was impossible. "Very well, I am Miss Lonsbury, of Greenoaks, I suppose. At any rate I live nearby."

"Allow me to see you to your door, my lady." He gently touched Charity's arm to escort her to his phaeton. The servant leapt nimbly down, handing the reins to Sir Oswald. Charity seated herself with pleasure.

The phaeton was turned around in a trice and they were off toward the cottage at a merry clip. "It is not very far, you see. I could have walked with no difficulty." She was on the verge of giggling like a green girl at this young man. Lord Kenrick believed in a variety of offerings, if Lord Powell and Sir Oswald were examples. They pulled up before the cottage, Sir Oswald handing her down with a flourish. She curtsied, then promised to see him before long.

Upon entering the cottage she found Lady Tavington

in a dither. Parton was hovering in the background, holding a Norwich shawl over one arm, a light-wool pelisse over the other.

"What think you, Charity? His lordship is graciously sending a carriage for us again to ride up to the great house for dinner. Should I wear the shawl or the pelisse?"

Considering the possibility of drafts in the saloon where the visiting might be done, Charity nodded toward the shawl. "This seems to be a day for shawls, Aunt." She walked past the two perplexed women up to her temporary room, unable to prevent her sagging spirits from showing. The painting episode came back to depress her after Sir Oswald slipped from her mind.

Aunt Tavington hurried up the stairs after her and paused by her door. "What is it, love? What has happened?"

"There was an accident. A pot of dirty water was spilled over my nearly completed painting. It left me feeling a bit blue-deviled."

"Oh, no! I should think so. Come, change into your pretty apple-green silk with the blond lace. You must be ready when the carriage arrives. Lord Kenrick has such consideration, does he not?"

Parton unobtrusively drew out the low-necked delicate silk with three deep flounces at the hem and elaborate puffed sleeves. Charity slipped into the dress, allowing Parton to do up the buttons, then the sash. Submissively seating herself before the dressing table, she watched Parton deftly arrange her hair, parting it in the center, then drawing the curls to each side. She wove silk blossoms in among the curls and laced apple-green ribbons to create a most fetching coiffure.

The vision in the mirror ought to have cheered Charity immensely. Perhaps a conversation with Sir Oswald would pull her from her doldrums. Her face brightened at the thought.

Lady Tavington had watched the too quiet young woman, obviously trying to figure out what had been left unsaid. More had occurred than Charity related. "I believe everyone will be at the house this evening. Even Squire Bigglesby and Miss Spencer are to attend. I suspect Lady Kenrick wants the local people to get acquainted with those who have come down from London. She is that thoughtful, dear woman."

Charity wondered aloud, "You do not mind being so far from your friends when you travel as you do? You fit in so well here. I should think you would miss all this."

Lady Tavington strolled to the window to look beyond the treetops into the distant clouds. For one moment she saw the misty hills of China, the slopes where she had searched for rare plants in the north of India, smelled all the pungent aromas of foreign places, saw the exotic sights denied to placid matrons in England. "Perhaps I miss a comfort or two, but I would not trade my travels for the peace of the hearth or the frivolity of society. I long for the adventure I have known." Realizing she was saying more than intended, and perhaps influencing Charity wrongly, she added, "But I do not desire you to be precipitate in choosing a husband. In the event that none of the gentlemen in attendance at the house party meets with your approval, we will journey to London for the Little Season, and if necessary, for the Season. I would not have you unhappy for my convenience."

Charity turned to the door, concealing her confusion. It seemed Lady Tavington had a mind to travel some more in the not too distant future. Would she possibly delay her trip simply to see Charity settled? Charity didn't have to question anyone, she knew that dear lady would forgo her own happiness to further that of her favorite niece.

Well, if Charity had to make a choice, surely there would be a gentleman present at the house party who would do. Sir Oswald seemed an agreeable man. Though, to admit the truth, she had wished to include love in her marital plans. But if that was not to be the case, she would try to choose wisely, a man who would be kind to her, tolerate her affection for the orchids and maybe her rabbit? Amused at the very idea of asking the man who sought her hand in marriage if he liked rabbits, and not only for stew, she joined Lady Tavington in the awaiting carriage.

Jameson greeted them with a less frosty mien as he surveyed the lovely gowns partially revealed beneath the large shawls each woman wore. Both ladies were quite up to snuff this evening. He announced them at the door of the Gold Saloon with gracious approval.

Charity braved the cluster of guests in the room, impressed by the charm of the saloon's decor. The walls were covered with cream damask, elegant paintings hung above the wainscoting. Kenrick must have been one of the many English nobles who took advantage of the peace to cross the channel and acquire works of art. Ignoring the knot of people at the far end of the long room, she turned her attention to her hostess.

The marchioness was dressed in a youthful silver-and-pink confection that strangely enough did not look foolish on the older woman. She embraced Lady Tavington with geniality and kissed Charity lightly on the cheek, a greeting signifying her warmest favor. She turned to the two gentlemen who had been at her side, urging them closer.

"Ladies, Sir Oswald Edgeworth and Lord Charles Fortesque, Earl of Harwood. Ozzie and Charles, I want you to meet my dearest friend, Lady Alice Tavington, lately returned from the Far East, and her niece, Miss Charity Lonsbury."

Charity's smile was genuinely warm, her eyes glowed with the intense gray light Lord Kenrick noted before on occasion. First she favored Sir Oswald with her hand, acknowledging his warm regard with a gracious tilt of her head. Then she unobtrusively studied Lord Harwood before extending her hand to him. He drew it to his lips, placing a butterfly kiss on the air above it. Still holding her hand, he looked up into Charity's eyes.

"This promises to be a most interesting party, Miss Lonsbury."

At Charity's side, Lady Tavington peeped at Charity, silently praising the demeanor and looks of her niece. If this chit didn't take with both of these smitten young men, she would turn in her traveling togs.

Charity floated off with a gentleman at either side, feeling the heady effects of sudden attention from two top-of-the-trees London beaus. Harwood, from the starched white of his intricately tied cravat, the elegant fit of his deep-blue superfine coat, to the tight black trousers revealed a fine muscular body, was a man any woman might admire. On the other side, Sir Oswald wore a corbeau jacket with gray trousers. Charity had no doubt that the buttons on their jackets were gold, not gilded brass. Both gentleman were of the first stare of elegance.

She eased the paisley shawl down one shoulder now that she was becoming accustomed to the gentle warmth of the room. The pleasantly husky voice of Lord Harwood reached her left ear. "Allow me, Miss Lonsbury. Kenrick tells me you paint quite well and raise orchids as a diversion. The latter is unusual for a young woman. Though I recall the Dowager Princess of Wales was ever interested in plants, was she not?" He adjusted her shawl as he spoke.

His words were so kindly spoken, Charity felt herself warming to the amiable gentleman. Sir Oswald spoke up before Charity could answer. "I say, saw her coming from the hothouses this afternoon, Charles. Like a vision from the gods floating over the lawn. Lady Kenrick said Miss Lonsbury is carrying on the work begun by her esteemed father."

Charity was determined to get her own words in this time and firmly interposed her answer. "It is true. I raise orchids and also do paintings of the blooms on occasion. Lord Kenrick is too kind with his estimate of my abilities."

A considering twist of the mouth preceded Lord

Harwood's reply. "Somehow I doubt that. Kenrick is an excellent judge of art, if one goes by the recent acquisitions to his collection. Have you see the oil he purchased lately, Ozzie? Chap named John Constable."

"Prefer Turner, myself. Like his splashes of color."

"Your aunt intends to settle here with you, Miss Lonsbury?" Lord Harwood smiled benignly down at her.

Charity was startled. She realized that she had no idea what her aunt's long-range plans might be. "I don't know, my lord. I suspect she longs to travel again."

Ozzie looked over to where Lady Tavington conversed with a very elegant gentleman in black breeches and coat, his waistcoat a dazzling white and a large diamond neatly centered upon his cravat. His white hair contrasted with a tanned and surprisingly young face. "Ought to get acquainted with the Earl of Dunstall, then. Understand he intends to sail off for Egypt before too long. Fancies himself some kind of expert."

Covertly studying the pleasant-faced gentleman so entranced with her dear aunt, Charity wondered if her aunt might be intrigued with the idea of travel to Egyptian sands. It was one area of the world she had not explored. "I'm certain they would find much to make conversation over with all the traveling Aunt Tavington has done. You gentlemen must persuade her to tell you of the Mongol attack on her party while she was traveling through China. She spent time in the emperor's court too, visiting with the imperial doctor."

Lady Kenrick fluttered up to introduce Charity to Lady Ann Rowe just as Jameson announced that dinner was served. Lady Ann smiled, her soft ash-brown curls shimmering in the candlelight as she nodded her greeting.

"I'm so happy to meet you all." While her soft, clear voice addressed them, her sherry-colored eyes darted to the elegant figure of Lord Powell not far away.

Lady Kenrick led the way on the arm of a not too

pleased Lord Harwood. Charity's aunt placed her hand on the arm of the Earl of Dunstall. Charity was shocked to see Euphremia claim the arm of the squire. Had they actually been in the room? She hadn't noticed! She usually had no difficulty in hearing Euphremia's slightly shrill voice. Sir Oswald followed with Charity. Lord Powell was attending the appealing Lady Ann, appearing greatly attracted to her. And Lord Kenrick was being most attentive to Lady Sylvia, Charity thought sourly. Then she reminded herself Lady Sylvia was no affair of hers, and returned her attention to the gentleman at her side.

At the table Charity found herself seated between Sir Oswald and Lord Harwood. She nibbled at boiled salmon while Lord Harwood discreetly questioned her about her family. Charity dithered between *canards à la rouenaise* and roast lamb while Sir Oswald tendered queries about orchids. Mayonnaise of chicken, green peas *à la française*, a helping of charlotte russe, with dabs of larded quail tempted her while Lord Harwood commented on current trends in watercolor painting. Iced pudding sat before her as she contemplated the poser of remaining slender if one ate such bounty frequently. Fortunately she had replied at modest length to each gentleman's inquiry, which gave less time for consumption of food. Also, she had been careful to observe her hostess, only a seat away, who ate with delicate nibbles and never very much of any one thing.

It was an exceptionally gay evening for Charity. She had never experienced anything remotely like it. The assemblies held at Orpington could not begin to compare, though, to be fair, she had attended very few of them.

While Sir Oswald and Lord Harwood concentrated on the last of their meal, she allowed herself a moment to reflect. Lord Kenrick had made it plain he was enamored of the elegant Lady Sylvia. Charity was pleased to note that Squire Bigglesby was being forced to address Miss Euphremia Spencer with something

approaching cordiality. And herself? She was not in the
least unhappy to observe Lord Powell attach himself to
Lady Ann. Indeed, a man who considered orchids of no
import was not for Charity. What a pity he could not
have shown the interest Lord Kenrick did in the
paintings she turned out from time to time. Lord
Powell's boredom had been all too evident.

The gentlemen decided to forgo their port this
evening. Charity was thankful, for it avoided possible
conversation with Lady Sylvia. She prudently ignored
the reasons for her feelings of hostility toward Lady
Sylvia. There were some things better overlooked.

So she practiced flirting with Sir Oswald,
complimented him on his fine equipage and skill with
the ribbons. Then she unfurled her ivory fan brought
from China by her dear aunt, and fluttered eyelashes at
Lord Harwood. Never had she thought to be such the
coquette. Nor had she expected it might be such fun!

Sir Oswald gave Lord Harwood a challenging look.
"Where do you think we will go on the outing Kenrick
said he's planned?"

Glancing warily at the two men, looking for all the
world like two strange dogs eyeing each other, neither
daring to bark first, Charity interposed a reply. "He has
not stated where he intends to lead us, but there are the
ruins of Lullingstone Castle to the east of us and to
thenorth are remains of a church at Ruxley." The two
gentlemen laughed sheepishly and relaxed against their
respective chairs. She added with a smile, "I'm afraid as
an attraction, they are somewhat lacking."

Leaning toward her in an attitude of intimacy, Lord
Harwood inquired, "Tell us more about the castle
ruins."

"I trust it would be more of a pleasant ride than
something to inspect. The castle was a fortified manor
with a moat and two gatehouses built in the sixteenth
century. It was constructed of bricks, but I neglect to
recall if it was Saxon or Norman design. There are only
modest remains now. However, it is a lovely excursion
at this time of year. I am certain the present owners

would not mind our visit to the park." Charity smiled demurely at his lordship.

"And the church ruins?" nudged Sir Oswald.

"Not much there, either, I'm afraid. One or the other would be the means of an outing on a lovely day in early fall, if you follow my thoughts."

Both gentlemen looked as though they would happily follow anything Miss Charity wished to cast out.

Not accustomed to such excess of gallantry, Charity rose and pleaded to be excused for a moment. She paused to speak with her hostess a minute, then headed for the ladies' retiring room.

The hall was cool after the considerably warmer environs of the Gold Saloon. Charity walked briskly to the stairs, only to find her way barred by Lord Kenrick.

"My lord." She made a small curtsy and waited for whatever was on his mind.

"What happened between you and Lord Powell?" He noted the charming way her gown clung to her, flowing as she walked while faithfully outlining her lovely figure.

"You don't mince words, do you, my lord?" His coat fit admirably, shoulders powerfully revealed in the smoothest of wool. But then he always looked so elegant.

He shrugged, and stood silently waiting for her reply.

Looking first at a painting of a Kenrick ancestor, then the carpet at her feet, she finally answered. "He is an attractive gentleman, one any woman could find interesting, I am sure. He showed great patience in teaching me to ride, and I find him pleasing to converse with, to be certain. But he seems to find orchids a dead bore, and I think he would relegate Roscoe to the stew pot faster than the squire. I will look elsewhere, my lord."

"I suppose you must be right. He will not do in that case. I hadn't realized you are such an accomplished flirt. First Geoff, then Ozzie and Charles." A strange moodiness seemed to settle over him as he spoke.

"I was always reckoned a good student, my lord. I do

not wish to place undue burden upon my aunt. She has offered further exposure to society if I am not pleased with your, ah, offerings.'' Charity knew she risked his censure at her pertness, but something drove her on, her eyelashes batting softly against her cheeks as she played the demure miss. Fortunately he ignored her acting.

''Are you aware your aunt yearns to travel again? She only remains here long enough for you to wed. She means to do the right by you.'' His gaze appeared troubled.

''I guessed as much, my lord. I *am* suitably appreciative. I suppose that means I must choose a husband as quickly as I can, so as to free her from her duty.'' Charity managed a strained smile and moved as though to pass the tall, lean body of the man she once considered her knight and had loved with all her girlish heart.

Her arm tensed as his hand clasped it, restraining her. She felt a warmth radiating out from his touch, reaching to all parts of her, sending a pink flush to her cheeks that all her flirtings with Sir Oswald and Lord Harwood had failed to do.

''Yes? Some instructions, perhaps? Do you not approve of my progress?''

He took a deep breath and muttered something softly before replying, ''Beware you do not overstep.''

Escaping from his loose clasp, Charity fled up the stairs and sought the retiring room. Glancing about the delicate green-and-ivory room, she observed pale-green velvet draperies hung at the alcove, and the polished floor gleamed in the soft light of many candles. It was empty. An enormous vase of flowers scented the air. She collapsed on a velvet stool and gazed at her reflection in the cheval glass. She didn't *look* any different. But she felt different. Very different.

Sinking into contemplation, she glanced at the door, beyond which spread the elegant house of Greenoaks containing such beauty and splendor. And Lord Kenrick.

What did she feel for him? Honestly, deep in her heart? She had loved him with girlhood love, deep admiration for qualities she had assigned him. His hard assessment had cut cruelly into her gentle heart. Yet could she deny there was still a *tendre* for him? With Lady Sylvia about to receive his offer of marriage, it would be the most stupid of all things.

Rising from the comfort of the velvet stool, she redraped the paisley shawl about her shoulders, wondering if she should allow the shawl to slide farther down to reveal that shocking neckline a bit more. Lord Kenrick? Well, she must turn her mind from him to someone else. There was no getting around that fact.

She took one bracing look in the glass, then marched to the door and down the stairs to the Gold Saloon. Someone was going to be her husband . . . and it wasn't going to be the squire.

8

THE FRAGRANCE OF CHOCOLATE drifted past Charity's nose, teasing her to wakefulness. The curtains of the many-paned windows were pushed apart, revealing another lovely day. Charity yawned and wondered how long this spell of nice weather could continue. The rains of autumn and winter ought to be plaguing them before long, she was sure.

The chocolate aroma wafted past her again. Charity struggled to sit up, puzzled. She was not accustomed to a pot of chocolate before rising. Usually she rose in the quiet of the morning to tend the garden before setting out for the hothouses. The deep, resonant voice Charity recognized instantly revealed the answer.

Parton poured steaming water into the hip bath. "You can sit in the tub while you sip your chocolate, Miss Charity. We let you sleep as long as possible, but the day is advancing at a spanking pace. Lady Tavington wants to see you dressed in the new salmon walking dress for your excursion today. Your hair needs tending. If you are to leave by eleven of the clock, we cannot tarry." The tall, very large woman placed a towel by the bath, then fixed Charity with a stern look, admonishing, "No loitering in bed, miss."

Charity permitted herself a languid stretch before slipping from her cozy bed. She tentatively dipped a toe in the bath, then eased her body into the blissfully hot water. So this was what it might be like to be one of the more privileged class. It certainly would not be difficult to become accustomed to in the least. The chocolate was to hand and she sipped it with appreciation. Lovely.

Drawing her knees up and sinking deeper into the

water, she reflected on the evening past. Lord Harwood had been so charming and attentive, not that Sir Oswald had not been kind. She smiled at his insistence that she call him Ozzie. He really hated his name, poor lamb.

Lord Harwood, with his fashionably tousled hair, longish nose, and seductive voice, had the sweetest expression, the most amiable disposition. Those hazel eyes crinkled so delightfully when he smiled, which seemed quite often when he was around her. She could not imagine *him* making such cutting remarks about her as Lord Kenrick had made. Charity could not understand Lord Kenrick. His warm glances in her direction seemed to war with his supposed purpose to wed Lady Sylvia. At times he was most puzzling. Lord Harwood had fair captured her heart with his laughing looks and softly murmured compliments. Reflecting on his stated desire to write an ode to her eyes, she giggled softly, then swallowed the last of her chocolate.

Dear Ozzie was her other gem of a beau. Now if she must choose—and it seemed she must—it might be rather difficult. She was just as glad Lord Powell had turned his attentions to Lady Ann Rowe. Ozzie informed her the young woman was a close friend of Lady Sylvia's and quite unexceptional as to fortune or beauty. She was welcome to Lord Geoffrey Powell. Since it seemed Lady Ann had no interest in either orchids or rabbits, other than in a stew, she appeared ideal for his attentions. Most convenient, actually.

Charity giggled again; then, reluctantly leaving the luxury of the bath now beginning to cool, she stepped from the water to vigorously dry herself.

When Parton reentered the bedroom, Charity was dressed in her cambric shift and petticoat, brushing her hair and wondering what the day might bring.

"Lady Travington said the Earl of Dunstall and Lady Kenrick will be arriving in his barouche in another hour, Miss Charity. That does not leave us with much time to perfect your hair." Parton took the brush from Charity's hand and nudged her toward the clothes press.

Wisely refraining from telling a scandalized Parton that she rarely did more than run a brush through her hair, then tie it back from her face, Charity allowed her aunt's abigail to slip her gown over her head and do it up, then propel her to the dressing table. Seated before it, she wondered anew on which of the two gentlemen she ought to fix her attentions. It was difficult when her whole heart was not available for the effort.

She had tried and tried to convince herself that she could subdue the emotion she felt for Lord Kenrick. Odious man. Well, she would simply put him behind her. He seemed to be absorbed in Lady Sylvia, at any rate. *They* would undoubtedly be riding.

"I suspect we will be in an open carriage, Parton. My bonnet ought to protect my hair." Charity firmed her lips in momentary rebellion as she contemplated herself riding sedately in a barouche while the exquisite Lady Sylvia would be elegantly perched on her mare. She cast a longing glance at the russet riding habit she could see in her small clothes press. She would be the only young person so imposed upon, she was sure. Euphremia would be riding if it killed her, given the squire's love for horses. Charity had observed her following the dinner last night for a brief time in the charming Gold Saloon. Euphremia had stuck to the Bigglesby's side like a limpet, the languishing looks from her large eyes totally unsuccessful in their attempt to capture the squire. Charity had to admire Euphremia's persistence. However, she *had* spared Charity the squire's prose.

"Good morning, dearest child. Do not forget a discreet touch of the lovely perfume his lordship brought you." Lady Tavington crossed from the doorway to peer into the mirror above the dainty dressing table where Charity sat under Parton's capable hands.

Charity managed a smile at the reflection in the mirror. "Of course, Aunt Alice. He said it was to be in aid of obtaining myself a husband, did he not? I must remember to use everything at my disposal." The slight bitterness she still felt in regard to the elegant Waterford container of her favorite scent could be heard in her voice, unfortunately. "I must remember to extend my appreciation to Lord Kenrick. I recollect I failed to do so in perhaps as proper a manner as I might when he presented it to me." She was relieved as Parton stepped back, surveying the finished product of her efforts.

"You look beautiful, dear girl. Parton has improved an already charming appearance. It is well you have a sensible heart, or I fear the compliments you will receive would turn your head." Lady Tavington moved aside to inspect Charity.

Picking up the scent bottle, Charity applied a rather generous amount below her ears, at the base of her throat, touched her hair and wrists, then turned to her aunt. "That ought to do the thing, don't you think? Do I have time for a bite of food before we depart? I did not believe I would ever be hungry again after that lavish dinner, but I find I am famished this morning."

"Ah, the appetite of the young." Lady Tavington put an arm around Charity's shoulders, wisely refraining from any comment on the excessive use of the lavender scent. They strolled down the stairs to where the plain deal table was spread with an ample breakfast.

Charity promptly slid onto a Windsor-backed chair and applied herself to toast with rashers of bacon to nibble between bites of scrambled egg.

Mrs. Woods hovered near the table, her hands clutching her crisp white apron. "When do ye have to get the plant off to London, miss? I'm that worried about it."

With a quick frown at her plate, Charity considered the instructions contained in the missive from the Horticultural Society. "There was no absolute date for delivery, only the presentation, which will be three weeks hence. They wanted me to have ample time to prepare the plant for the Prince."

"Have you any further thoughts about the presentation? You are aware you cannot be there in person."

Lady Tavington helped herself to a warm scone, buttered it, then spread wild-strawberry preserves on top. She studied the suddenly angry face across the table from her. "You would not do anything foolish, would you, Charity, dearest child?"

"Of course not, Aunt." Charity compressed her lips a few moments before continuing. "It is all so nonsensical! I do not see why a woman cannot receive the accolade for growing the orchid for the Prince. As much as I adore growing the plants, it would be nice to have the acknowledgment of the other orchid growers."

"I believe I hear the earl's barouche approachng. Wipe your mouth and fingers and let Parton settle that lovely bonnet just so upon your curls. We desire you to be the elegant, proper lady you can be, you know."

Charity recalled the words that had cut so deeply into her sensitive heart. "Of course. I must countermand the notion I am anything but the perfect lady, eliminate the idea that I grow orchids. Heaven forbid I actually put my hands in the dirt. Though I confess, Ozzie does not seem to mind and Lord Harwood actually appeared to find the subject of interest."

"Good. Do you really call him Ozzie, my dear? These modern young people! Seems most improper to me."

Smiling as her aunt sailed forth down the flower-bordered path to the picket gate, Charity walked toward the earl's barouche with a lighter heart. If she must select a husband, at least these two would not object to her raising orchids. She would have to find out which man might build her the kind of hothouse that she desired, one with the very latest improvements.

She greeted the earl and Lady Kenrick with proper deference. Slipping in across from Lady Kenrick, she felt herself turning pink under that lady's nod of approval.

They were to all meet at the village green and proceed from there. It was to be a relaxed, easygoing jaunt. There was likely more interest in the relationships between the various members of the party than in the supposed attractions of the ruin of Lullingstone Castle, such as it was.

The sight of Lady Sylvia superbly seated upon her gray mare, wearing a sapphire-blue riding habit, was quite enough to make any young lady's teeth gnash in frustration. Coupled with the attentions of the elegant Lord Kenrick, it was not to be borne. He looked so commanding as he rode into view. Charity wished her esteemed papa had not had such a pronounced aversion to horses. Perhaps if she had acquired a good seat, with her charming riding habit, she too . . . Ah, well, she must do what had to be done. What else could she do? After the information imparted by Lord Kenrick last night—that Lady Tavington was here only as long as need be, that she yearned to be traveling again—Charity felt *compelled* to fall in with the plan for her to wed. And soon, if Lady Tavington was to be pleased. Considering the warm generosity of that dear lady, Charity wished to comply if at all possible.

Twirling her matching salmon parasol with dainty tassels as the pair of chestnuts was tooled down the lane, Charity smiled happily at Ozzie, seated on a roan of impressive size, came up to the barouche. He was a dear, she reflected. She sensed he was not enthusiastic about her orchids, but was willing to tolerate anything she liked. He had such a delightful personality, tried so hard to please her, it was impossible not to like him. Never mind, she sighed to herself, that she had so long ago dreamed of finding love in her marriage as her mama had.

His light-blue eyes beamed at her with obvious pleasure that he had arrived at the barouche before Lord Harwood. "I say, you look most fetching this morning, Miss Lonsbury. Good day, Lady Kenrick, Lady Tavington, my lord. Another marvelous day, ain't it? We are to join the others up ahead. Thought I might greet the fair Miss Lonsbury before the press of the crowd and all that, you know."

Charity gave another twirl of her parasol and

accepted his homage with grace. There was much to be said for the gallantry of beaus. It gave one such a sense of well-being. She suppressed a smile when Ozzie grimaced as Lord Harwood rode up to the barouche.

"Lovely day, ladies, my lord. Miss Lonsbury, you put all the flowers in the gardens to shame this fine moring. I daresay not even your orchids could match your beauty today," he said with an attractive sparkle in his eyes.

If they were going to keep on in this vein, Charity was afraid her bonnet would become too tight. Next to her, Chico stirred restlessly and Charity glanced at the little monkey. Why Aunt Tavington insisted upon bringing her pet was beyond her, but the comical expression on its face promptly put Charity in her place. It had placed its tiny paws over its ears and screwed up its mouth. How right it was, she thought.

"You will put me to the blush with your extravagant words, gentlemen." The others were close now, all on horseback, even the redoubtable Euphremia Spencer. Charity caught a stare of displeasure from Squire Bigglesby and hoped he wasn't going to be tiresome. He had clearly stated he did not intend to cease his attentions. Would that he might take her "no" as a final answer.

With the barouche in the center, the party began its leisurely way in the vague direction of the remains of Lullingstone. Lord Kenrick had sent grooms on ahead with the alfresco repast. All would be in readiness when they arrived, complete to cushions and rugs upon which to rest, chilled wine, and delectable tidbits prepared by his lordship's fine French chef.

It was a wonderful day for a picnic. The light breeze stirred the ribbons on Charity's bonnet as well as the tassels on the elegant parasol sent down from London with all the other things. Even her feet, in her dyed-to-match-her-dress kid slippers, tapped with restless enthusiasm for the day.

The only cloud was the two figures off to the left, Lady Sylvia and Lord Kenrick. She was so beautifully fair and he so handsomely dark. Depressing, it was. It was quite clear to Charity that Lady Sylvia was secure in his regard. She seemed so composed, so certain she would be the next marchioness. Undoubtedly she would. Charity had the sinking feeling that the marquess would make a declaration at the forthcoming ball. Would Lady Sylvia accept the family ring Lady Tavington described to Charity, the one with the sapphire surrounded by diamonds. The stone would undoubtedly match the blue of the marchioness's eyes. Or something. Perhaps it was intended to match the eyes of the man who bestowed it? His eyes were such an intense, romantic blue. Bah! Odious man that he was, she must contrive to dismiss him from her mind completely. Which undertaking was distressingly difficult to accomplish while he remained within sight and looked so disgustingly handsome.

As they neared Lullingstone Park, Charity gasped, "Oh, look, Aunt! What lovely wild flowers. My lord, could we stop so I might gather a nosegay for my aunt? She said she has missed the autumn blooms while far away."

The barouche was halted and Charity was assisted down by the Earl of Dunstall's groom. The earl seemed quite content to see Charity sweetly skimming across the meadow to the bank of a creek to gather flowers. Rather, he looked as though he wished she might stay there so he could have the complete attentions of the lady he found so fascinating. He totally ignored the other lady seated at his side.

Ozzie was off his horse in a trice, followed by Lord Harwood. Their horses trailed along behind as the two gentlemen offered to assist Charity in the gathering.

"Lovely, aren't they?" she beamed up at them as they joined her. Oxeye daisies and the last of the clustered bellflowers combined with autumn gentian and wisps of yellow-flowered horseshoe vetch to create a delicate bunch of purple, yellow, and white blooms. The admiration from the two gentlemen was not for the blooms in her hands, but for the attractive face shining above them. Her delight in such a simple thing was a joy to behold.

Charity walked purposefully to the barouche to hand the flowers to her aunt, plus a posy of blooms for Lady Kenrick. "Are they not pretty?"

Lady Tavington was appropriately pleased. Lady Kenrick bestowed a look of approval at Charity's charming manners.

Euphremia urged the squire forward when he scowled at Charity, mumbling something about a frivolous miss whose ways needed changing. The squire obviously was disgruntled at being excluded from the sociability shared by the others of the group. His ways did not endear him.

Restored to the barouche, to the patient resignation of the Earl of Dunstall, Charity settled in next to her aunt. The little group continued on its way. Lord Kenrick and Lady Sylvia were far ahead, probably thanks to that lady's careful maneuvering. Euphremia had captured the squire's attention with a question about a hunt he had attended. Charity felt a relief at being spared a few of his black looks. Perhaps Euphremia might not mind his interminable stories, which had a lamentable tendency to sound alike.

The winter winds had not yet torn the leaves from the trees. The sun was mildly warm, a subtle hint that autumn was nearly upon them in its angle to the ground. A cloud or two drifted in the cerulean sky. As they approached the grounds of the ruined castle, Charity tried to convince herself she was content with her decision to accept marriage. She could come to love her choice in time. Couldn't she?

The barouche drew to a stop, the groom hurriedly assisting the ladies to the ground one at a time. Charity waited patiently, amused to see the earl leap nimbly to give his hand to Lady Tavington. The two sauntered off toward the ruins while Charity smiled at Lady Kenrick.

"I wonder if my aunt will find a new partner in her travels, my lady?" Charity glanced at the pair, then respectfully back to Lady Kenrick.

"Anything is possible. And you, child? What of you? Your aunt talks of her desire to see you wed before she departs. I cannot help but observe those two gallants coming our way. Will one of them perhaps be your choice?"

Charity reflected that if she had her choice, her groom would be neither. "I do not know, my lady. I had not anticipated such an upheaval in my life as has occurred since my aunt joined me. It is difficult to become accustomed to the idea I must wed, and soon."

"It is every woman's duty to wed, create a home for her husband, bring forth sons to secure the line. You seem a charming young woman. Either gentleman should be honored to claim you as his bride. My son has promised me to wed soon. It is past time he set up a nursery and provide himself with an heir. His present heir is a distinctly vexatious nephew, son of my brother-in-law. That young man would decimate the fortune in no time at all, I'm sure." Lady Kenrick spoke softly, with no idea of her dry words impact on Charity.

Charity seemed unaware of the scrutiny she was under from Lady Kenrick's very blue eyes, eyes very like her son's. "How nice to have a dutiful son, my lady. I only pray I can be as fortunate in the future." That she would be required to bear an heir for Ozzie or Lord Harwood flashed through her head. Well, as Lady Kenrick intimated, it was all part of a woman's duty to her husband. Charity considered the two men striding toward her with a measuring look. They were fine men, both pleasing in appearance. Lord Harwood might have the edge over Ozzie's dandified garb. Lord Harwood more closely resembled Lord Kenrick in his manners and dress. Was that a plus or a minus?

Fortunately neither of them resembled Lord Kenrick in looks. Ozzie, with his blond hair, light-blue eyes, and thin figure, and Charles Fortesque with his light-brown hair and hazel eyes with that longish nose (not objectionable, mind you) were pleasant enough. What a pity she had grown to admire dark hair with a tendency to flop over a forehead, intensely blue eyes, and a lean

form elegantly clothed at all times. Odious, maddening
man. The least he might do if he was going to marry the
beauteous Lady Sylvia is be utterly beastly to Charity,
give her a disgust of him. But even the harsh words
uttered to Lady Tavington had not completely done him
to disgrace, alas.

They all strolled about, not really paying much
attention to the remains of the castle they had
supposedly come to view. Lady Sylvia clung to Lord
Kenrick's arm after stumbling on a hummock of grass.
Charity thought it a great pity water was no longer
diverted to the moat. It would have been interesting to
observe the impeccable Lady Sylvia in less than perfect
condition. A vision of Lady Sylvia with dripping hair,
sagging habit, and wilting demeanor drew a wicked
smile from Charity.

She turned to Lord Harwood, whose arm had been
offered to lend her support. "You inquired about the
castle before. I think they received a license to crenellate
at the time of construction. The two gatehouses date
from 1460. Some of the brick may have been taken from
a Roman site north of here, though it's possible they
produced their own. I'm afraid there isn't much to be
seen now, and I can't tell you anything more about it."
She had never been one for studying ruins, much pre-
ferring living plants for her attention.

After surveying the modest remains, Lord Harwood
drew her along with him toward the pile of cushions
near the baskets of food. "I can think of else to do with
our time. But first let us replenish our energy."

Charity wasn't particularly interested in a pile of
ancient brick and mortar. She was only too glad to
gracefully (she hoped) sink down on a cushion and
accept a glass of lemonade from her escort.

Leaning against the convenient oak tree, Lord
Harwood gazed at Charity with serious intent in his
eyes. "You enjoy living in the country, Charity? You
don't hanker for the gaiety of a Season in London?
Would you be unhappy there?"

She ran a finger around the rim of the glass. "While I enjoy living in the country, it is not a must. I daresay I could be happy most any place"—she grinned at him—"even in London. There are gardens to be seen, and I believe Kew is close enough to be pleasing. And . . . it is not a permanent residence for most people, is it? I mean, many have estates they repair to after the Season is over." She accepted a plate of food from him.

Charles gave Ozzie an annoyed glare as the younger man intruded on their solitude. "Dashed interesting place, this Lullingstone. Saw Roman bricks over there, sure of it. You two give up so quickly?" Then Ozzie noted their rather intimate position and frowned. He said nothing, but Charity had a feeling Ozzie would not be far removed from Lord Harwood the remainder of the trip.

"Oh, dear! Chico? Where are you, pet? Charity, have you seen little Chico? He has slipped away from me. I thought it would be so good for him to be out in the fresh air with us." Lady Tavington rushed up to the trio, anxiously wringing her hands.

Charity forbade reminding her aunt that the little monkey could have had all the fresh air he desired back at the cottage. With Parton to keep an eye on him as well. Nothing would do but everyone scatter in every direction to hunt for the spider monkey. Knowing his propensity for climbing, Charity did not bother to look down, concentrating on the branches of trees about her.

"Botheration," she exclaimed softly in disgust. "I was afraid of something like this." Her aunt doted on the little fellow so much. Knowing how Charity would feel if Roscoe were to turn up missing, she kept her voiced irritation to a minimum. It was just that Lord Harwood had become so serious. If Ozzie hadn't turned up at that moment, and Chico stayed by her aunt, well, she didn't think Lord Harwood had an ode to her eyes on his mind. She watched the others head off on various paths.

An acorn fell to her head and she peered up at a

gnarled oak tree. She was certain she espied the monkey perched on a branch. Looking in all directions, she could see no one was anywhere in sight. Now, when she could use assistance, no one was near. She didn't want to call out. For one thing it might frighten Chico. For another, she hated to sound like a village maid.

Again searching the area, she decided she couldn't wait. She hitched her skirts up and climbed up to the low-hanging branch, then the next. It was a simple tree to climb. As a girl, she would have enjoyed many an hour in this leafy abode. Her bonnet slid back, dangling by a ribbon, as she reached for the monkey, calling softly, coaxing it to her arms. She ignored the curl that brushed her cheek in disarray. Her lace-trimmed petticoats were hitched up, revealing a shapely ankle and the hint of the curves beyond. Her kid-shod feet swung in an effort to balance herself.

A smug smile on her lips, Charity contemplated how she was going to get down from the tree. The smile faded as she realized it was one thing to climb up the branches, using both hands. It was entirely another matter to get down with a squirming monkey held in both hands, no help below.

Why hadn't she waited for help? What a foolish thing to do, to climb up here in such a hoydenish manner. And *she* was the one who was going to be such a lady today.

Bracing her shoulders, using her feet carefully so as not to rip her gown and further disgrace herself, Charity edged down from branch to branch until she was on the lowest one. Biting her lip in concentration, she nearly lost her balance as a deep, rich voice, in the unmistakable accents belonging to Lord Kenrick, spoke.

"What are you doing up there?"

A resigned sigh escaped her. "I was getting the monkey."

Lord Kenrick was on foot and stood directly below the branch where Charity was perched. The amused expression on his face was too much to endure. There

was an unseemly amount of feminine leg on view, hers!
All that ruffled lace on her petticoat was visible as well.
She was about to give him a scold when Chico gave a
squirm and Charity attempted to hold on to it. Her
balance, precarious at best, was lost and she tumbled
from the branch.

Strong arms caught her and held her tightly to a very
broad chest. Charity looked into a pair of intensely blue
eyes and was completely past praying for.

"Oh," she breathed, "I *am* sorry."

"I don't think I am. You deserve a scold, my dear
Charity. You have this age." The twinkle in his eyes
seemed to belie his words. That tender regard she had
noted before had returned to light his eyes with a
warmth that melted her right down to her toes.

"I meant to thank you again for the lovely scent
bottle and perfume." She ignored it had nothing to do
with the monkey or the picnic, for that matter.

"I notice you used it. It suits you." He breathed in
deeply, enjoying her scent, the feel of her body pressed
against his so intimately.

Charity forgot all about the monkey she had rescued,
allowing him to escape again, to scamper across the
meadow toward the pile of cushions and food where he
found a bunch of grapes to his liking. "Thank you,"
she whispered.

Lord Kenrick's arms were so strong, his body warm
through his elegant bottle-green superfine coat. His
hands were gentle as they cradled her tightly to him. It
was lovely. Breathtaking. She could feel the beat of his
heart. My, those eyes of his were blue. She could smell
the clean soap-scrubbed scent of him, a faint tang of
lime as well. Her fingers longed to slip through his dark
hair, caress his firm skin, touch that mouth. She raised
her eyes from contemplation of his face to meet his eyes.
Was she betraying her feelings to him?

Her bonnet fell to the ground as his face neared hers.

9

"NAUGHTY, NAUGHTY, NAUGHTY!" LADY Tavington's voice carried over the meadow where the members of the picnic were straggling back to the oak tree and their interrupted lunch.

Lord Kenrick gave a startled glance over his shoulder, saw that Lady Tavington was shaking a gloved finger at the monkey, then abruptly placed Charity on her somewhat shaken feet. "Er . . . there you are, safe and hopefully sound. You weren't injured in your fall, were you?" He surveyed her as she brushed bark from her gown, pulled a leaf from her curls, and gathered her fractured poise about her.

Charity was not quite certain if she ought to be thankful for the interruption or not. She mentally checked all her limbs—not to mention other areas—and shook her head. "I daresay I am fine, my lord. No damage done. Not even my dress suffered." She turned aside from those penetrating eyes of his, the romantic blue now dark with concern, she supposed. She wouldn't vouch for the condition of her heart. She had never before been held so close in a man's tight and wonderfully satisfying embrace. His arms had been like bands of strongest hemp, only much nicer. No inanimate object could possibly stir her as his touch.

"That was a stupid, fool thing to do. You could have been killed if I had not caught you," he said suddenly. His voice was cold and cutting. He looked as though he might breathe fire like some mythical dragon, however.

"I only did what I had to do, my lord. Excuse me, I must go to my aunt." Ignoring the fast beat of her heart, she snatched her bonnet before she fled to Lady

Tavington, avoiding a censorious look from those knowing blue eyes.

Across the meadow, Lady Sylvia stared thoughtfully at the two figures who had been in such a strangely close attitude. A dark frown briefly marred the perfection of her forehead. She smiled graciously at Lord Harwood, who had been assisting her as they wandered along the River Darent. Tapping him playfully on the arm, she urged him toward the group clustered beneath the oak tree where Lord Kenrick now stood. Her smile was strained as they neared the others.

"You found the dear little animal! How lovely." Lady Sylvia's voice lacked a certain quality of enthusiasm to make her words totally believable, but no one paid attention to her. Lord Harwood gave her an odd look, one Sylvia did not observe.

"Miss Lonsbury can lay claim to that feat. Quite a daring rescue." Lord Kenrick gazed at the muslin-covered figure with an inscrutable expression neither woman could fathom. "If I was able to be of assistance in my small way, I am most happy."

Lady Tavington arched an eyebrow as she coolly listened to Lord Kenrick. Her eyes questioned him, but she remained silent.

Charity wanted no part of any deception. She had enough of that on her plate as it was. "Lord Kenrick saved me from a nasty fall, Aunt. I espied Chico in that oak tree"—she gestured vaguely in the direction of the tree from which she had fallen into Lord Kenrick's arms—"and since there was no one else present, I attempted to capture him. I suspect the rascal would have made his way to the ground if only I had had the sense to offer him the grapes he now eats." She gave a disgusted glance at the obviously unrepentant Chico.

"You were not injured?" Lady Tavington's voice was calm, almost bland. Certainly she was not terribly anxious.

"Not a scratch, thanks to his lordship." Charity ignored the cool stare from Lady Sylvia. Lord Kenrick was watching her with that strange expression again. How she would like to know his thoughts. And then again, perhaps it was as well she didn't.

"I thought I saw a patch of color in among the oak leaves and decided to investigate. I found Miss Lonsbury up in the boughs, so to speak." He bestowed a bland look on Lady Tavington, who merely nodded in return.

"Had I been here, I would gladly have played the hero." Lord Harwood smiled roguishly at Charity, who couldn't repress an answering chuckle.

"You are far too amiable to be a hero, my lord." Lady Sylvia sparkled up at Lord Harwood, clinging to his arm in a fragile, ladylike manner. Apparently she had not given up her attempt to cause a spark of jealousy in Lord Kenrick's heart. Charity couldn't see if anything had caught fire in that well-guarded area. Rather, it seemed to her that Lord Harwood didn't seem to mind the flirtation with Lady Sylvia in the least— nor, for that matter, did Lord Kenrick!

"Charles, call the others back, let them know the animal is found. Miss Lonsbury, a word, please." Lord Kenrick touched her elbow with a firm grip, one she couldn't have easily shaken.

Lady Sylvia gave a vexed sigh as she watched them move apart from the others. She remained beneath the tree for a moment, watching with narrowed eyes as Charity and Lord Kenrick walked away from the group. Firming her mouth into a hard, unattractive line, she walked to her horse, obviously deep in thought.

Lord Harwood found her there minutes later when he returned. "Problems, Sylvia?" he softly taunted.

Across the meadow Charity balked in a second of rebellion. "What do you want?" She was proud of her cool, distant sound. He expected her to obey or else, did he? She was no milk-and-water miss.

"This is your idea of being a lady? I was right when I told your aunt I felt you lacked in certain areas. I do not see how you can please your aunt by forming a desirable *parti* when you conduct yourself with such abandon.''

His air of righteous indignation was more than Charity could bear. Anger flared within her deliciously dressed frame. It boiled, seethed, overflowing in deceptively sweet words. "I do not behave with seemly modesty? Well, that is really no concern of yours, is it? I *will* marry, my lord—the first man who asks me." Then she realized that might bring disastrous results. "Except the squire, of course." Seeking to justify that statement, she added, "I am persuaded he would suit Miss Spencer far better than me." Her smile would have frosted grapes off a vine at twenty paces.

Ozzie came striding up at the moment, a mystified look on his face. "I say, are you all right, Miss Lonsbury? Lady Tavington said Kenrick had saved you from a nasty fall. Dashed havey-cavey thing, seems to me." His eyes narrowed at his friend. "Shouldn't say anything, I expect, but oughtn't you be with Lady Sylvia instead of Charles? I am most pleased to be of assistance to Miss Lonsbury."

Charity observed the hostile look exchanged between the two men with growing amusement. It was as if Ozzie had, much like the village lads, informed Lord Kenrick he was poaching on another's territory. If he but knew that Lord Kenrick was lecturing her on her unseemly deportment!

Charity smiled guilelessly up at Ozzie, looking like an entire box of comfits. "Lord Kenrick merely wished to ascertain I was not injured in the fall, Ozzie. I daresay he can return his attentions to Lady Sylvia immediately. He is not needed here. Although I do thank you, my lord, for breaking my fall. My bonnet would have been quite crushed had I fallen on it." Charity patted the elegant straw bonnet swathed in salmon-colored riband and trimmed with cream silk flowers.

Lady Ann strolled into the meadow on the arm of Lord Powell looking demurely pleased with herself. They joined Lord Charles and Lady Sylvia, moving toward their horses with casual intent. Lady Ann's soft,

sweet voice drifted across to where Charity stood. "I'm
so happy they found the little monkey. I am persuaded
Lady Tavington would miss him greatly if he was lost."
Her voice held a genuine concern missing in the honeyed
words from Lady Sylvia.

The footmen sent to wait upon the group were
hovering near the large oak tree, tucking unwanted food
in the hampers, discreetly preparing to leave.

Ozzie glanced up at the darkening heavens, brows
furrowing in dismay. His concern was not noticed. The
two combatants glared at each other with furious
disdain. Charity clutched Ozzie's comforting arm with
militant fervor as she refused to break away from Lord
Kenrick's penetrating stare. The melting sensation that
had spread through her from those previous looks of
tender regard was forgotten as she searched the intensity
of those deeply blue eyes.

"I say, dashed if I don't think it's going to rain. Wish
I'd eaten more before that animal took off." His words
were ignored by the two locked in silent conflict.

The Earl of Dunstall spoke quietly to his coachman
and soon the top was up on the barouche. Lady
Tavington nodded to his softly spoken suggestion and
followed him to the carriage along with Lady Kenrick.

"Charity, dearest girl, we must return. It appears it is
going to rain. I am persuaded none of us wants a
wetting, especially those on horseback. It would be such
a shame if the ladies got those lovely riding habits wet."
Lady Tavington's words woke Charity from the spell
that seemed to grip her.

Ozzie walked Charity toward the barouche while the
others hastily scattered toward their mounts. Lord
Kenrick had taken one last look at Charity before he
strode toward his horse and Lady Sylvia. Squire
Bigglesby marched up to Charity, begging Sir Oswald
for a word with his old friend.

Giving her a curious look, Ozzie patted her hand
before leaving them. "Of course, Bigglesby."

Charity was not pleased. Euphremia was glaring

daggers at her, and Charity had no desire to endure either another scold or one of his tedious proposals.

"Well, what is it you wish to say?" she said ungraciously. She could barely see the sapphire-blue riding habit Lady Sylvia wore, trees obscuring her as she cantered toward home. Ozzie took another look at the sky, and he also aimed his horse toward Greenoaks. Only Euphremia waited, an anxious expression settling on her face.

"I will not have this unseemly behavior in my intended, Miss Lonsbury," the squire blustered, his face growing more red by the moment as he glowered at the defiant Charity.

"What an uncommonly fertile imagination you have. I am not your intended. I have no intentions of wedding you, now or ever, sir. You believe in plain speaking? So do I! Mark my words. I will not marry you. My aunt is now my protector. Believe me, your suit will not prosper with her. Better that you look elsewhere, sir." She whirled, marched to the waiting groom, and slipped inside the barouche before Bigglesby could recover his astounded wits.

The carriage began to move down the lane as Miss Spencer called to him. With the reins of his horse in her hands, she joined him. "A problem, Squire? You can tell me about it while we ride, if you wish."

Euphremia might not have the charming countenance Miss Lonsbury had, but she gave flattering attention to the squire. It soothed his wounded ego some to have such regard bestowed in his direction. Still, he was determined to wed Miss Lonsbury. Only a blind, stubborn man would attempt such a thing, but then the squire had never been given high marks for perception.

A gentle rain was falling by the time the barouche reached the front door of the great house. Jameson ushered each person in from the carriage with the aid of a great black umbrella. Lord Kenrick met the group as they made their way toward the Rose Drawing room, the older ladies twittering like a cage of canaries.

Taking advantage of the confusion as the remainder of the party joined them, Lady Sylvia and Euphremia fussing at their presently improper attire in riding habits, Charity examined the lovely room. The Adam carpet, its great star and circle complementing the design of the ceiling, echoed the rose of the velvet chairs and sofa. Ivory-silk-hung walls displayed a wealth of oils. Moving closer, she admired a Bellini and the view of Greenoaks painted by Turner. The remainder of the oil paintings appeared to be of the Italian school. Several landscapes in watercolor, also possibly Italian, were grouped near the door on the far side of the room. She was certain she could spend days studying the art contained in this house. Quietly stepping to the warmth of a crackling blaze in the fireplace, she sought to rid herself of the penetrating chill from the rain.

"I believe your aunt might enjoy that bit of work." Lord Kenrick indicated a monkey orchestra of fine Meissen that was arranged on the chimneypiece. "I take it you suffer no ill effects from the rain?"

"No," Charity replied, warily observing Lady Sylvia studying her with a patently hostile expression on her face. "I was stopped by the squire for a moment, but gained the carriage before the rain began to fall." She drew her paisley shawl more closely around her shoulders. There was something in Lady Sylvia's look that chilled her.

His knitted brows revealing either puzzlement or deep thought, Charity wondered if he believed her determination to refuse the squire.

"What did he want, if I may ask?"

Charity allowed an amused look into her eyes. "He gave me a scold, my lord. You might have applauded him." An unconscious sigh slipped out.

"And?" Lord Kenrick was nothing if not persistent.

"He informed me my behavior was not seemly for his intended. I again told him I will not be his bride, but he seems to have a distinct difficulty with his hearing. Pity. Miss Spencer would undoubtedly snap up his proposal in a trice."

"But then we all have our little problems, do we not?" The sober expression was not the sort to send a girl's heart fluttering, yet Charity found that, in spite of his unsmiling face, she treasured the moment with him. What could be the source of *his* problems? All he had to do was toss the handkerchief and Lady Sylvia would be his.

The Earl of Dunstall joined them and Charity stood quietly as the gentlemen conversed until the butler entered the room with a tea tray overflowing with delicate pastries, some of the provender from the aborted picnic, plus pots of tea and coffee as well.

Lord Kenrick offered the men something more to their possible liking. They regrouped, the ladies fluttering toward the tea table, where Lady Kenrick presided. Lord Kenrick drew the men to the far side of the room, where several decanters towered over an arrangement of crystal glasses. Ozzie took a plate heaped with food over to where the men stood and calmly munched as he listened.

Charity found herself seated between Euphremia and Lady Sylvia. It was possibly the most disconcerting arrangement she could conceive at the moment. Both women eyed her teacup as though they would be only to happy to slip the contents of a Borgia ring into it. That perfume would most likely now fill the popular "fountain" rings did not reassure her. She had the uneasy feeling that instead of a fine spray of scent released at the least pressure, she would receive a dose of poison. How nice it would be to promise each of them she had no designs on Kenrick or Bigglesby.

Lady Ann slipped into the room, apologizing sweetly for her absence. "I simply had to slip up to my room to change. My skirts were dreadfully muddied, I couldn't wait to get out of them. I've been longing for a restoring dish of tea. Do forgive me if I have kept you waiting."

"Not at all, Lady Ann," said Lady Kenrick.

The ladies ate sparingly, Charity not at all. She couldn't help but think she enjoyed her times with Lord Harwood more than with the ladies, though Lady Ann seemed much to her liking with her soft voice and smiling eyes.

Charity covertly examined the quietly sweet woman. She was few years older than herself, just a bit on the plump side, with ash-brown hair becomingly arranged in curls and braids. Her brown eyes showed lively intelligence as well as a tendency to stray in the direction of Lord Powell. Charity wished her well if her interest lay there.

With the addition of another woman, the atmosphere altered subtly. Charity sensed that somehow Lady Ann was the moderating influence. Perhaps the others relaxed, knowing Lady Ann harbored no interest in their respective gentlemen. At least none of the others was under pressure to select a husband as speedily as possible. Charity shifted her position so she could watch the gentlemen on the far side of the room by the tall windows that looked out on the view. Ozzie and Lord Harwood were arguing amiably with Lord Kenrick while Lord Powell, his shirt points unwilted even after being in the damp, chatted with the Earl of Dunstall and the pompous squire.

Lord Harwood was well-groomed, had a pleasing voice and manners. Ozzie was a delight, though a bit of a rattle. She had rashly promised Lord Kenrick to wed the first man who asked her. As long as it wasn't the squire, she supposed it didn't really matter all that much. She was not so foolish as to consider her *preux chevalier* as one of her prospects. If she couldn't have her heart's desire, what difference did it make? She would do her best to be a good wife and mother. Startled with the direction of her thoughts, she stole a glance at the gentlemen again. She knew precious little of the intimacies of marriage. Her father had never spoken of it, and her mother had died while Charity was too young to discuss such a thing. Perhaps a caring and civilized husband was all that was required to make it tolerable?

Lady Tavington peered at the dainty watch pinned on her ample bosom, then murmured a few words to her dear friend, Lady Kenrick, who nodded in return.

Lady Tavington rose gracefully, the younger women of necessity following suit. She motioned to Charity. "It is time we departed. A little rest and time to change our clothes will be most welcome. I am persuaded it will also give Lady Kenrick a few moments to relax."

Charity gathered her gloves and parasol after bestowing a light kiss on Lady Kenrick's soft scented cheek. Such a dear woman. Still, she had made her son promise to marry soon, just as Aunt Tavington had convinced Charity marriage was necessary. Would Charity, once married, with grown children, force them into a path not of their choosing? She devoutly hoped not.

Since the rain had dwindled to a fine mist, the squire and Euphremia insisted on riding to their homes. Euphremia seemed bent on showing Bigglesby she was not a wilting lily.

Lady Ann and Lady Sylvia hurried to their rooms after a polite good-bye. Lady Tavington paused a moment for a word with her dear friend, to be joined by the earl. Charity strolled to the entry hall to wait with impatience for Lord Kenrick's carriage to be brought to the front door.

The marble of the entry floor echoed with the click of heels as Lord Kenrick walked briskly to join her. She couldn't help but think he looked at home here among the carved alabaster, the simulated porphyry columns, and the austere blue of the walls. Though the decorative ivory-tinted Chippendale chairs did not look as though they were meant to hold his weight, nor, indeed, the weight of so slight a person as herself. No fires burned in the grates of the marble fireplaces and she shivered, whether from his look or the chill she couldn't say.

"A word, Miss Lonsbury." There was no warmth in his voice.

"Since I do not see my aunt in your trail, nor do I hear the approach of the carriage, I am at your disposal until one or the other arrives." She stood stiffly erect, her hands held properly before her, chin tilted up. Of course the latter was necessary, considering his height and all.

"You will have to do better this evening at dinner, my dear. You certainly do not wish to put your aunt to the bother and expense of a Season. I'm sure if you try . . ." He gave an impatient wave of his hand.

Odious man. "I am a lady, my lord. As such, there is a limit to what I can or will do. I must have time. Surely you will grant me that? Lady Tavington has stated I am to be content with my choice."

"Curious," he reflected aloud, "I would have thought a young woman as yourself might harbor notions of devoted romantic love." His intent look disconcerted her to no little degree. What did he hope to discover?

She fastened her gaze on the top button of his waistcoat. "That is a luxury not permitted to everyone, my lord."

"You don't insist on that?" His voice seemed to contain more than curiosity. He appeared bent on challenging her, almost disappointed in her lack of argument concerning the subject. Did he really expect a well-bred young lady who certainly knew what was expected of her to rebel?

She didn't know the purpose of this conversation. What difference could it make to him whether she was in love or not? "Most marriages today are those of convenience. If I receive an offer from an eligible man and my aunt gives her approval, I shall marry, like most any other dutiful young woman does in the same circumstances." She was fast losing what little enthusiasm she had for marriage.

"I would . . ." Whatever he was going to tell her he might do or approve was lost as Lady Tavington bustled into the entry followed by the earl, and the carriage drew up outside.

Charity was pleased the earl elected to ride with them. She was quite certain it saved her from another scold.

Or at least a quizzing from her curious aunt. She settled back against the squabs and turned her mind to Sir Ozzie and Lord Harwood.

The earl broke in on her thoughts. "Miss Lonsbury, I should very much like to view the orchids you cultivate. Lady Tavington informs me they are rare and exceedingly beautiful. Would we have time to have a look-in now?"

First glancing at her aunt to get approval, Charity nodded. "If you wish, we can stop awhile. You can always view them at your leisure tomorrow if they interest you."

The carriage drew to a halt at the point closest to the hothouses, and the three walked up the narrow path in a single file, Charity first. She was grateful the rain had ceased, with a sun peering around fitful clouds. The temperature had dropped: it was a good thing there was heat for her plants to protect them. There was a hint of chill in the air that spoke of the winds of winter to come.

A few drops of rain spattered down from a spreading beech and she brushed the water from her shawl as she considered the day. Lady Sylvia made her feel uneasy, unlike the sunny Lady Ann Rowe. Why the elegant blonde should have an antipathy toward Charity was beyond her.

She approached the hothouses, taking care to mind her steps. Josiah was to have scythed the grass along here today, but it had been left undone. Poor man, likely he had far more to do now what with fetching flowers to the great house and all.

The door made a mournful rasp as the earl opened it for the ladies. Charity stepped in first, smiling at Roscoe as it hopped forward to meet her. The rabbit seemed upset, whiskers all aquiver and ears not their usual placid selves. Then she observed it was not as warm as normal. A shiver ran down her spine that had nothing to do with temperature.

"Is something amiss, Charity dearest? You have such a perplexed look on your face." Lady Tavington lightly touched Charity on the arm, startling her from her thoughts.

"It is too cool in here. It ought to be warmer. Excuse me a moment while I check on the stove." She began to make her way to the back of the hothouse where the stove was located. As she walked, her fears increased. It was cold and damp. She might have known Josiah would forget when there was so much to do with all the guests as the great house. A sudden sprinkling of chilling drops of water brought her eyes to the top of the hothouse. Sharply glancing at the floor ahead of her, then the benches, she saw shards of glass lying scattered here and there.

"What is it, Miss Lonsbury?" The earl was hurrying down the slatted boards of the aisle to where Charity had frozen in horror.

"The roof! Several panes are broken! I could lose all my orchids!"

10

"MERCIFUL HEAVENS!" LADY TAVINGTON rushed to
Charity's side and gazed with horror at the large
fragments of glass scattered around the area. Looking
up to the roof, several broken panes of glass could be
seen, sharp points protruding from the frames.

Charity made to move forward, compelled to do
something to save her precious orchids, but the earl
cried out in alarm, pulling her back from the piece of
glass she was about to pick up. "Don't touch that! You
could do yourself serious injury, my dear. Allow me to
summon help." The earl hurried from the hothouse,
heading toward the spot where the carriage remained
waiting for them to return.

"I must take these plants and transfer them to the
smaller hothouse. The stove does not work so well in
there," Charity fretted. "Not only are these poor dears
going to be dreadfully squashed together, the heat may
be uncertain at best. Oh, Aunt Alice, nothing must be
allowed to happen to the orchid for the Prince!"

Taking several of the smaller pots, Charity ignored
her delicate salmon walking dress to begin moving the
plants from the chilled air to the smaller, but safer
hothouse. She worked swiftly, rushing back and forth,
welcoming Aunt Alice's assistance in gathering up a few
of the many pots to be transferred.

After several trips, Charity looked around her in
dismay. "I begin to wonder why I have *quite* so many
orchids, dear Aunt. I can only hope the earl is able to
find help, and soon."

She whirled around as the door gave its customary

wheeze, like a dying gasp from an about to expire ancient.

"I say, what a tempest! Can I be of assistance?" Sir Oswald looked around the hothouse, now partially emptied of its exotic contents. It was obvious to Charity he wasn't particularly eager to handle the pots, but she felt it a measure of his devotion that he was willing.

Behind him Lord Harwood stood in the entry, surveying the damage. The waning afternoon light picked out points of glass. "We had best all take as many of the plants as we can. Jameson was sending for the glazier, but I doubt if he will be able to do much more than take measurements until tomorrow. You realize the glass may have to be sent down from London?"

Two under-gardeners came up to Charity at that moment, looking confused. Ned spoke first. "Ol' Joshua ain't nowhere aroun', miss. Wot kin we do for ye?"

The earl interrupted. "Better see to the broken glass. Mind how you pick it up. We don't want casualties."

The two young men touched their forelocks in recognition of authority and respect for the earl's wisdom. A lantern was brought to the bench, illuminating the scene more clearly.

Charity turned to thank the bearer of the lantern and found herself face to face with Lord Kenrick. "Oh, dear. It's you. Thank you for the lantern." Unable to think of what to say next, she thrust two pots of orchids at him and pointed toward the other hothouse. "Hurry! The cold cannot be good for them."

Lord Kenrick gave a rueful grimace at the dust that was bound to find its way to his cream waistcoat, and left the hothouse at once.

Lady Tavington sang out gaily, "This is quite an experience, is it not, my lord? We shall have all these plants moved in no time. Willing hands make light work, my mother was used to say."

Lord Harwood reached up to remove several hanging

baskets and queried Charity before leaving. "Once I have these in the other hothouse, there remains the orchids attached to the wood poles. Perhaps you ought to see to those yourself. Does anyone else know the secret of how they grow up there?"

Charity shook her head, wondering how she was to avoid disgrace while climbing up the ladder to shift the air plants. She had the ladder in place and was at the top, removing one creamy-petaled bloom from its perch, when strong hands grasped her about her waist. She glanced down with a growing sense of resignation. "You again! I thought you were in the other hothouse." The words erupted before she could give thought. It was hardly the manner in which to speak to her landlord, especially the man whose initials she had been using in her business.

"So it seems. You must be part bird with your liking for high places. I don't suppose you will permit one of the under-gardeners to handle those plants?" There was a trace of amusement in Kenrick's voice, although his eyes were the only other thing about him that gave her courage. A hint of a sparkle lurked in the brilliant blue. Charity had the awful feeling that it was deceiving. He was bound to ring a peal over her head, though why he felt it to be his duty was more than she could fathom.

"Certainly not!" Her indignant words rang out with great fervor. "Those ham-fisted men would only ruin them. Joshua could do this, but no one seems to know where he is." She was able to remove the pole from its slot and offered the plant and pole to the elegant man who was her host. Her voice faded as she looked at him. How foolish could she be, to put this man to work as though he were a servant.

"I was afraid you might say that. Ozzie, old friend, take this plant and pole and find a place for it in the other building."

Charity found herself soaring through the air to be set firmly on the slatted wood floor. She resolved to ignore the feelings that radiated out from the warm touch of his hands through her muslin. A futile effort, at best!

"Now, I will see to the remaining plants while you supervise. I am considered to have a light touch with . . . things." His eyes held a wicked gleam, and Charity held a rising hope that she might escape with no scold at all. She paid no thought to what he might have a light touch with. Could it be the ribbons?

"Miss, we found ol' Joshua. He was all of a heap behind the hothouse. Right near the stove, 'e was."

Charity forgot the air plants for the moment, dashing out of the hothouse and around to the back. There she found Ned kneeling by Joshua. The older man was half sitting up, his right hand gingerly exploring his head.

"How badly are you hurt, Joshua?" She was set to kneel by his side when she was nudged aside by a larger figure.

Lord Kenrick bent over the injured man, his hands expertly checking to see if there was any bleeding.

Lady Tavington bustled up to them, exclaiming in dismay as she observed the scene. "Bring him to the cottage and I shall see to his wound." She inspected the poor man's head, adding, "I am persuaded it is not serious, my lord."

Lord Harwood came to stand beside Charity, gently touching her arm in inquiry. "We have the last of the plants moved if you wil come to check them. Not knowing just how they should be, I'm afraid they have been placed in any old spot."

Charity gave a lingering look at the tall figure of Lord Kenrick as he walked Lady Tavington to where the carriage waited. Ned and Tom carried Joshua. Charity felt she ought to have been tending him, but she knew her aunt was far more capable. It might be wise to take lessons from Aunt regarding Wang Fu's treatments.

"I'll do what I can, my lord. I appreciate what everyone has done. I cannot believe someone would be so careless as to be tossing balls near the hothouse. We have never had problems in the past that I recall." Charity's voice was soft, her distress apparent in her troubled eyes.

He walked back into the damaged hothouse and
prowled around while Charity checked the condition of
the stove. "I do not think it was the work of boys
playing ball, Miss Lonsbury. There is no sign of a ball,
but there are several bricks where I do not think bricks
belong."

Charity left the stove, its fire about out. Walking to
where Lord Harwood stood looking down at a number
of randomly tumbled bricks, she nodded in agreement
with his assessment. She had never tossed bricks about
in that fashion. The few she had were neatly stacked by
the bench. She took a deep breath and voiced the
unpleasant thought that came to her. "It was deliberate,
then, wasn't it? But who? What could this mischief
accomplish?" The wanton destruction made no sense at
all to her, and she shook her head in confusion.

His arm gently around her, Lord Harwood
shepherded Charity from the hothouse to join the
remaining helpers. Lady Ann Rowe came hurrying
down the path from the great house to meet them.

"What has occurred? We came down from our rooms
to find most of you missing, the footman telling some
dire tale about damage. Jameson is in what is for him, I
daresay, a flap. What is the mystery?"

Charity pressed the arm that helped support her,
shaking her head slightly to caution Lord Harwood.
"Bothersome children, I have no doubt. Several panes
of glass were broken in the hothouse. The gentlemen
were so kind to help me move my orchids so they would
not be killed by the chill. The panes will be replaced as
soon as possible, I am sure." Then, attempting to
change the subject, she tried a smile at Lady Ann. "But
you are dressed for dinner and I have not yet been
home. Pray excuse me, that I might change my clothes.
I do not desire to be late." To Lord Harwood, she
pleaded *sotto voce*, "Say nothing for now about what
you discovered."

The cottage appeared surprisingly quiet when she
hurried down the path and through the gate. All signs of
the carriage, Lord Kenrick, and the under-gardeners

were gone. Mrs. Woods opened the front door for her, her hands as usual twisting her white apron.

"Joshua? My aunt? Where is everyone?" The house was silent. Charity searched the rooms for her aunt, not admitting to herself she also hoped to see the tall figure of Lord Kenrick as well.

"Joshua wanted to be home, he did. Said he wouldn't rest in naught but his own house." Mrs. Woods sniffed with approval at his sense of what was proper. "Your aunt did what was necessary and told him he could go iffen he was careful."

At that moment Parton came from the best bed-chamber, where Lady Tavington could be heard softly chattering to Chico, once the door was opened. "Your dress is laid out, Miss Charity. Come, let me help you. You must be near frazzled with all these goings-on."

Charity was grateful to have assistance, especially at the moment. All the way home she had been mulling over the deliberate smashing of the hothouse roof until she was near dizzy with the effort. She could think of no reason for such behavior. The local lads all knew she raised the orchids, and she didn't think she had any enemies there. Respect for his lordship was high, so that was ruled out. Unless it might be some crazed soul with a grievance against Lord Kenrick that had not come to light.

The only strangers she knew to be in the area were the group here for the house party. But that couldn't be. Who among them would want the hothouse and its contents ruined? Lord Powell? He might not care for growing plants, but he didn't care sufficiently to ruin the place. Sir Oswald? He was obviously not enamored of orchids, but he was far too good-natured to do such a thing. Lord Harwood? Never. He was, as Lady Sylvia said, too amiable a person for such a deed, and had shown interest in Charity's efforts.

The ladies were not considered. No *lady* would do such a thing, *if* she would soil her hands to pick up a brick, then had the strength and power to toss it.

"I do not know what to make of it, Parton. It is indeed strange, and not a little worrying."

Parton nodded, keeping her thoughts to herself, then helped her from the hasty bath, into her chemise, petticoat, and then her lovely evening dress of sea-green satin embroidered daintily at the scalloped edges of the hem. Charity pulled at the beret sleeves, wishing they were not quite so short or her décolletage quite so low. Her aunt entered the room as Charity inquired of Parton, "Do you not think I ought to wear gauze sleeves over these?"

"Never give it a thought, dearest," her aunt interposed. "You have lovely arms, and if you fear a chill, you may take a shawl along. Your white cashmere de laine with the colored border would be nice with that gown. It has the same shade of green, does it not?"

Surveying her niece with great satisfaction, Lady Tavington cocked her head as she studied her. She was enjoying her foray into a kind of belated motherhood. Charity was the sweetest girl imaginable and certainly paid for dressing. Now, if she could only be guided in the right direction, all would go well.

Alice had watched with great care as each of the gentlemen spoke with Charity. Only one man brought true roses to her cheeks, only one brought a brilliant sparkle to those intriguing gray eyes. Lady Tavington meant to do all she could to see to it *that* man was the one who offered for her dearest girl. Lady Tavington had known great happiness in her marriage. It was unthinkable Charity must settle for less.

Charity studied the shawl, then agreed. "I suppose you are right, Aunt." Nodding at Parton, for, truly, she didn't care one jot which shawl she took, she turned to the point that had been plaguing her the past hour or so.

"Aunt, can you conceive who might wish his lordship ill? Or resent my growing the orchids enough to do damage?"

"I have no knowledge of these things, but I daresay

the culprit will come to light before too long." Lady
Tavington sounded supremely confident.

Charity wasn't so sure. And she feared revelation of
her own activities if the investigation was too complete.

The carriage awaited at the front gate when Charity
peeked out the window. Her aunt went out the door,
followed by Charity. Until now, Charity had been too
occupied to think of the evening ahead. Another dinner,
another opportunity to consider the gentlemen who
exhibited such an interest in her. She had to confess it
was exciting for one who in the past had considered a
subdued dinner with the Spencer family as the height of
local society. She resolved to set aside the disturbing
incident of the hothouse for the moment. She had no
doubt it would intrude again too soon.

Lady Sylvia made Charity feel ill at ease. How could
any woman as beautiful as she resent Charity? She
voiced this thought to her aunt, who was looking out of
the carriage window to see the great house ablaze with
the light of hundreds of candles.

"She is not blind, dearest. You are a lovely woman,
and as such, competition. She will not feel easy until she
has brought Kenrick up to scratch. I have developed a
feeling that it may not be as simple a matter as she
thought at first. We can but observe. It is nearly like a
play at Drury Lane. One waits for the ending of the
story."

With that their exchanged ceased, for the carriage
drew up before the broad steps leading up to the front
doors. Jameson had one tall, burnished oak door open,
welcoming them into the house before Charity had time
to reflect on her aunt's words.

The others were all gathered in the Gold Saloon when
Charity and Lady Tavington entered the long room. At
the far end, Charity could see Lady Ann Rowe and Lord
Powell conversing with the Earl of Dunstall. Closer by,
Euphremia clung to the arm of Squire Bigglesby, who
nattered on at Lord Kenrick. Lord Harwood and Sir
Oswald were crossing the polished wood floor, skirting

the Aubusson rugs where clusters of ivory upholstered gold chairs got in their way. Behind them, Charity could see several elegant Roman inspired torchères ablaze with light. It seemed to her like a page from a storybook. What a pity her knight was not real, nor was she a fair maiden in distress . . . Yet.

"At last. We have been waiting impatiently for your lovely presence to cheer the evening for us, Miss Lonsbury." Lord Harwood smiled, his eyes sending a message of his regard for her. "May I add you look charming? That shade of green is vastl becoming to you." He narrowed his eyes with consideration, then added, "But then, I suspect anyone with your sensitivity to color would choose with care."

Charity cast a demure look at the floor before daring to meet his eyes. What a hand he was. Or were his words genuine? She was too unused to compliments from polished gentlemen, she could see that. She sparkled up at him. "La, sir, you are too kind."

"I say, dashed if Charles hasn't said the thing exactly. You are quite the prettiest, Miss Lonsbury." Sir Oswald beamed his amiable smile at her, making her feel warm with their friendship.

Lord Kenrick excused himself from the squire, leaving that man in the belief he had been eloquently convincing in his assertion Lord Kenrick ought to spend more of his time at Greenoaks.

Near the door, Charity was aware of every step he took toward her and the group which was so gay. Lady Tavington nudged her arm just before Charity dropped a deep curtsy to the marquess.

"So kind of you to include us in the evening festivities, my lord." Lady Tavington nodded regally, then turned to greet her dear Lady Kenrick with affection.

Just as they were about to be joined by Euphremia and Bigglesby, Jameson entered to announce dinner was served.

Lady Kenrick accepted Lord Harwood's arm while

Lord Kenrick took Lady Sylvia and the Earl of Dunstall beamed his smile of welcome on Lady Tavington. Protocol might have been a bit confused, but Charity was certain most everyone was pleased. Lady Ann certainly glowed as she lightly touched Lord Powell's black-sheathed arm. Sir Oswald approached Charity with evident satisfaction.

"Glad I'm a sir and not a lord. Get to offer you my arm. Much better." Charity bit back a grin as they followed the others, then gracefully slipped into her chair. Of mahogany, the Chippendale design had unusual curved seats she found tolerably comfortable. Above the marble fireplace across from where she sat, she noticed the portrait of yet another of the Kenrick ancestors, a lovely woman in eighteenth-century dress with a faintly melancholy expression.

Conversation was lively and Charity did her best to join in. But at odd moments she found herself examining the faces around her, wondering who of this group might have had motive to toss bricks through the glass of the hothouse. The thought came to her that even if a lady did not throw a brick, she might put someone else up to doing the job. That brought Lady Ann and Lady Sylvia in focus.

Lady Ann was dismissed immediately, being far too kind and sweet in nature. Lady Kenrick was never considered. However, Lady Sylvia might bear thinking about. Charity would have to watch her this evening.

When Lady Kenrick signaled the ladies to retire to the Gold Saloon, Charity was prepared to begin her observations.

"Do you play the pianoforte, dear Charity?" Lady Kenrick gave Charity a quizzical look. "Perhaps you sing?"

"I fear my talents lie in a different direction, my lady. I find expression in painting watercolors. Alas, it is not something that can be trotted out for display, thank heavens." Charity smiled demurely at Lady Kenrick, finding an answering smile of understanding much to her liking.

"Lady Sylvia is going to favor us with a harp selection while Lady Ann plays the pianoforte for her."
Lady Kenrick nodded in the vague direction of the two
exquisitely groomed ladies fussing about the
instruments.

For the first time, Charity noticed a harp placed by
the second of the marble fireplaces in the room, at the
far end from where she had entered. Lady Sylvia,
dressed in a frock of sapphire-blue crape over a slip of
white satin, seated herself by the harp and softly began
to tune it. It would take strong fingers, firm wrists to
play the harp, Charity noted. Lady Sylvia was not your
usual frail woman.

When the gentlemen joined the ladies, it was to find
Lady Sylvia playing, with delicate fervor, a light French
air. Lord Harwood came to sit in the chair next to
Charity. Sir Oswald stood restlessly behind her, tapping
a foot on the hearth, then his fingers on the mantel.

While pleasant music flowed from the golden harp,
Charity studied the men in the room. She doubted the
Earl of Dunstall would be involved. He seemed to have
shown genuine interest in the orchids as well as concern
for possible damage. In his black dress with the white
waistcoat and the diamond sparkling from his
immaculate linen, he looked about as far as one could
get from someone who might throw bricks through
windows.

Lord Harwood she could observe with an oblique
inspection. His dark-blue coat was perfection itself. The
fawn pantaloons with straps under his polished shoes
and the exquisitely tied cravat bespoke a gentleman of
the very highest order. He, too, seemed an unlikely
candidate. Besides, she liked him.

She sighed and shifted her gaze to Sir Oswald. He,
too, was elegantly garbed, while more dazzling with his
neat fobs and fancy tied cravat, he wouldn't do
anything so low.

Further on, leaning over the piano to turn pages for
Lady Ann, stood Lord Powell, a gentleman of the first
stare. The high starched points of his collar must make

it difficult for him to bend as he now did, much less pick up a brick. She was very positive *he* would not deign to soil his hands picking up a brick. Charity hadn't forgotten his distaste for the soil on the potting bench. He had been notably absent from the crew of helpers who came to her assistance earlier. He was too fastidious to concern himself with an intrigue that might involve dirt.

Lady Sylvia finished her selection on the harp and joined Lady Ann by the pianoforte. She very prettily persuaded Lord Powell to join her in a duet. They sang well together, Charity admitted, wishing she could manage to carry a tune as nicely.

Once the singing was over, Lady Kenrick insisted Lady Tavington join her, the earl, and a reluctant Lord Harwood in a game of whist. Since Charity was an indifferent player at best, she wandered as far from the card table as she could. She stood silently contemplating another of Kenrick's female ancestors who stared gloomily down from the frame hung above one of the marble chimneypieces.

"That was my great-grandmother. Formidable woman, wasn't she?" Lord Kenrick's voice reached her from very close to her left ear. "She looks as though she spent most of her time giving a scold."

"Must run in the family," Charity muttered as she took another look at the face to see if other traits had been passed along.

"I must show you her husband." He turned to his friend. "Ozzie, we will return shortly. I'm going to show her Great-grandfather."

Lord Kenrick touched Charity's elbow to guide her from the room. She had the distinct impression his touch would become a grasp if she didn't meekly follow him along. How comforting he couldn't know how her knees trembled when she drew close to him.

Sir Oswald nodded, then joined Euphremia, the squire, and the others who were not playing cards. The six sat close togther, conversing more agreeably than Charity expected, given the squire was a member of the party. Kenrick drew her from the room.

They walked quickly through the adjoining rooms until they reached the central hall. The Rose Drawing Room and the Green Drawing Room were skimmed past with unseemly haste. They entered the library, lit with very few candles and a comfortable fire. A footman bestirred himself to bring more light to the room.

"So, tell me about this great-grandfather of yours." Charity gazed up at the painting above the mantel. It was barely discernible in the dim light of the room.

"He was the one who built Greenoaks. Earned his money in Barbados through customs and governments contracts, dealings with sugar planters. His son was given the title."

The footman lighted a few more candles, then retired at a signal from Lord Kenrick.

Charity looked about with great curiosity. The room had a warmth she supposed came from the rich glow of the row upon row of dark wood bookshelves and colorful bindings. Green-tinted, leather-embossed wall covering hung above and at either side of the shelves.

With more light, Charity returned her attention to the painting. He was a kindly-looking man, in contrast to his wife. The white wig revealed an intelligent forehead, with keen eyes and a temperate mouth below. Charity glanced up at the ceiling before finding the words for her response. "I find I quite like him. Rather opposite to his wife, I take it. She looks to be . . ." Here words failed her.

"A dragon," Kenrick supplied. "I didn't bring you in here just to see the portrait. Charles tells me he believes the windows were broken deliberately. You did not plan to inform me, did you?" The amusement had left his face, replaced by an expression she found hard to fathom.

Swallowing with difficulty, Charity shook her head, her tongue seemingly still having a problem with speech. Her voice was raspy when she at last found it. "It is mere speculation. Will it be difficult to repair the roof, my lord?"

"Why didn't you want me to find out about this? Charles seemed to think you were very upset when he told you of his find."

His persistence was unnerving. Those blue eyes were able to search out too many things. Charity feared all could be known merely by looking at her guilty face. She shrugged. "Only a natural reaction, to be sure. I have never been involved in malicious action before."

His lean fingers caressed his chin while he studied Charity thoughtfully in the flickering light of the fire and two branches of candles. She was being evasive, he felt certain. He stepped closer to her, trying to pierce that demure calm. "Was there something to what the squire said during his rambling speech? Is there unusual activity going on in the hothouses? A matter I ought know about?"

This was the last subject Charity wished to discuss. Her salvation came in the form of a smiling Lady Sylvia peeping around the open door.

"I vow you have spent an age inspecting David's great-grandfather. A charming-looking gentleman, was he not?" Lady Sylvia floated across the room to Lord Kenrick, knowing full well what her use of his Christian name implied. She dimpled sweetly up at Lord Kenrick as she clung to his arm. Her normally cool voice had assumed a sensuous warmth that surprised Charity. Apparently all was not as seemed with Lady Sylvia.

The smie directed at Charity had not quite the same intensity as the one to David. It was more in the nature of a warning. And it made Charity think all the harder.

11

" 'TIS A BLESSING I kept two of the special orchids in the other hothouse, Aunt. If the one I intended to present to the Prince Regent is damaged, I have the others to fall back upon.'' Charity sipped her morning chocolate while perched on her chair at the side of the deal table. Her aunt murmured some kind of a reply as she glanced over the paper sent down for her perusal by Lady Kenrick. Charity looked out the window again, to see if Lord Harwood had arrived on his horse as yet. They had arranged to go riding together after Charity returned to the Gold Saloon the previous night following the episode in the library.

The storm signals that she thought flashed in Lord Kenrick's eyes just before she sailed from the library, haunted by the low, intimate laughter of Lady Sylvia, had subsided by the time they all resumed their places in the saloon. Charity had discreetly flirted with both Lord Harwood and Sir Oswald, ignoring the narrow look Lord Kenrick directed toward her. Let him furrow his brow if he please. She was not required to ask his permission to flirt with the gentlemen who sought her company. Abominable man. Let him pay attention to Lady Sylvia. Though, upon reflection, he had spent more time in general company, visiting with every person in turn, than courting his lady. But perhaps that was proper. Poor Lady Sylvia, the only way she seemed to capture his time was to canter out with him in the morning.

Rising from the table, Charity impatiently paced the worn but polished boards of the parlor. "He is late.'' Her tone was as vexed as she felt. The morning was

clear, though cool, just right for a bit of activity. She
could spend some hours later on with her flowers. Never
would she admit she hoped a group would form so she
could see Lord Kenrick as well as the others.

The clattering of horses in the lane drew her to the
window to peep once again. She pulled back, unwilling
any see her so anxious. They were all in the party today.
Even Lady Ann and Lord Powell joined the riders.

"I see everyone decided to risk this uncertain sun. If it
is to rain, they might as well get out while they can."
Lady Tavington studied the trim lines of her niece as set
off by the russet habit. "It can get beastly dull cooped
up in the house, even one such as the great house. I
believe we should send to Madame Clotilde for another
habit, this one in jade kerseymere. What do you
think?"

"I think you have already spent too much on me,
dear Aunt." Charity gave her aunt an affectionate hug
before leaving the cottage to join the group.

Lady Tavington watched from the bay window as the
groom tossed Charity up to her saddle. She particularly
observed the expressions on a couple of faces. Most
interesting. With a wave of a hand, Charity was off, and
Lady Tavington walked to her room to locate some
writing paper.

The brisk autumn air was exhilarating, Charity
decided. She spent so many hours in the confines of the
hothouses, she missed a great many things. Of course,
she mused, there would have been no horse for her to
ride. She must ask Lord Kenrick if she might exercise
one of his mares after he departed. Then she recalled
that she, too, would be leaving. The thought held little
joy for her.

Ashamed of herself for wanting to have love instead
of being content with being allowed somewhat of a
choice in a husband, Charity turned a sunny smile
toward Lord Harwood and wished him the best of
mornings.

"I'm pleased you have given over your tutelage in
riding to me, Miss Lonsbury. Geoff seems to have his

time occupied. Odd, I have never observed Geoff to be so attentive to any lady.'' The last sentence was murmured in a voice Charity barely caught.

Tossing him a glance full of mischief, she turned to greet Sir Oswald on her other side. With the group setting such a leisurely pace, Charity had no difficulty at all in feeling comfortable with her abilities.

In front of her and to her far right, Lady Sylvia rode next to Lord Kenrick. She was dressed this day in a habit of darkest gray, set off by frills of cream lace at her throat and wrists. She looked very elegant and sure of herself. She spoke only to Lord Kenrick.

Lord Kenrick was as ever, Charity ruefully decided, trying not to look at him. That dark hair of his still wanted to tumble over his brow and she longed to smooth it back. That one glance she'd had from him reminded her his eyes were just as blue and just as piercing as ever in their regard. Every feature on that arrogant face, from the distinguished brow, those unusual eyes, to the lips, which had done such delightful things to her senses, was etched in her heart. His build, revealed so nobly by the fit of his coat, was intensely masculine, as were the well-muscled thighs and legs she wasn't suppose to notice. There was that about him that made him appear in command, to stand above others, even his well-appearing friends.

And that returned her to consider Lord Harwood and Sir Oswald. Kind, gentle men, both of them, they failed to completely capture her heart. Why? Why couldn't she simply fix her attentions on one of them, and let it be? She would have to make up her mind by the end of the week one way or the other. The house party would be breaking up on Sunday, with everyone returning to their respective homes. Each of the men was becoming more particular in his attentions. Charity couldn't figure out if Kenrick—or David, as Lady Sylvia called him—didn't approve of her flirting or if he felt she should choose one man and be done with it. It made life very difficult.

It was pleasant to ride along in the mild sun, admiring

the leaves, which had turned color. For a moment she
could forget about the pressures and secrets she must
hide from the others. Charity smiled absently at Lord
Harwood as she considered the watercolor she intended
to include with the orchid. With so many people
around, Lord Kenrick would not be apt to concern
himself with her. If he did not present himself at the
hothouse, neither would Lady Sylvia. It should be safe
to paint.

The workmen would be at the hothouse this morning
to tend to the repairs. If the glass was available and
could be set immediately, she could return her plants to
their proper shelves and possibly do some painting as
well. She had no idea what the others planned for the
afternoon.

"I say, a shilling for your thoughts."

Charity bestowed a cordial smile on Sir Oswald. "I
was admiring the scenery, enjoying the air."

Lady Sylvia murmured something to Lord Kenrick,
gave a bubble of laughter, then spurred her horse into a
canter, which soon became a gallop. Lord Kenrick was
after her in a flash, followed by Lady Ann and Lord
Powell.

Feeling as though she was holding Lord Harwood and
Sir Oswald back, Charity urged them to go as well. "I
am quite sure you are bored to death, trotting along
with me at this pace." She reached over to give her
horse a reassuring pat, though whether it was to assure
her horse or herself, it wasn't positive. "I have the
groom to stay with me. I'm sure you must be longing for
a dashing race."

Lord Harwood watched the flying scarf that whipped
back from Lady Sylvia's hat as she skimmed over the
field. His voice held a trace of bitterness as he spoke. "I
doubt they miss us overmuch." He turned to Charity
and his smile held genuine warmth. "Why not explore
this path to the right?"

There was something puzzling about this all, Charity
concluded. Saying nothing of her confusion, she

nodded her agreement, only adding that she wished to return to the cottage before too long, as she had a few tasks to complete.

It all reminded her of how the village children would play games and exclude the ones out of favor at the moment. Well, she had no use for such childish behavior. Her eyes danced with merriment as she considered how those others, particularly Lady Sylvia, had not the faintest notion how they were perceived.

The ride was over too soon. Charity paused by the gate as she watched Lord Harwood, Sir Oswald, and the groom with her mare in tow disappear up the lane toward the stables. Lord Harwood checked his horse, said something to Sir Oswald, then wheeled around and rode off to the south, followed seconds later by Sir Oswald. Both men galloped across the fields, disappearing from sight behind the trees.

It was lowering to feel she had been keeping them from a bruising ride, since that is what they appeared to want. Her spirits were down when she entered the cottage and went up to her room. Aunt Tavington was absent, no doubt with Lady Kenrick. Parton had walked to the village, according to a bustling Mrs. Woods.

Charity ate a light luncheon, absently staring out the window. Her deep sigh, crumbled bread on her plate, brought Mrs. Woods' attention more than once. She said nothing to the girl, simply kept her eyes open.

The hothouse roof shone in the filtered sun. Leaves of the tall beech trees danced in the afternoon breeze. The glazier had been and gone. Apparently it had not been necessary to send up to London for glass, after all.

Charity walked into the hothouse, inspected the stove, in which someone had thoughtfully started a good fire, then looked around. The floor was swept clean and all the benches had been scrubbed thoroughly. The windows had never looked so clear. It was obvious an army of cleaners had been here while she had been riding, and gone over everything from the ridgepole to the wooden slats beneath her feet.

Here was where she belonged. Trying to fit into the elegant London society would never suit her. A blue-deviled mood settled over her, refusing to go away. Nothing was right. With resolution, she turned her attention to the plants. Just as she was about to begin moving them once again, several under-gardeners approached with the orchids from the other hothouse. She stood in silent amazement as they marched in the door, which no longer wheezed as though it was going to die, then out again.

The door hinges had been oiled and the door repaired so it no longer sagged. There were no wheezes or squeaks when she pushed it to and fro. Roscoe hopped around the corner and peered up. "You look as confused as I am, dear bunny. Who gave the orders for all this to be done?" She could think of no one who would have the authority save Lord Kenrick, and why would he do such a thing? Joshua knew Charity didn't mind the conditions here. Perhaps Lord Kenrick decided it was time the place had a going-over. Certainly the plants would do better in a spanking-clean environment.

Deciding it was better not to interfere with the brisk transfer of the orchids, she relegated herself the task of directing the under-gardeners where to place various plants, and climbing the ladder to restore the orchids that had grown high in the air. This time there was no Lord Kenrick to put his strong warm hands at her waist and tease her about being a bird.

Before she knew it, the plants were back as they had been and she was once again alone. Roscoe hopped to its usual place at her feet, beneath the bench, while Charity set out her paper and paints. She found the original sketch and pinned it up so she could compare as she went along.

The black mood that had slipped over her when she

returned from the ride gradually dissipated. She loved working with first the pencil sketch, then the flow of color over the white paper. She was accomplished at it, too, she thought with honesty. The bloom on the flower she painted the day Lord Kenrick watched her was still in fine condition, in spite of all that had transpired in the meantime.

There was no wheeze of the door to warn her now, but the sound of Roscue shuffling farther under the bench alerted her to the presence of someone or something. She raised her head in query. "Oh, dear. Lord Kenrick."

"You didn't come up to the house to join us for lunch. Why?" He appeared concerned, searching her face intently as if determined to learn the truth.

"No one said a word about it to me, my lord. I told Charles I had a number of tasks to do. He and Ozzie went tearing off across the fields after they left me. Nothing happened to them, did it?" For a moment she had a vision of two men lying in a ditch, limbs awry, bloodied heads.

"He made an impatient dismissal with his hand. "No, no, they are fine. I, that is, we missed you at lunch. I think they went with the squire to look at some horses or some such thing."

She nibbled at the end of her paintbrush before commenting. "I suppose you cannot be together every moment of the day, can you? I had to complete this painting and it seemed like a good time to get it done."

"Had to complete it?" His voice was smooth, soft as velvet, dangerous in intent.

Charity nodded as she bent over the paper to resume her work. "The sun is just right today and I need to finish this, if you will excuse me, my lord."

"Do you mind if I stay to watch as I did last time? I think the guests at the house can find their own amusements for a short time."

A troubled look entered her eyes as she sought out his. "Do you find this all vastly boring, wearying? You are an unexceptional host, my lord. I am certain your guests have nothing to complain about.''

"When I left, the older ladies were in the Rose Drawing room discussing the latest London fashions. I believe Lady Sylvia intended to practice on her harp and Lady Ann mentioned the idea of planning charades.''

A chuckle found its way past the tightness in her throat. "I gather you do not have to worry about them —at least for now.''

"Not them. I do have a concern about you, however. Should you be alone out here?''

"Roscoe is with me. It seems one or another of the under-gardeners are about the place most every day. There has never been any trouble here in the past. I cannot think why now.''

"There is nothing you wish to discuss with me regarding the hothouse? Last night I mentioned Charles seemed to think there might be something amiss.''

"Amiss?'' She winced internally at the hint of a squeak in her voice. She sounded like a frightened mouse. "No, nothing is the matter. Nothing at all.'' It was a blessing her father could not hear his beloved daughter telling such taradiddles.

"Have you decided who it is to be?'' His voice was a low growl. It brought her head up to look at him, totally disconcerted by his words.

"I have no idea who it might be.''

"I think you misunderstand. I am talking about your future husband.''

"Oh.'' Her face fell in dejection, then brightened. "I am sure I can decide before long. Both of the gentlemen are kind and would allow me to continue with my diversion of growing orchids. Lord Harwood mentioned he has an aunt who has a large greenhouse at her home near Bath. He is her heir, I understand. That would work out well, don't you think?''

"Of course. What would you do with them in the meantime?'' he snapped out with a curtness that was most alarming.

Charity paled and dropped her gaze back to her paper, where no progress was being made on her painting. Bravely she decided to ask him the favor she intended to ask . . . sometime. "I was wondering . . . Once I am betrothed, there is no hurry, is there? Couldn't I remain here at the cottage and tend the orchids as I always have? When Aunt knows I am settled, she will be free to travel as she pleases." She took a valiant breath. "I am in no rush to marry." She didn't dare meet his eyes.

"Has either of them kissed you?" His words were idly spoken in a neutral manner, yet as though with great care.

His question took her by surprise. Her startled gray eyes met his intense gaze. "No. Most certainly not! It would be most improper." She neglected to mention she had no particular desire to kiss either gentleman, not even from curiosity.

"Don't you think it might be wise? It would give you a comparison you have lacked heretofore," Lord Kenrick said with an amused smile.

"I believe I can survive without it, my lord," she answered in a strangled voice.

"I think you are leading them both on too much. You ought to decide on one or the other and let it be. Does it make so great a difference? Aren't you merely seeking a husband, any husband?" His voice had now hardened and his incredible eyes looked like chips of lapis lazuli she had seen set in one of the tables at the great house.

Charity longed to toss a pot at his head again. Heartless man. "It matters to me very much whom I spend the rest of my life with, my lord. I realize I have to wait until one of them actually offers for me . . ." She broke off as he stood upright, moving away from the bench from where he had leaned so casually. "My lord?"

"Neither of them has offered as yet?" There was a tense quality about his voice, a taut set to his shoulders.

She shrugged. "It seems if one of them comes, the

other is not far behind. I rarely see one without the other. I should think it difficult to propose with an audience."

"That is why neither has kissed you."

"I would not allow it, in any event," she declared stoutly, clear *she* was convinced, at any rate.

"My dear innocent, if a man desired to kiss you, I fear you would not have a great deal to say about it. How would you prevent it? Especially in the seclusion of the hothouse, as you are now?" To prove his point, he grasped her shoulders and drew her up. His hands held her firmly before him, drawing her closer and closer. His eyes had a peculiar glint in them, like sunlight on a summer lake.

His words had softly taunted her, teased her in her helplessness. His grip was like iron and she hoped her dress would cover the bruise his hands would surely leave. There seemed to be a sort of anger within him and she wondered what she had done to bring this on.

Charity shook her head, wanting yet fearing his kiss. He was utterly correct. She had no protection, even counting Roscoe, who offered precious little if truth be told.

"Oh, yes, my dear girl." The fragile scent of the orchids drifted about them as his face neared her. She was like a fly about to be trapped in the spider's web.

The feel of his mouth was just as she remembered. Her dreams had been pale reflections of it. At first he was rough, demanding, his mouth hungrily seeking hers, as though he were punishing her for something she had done. But that was impossible, she had done nothing to him he knew about.

She whimpered as he demanded more, and he groaned in response. Charity leaned against him with those strange longings welling up again inside her. Then, as though his mood shifted, he gentled his caress, easing his mouth against hers, molding it to his with tender passion. For long moments they clung together, exploring the touch, the taste of each other.

Charity tore her lips from his, horrified she had permitted the kiss to continue as long as it had. A shamed blush crept into her cheeks. "You have no right to do this."

"You are a little flirt, my dear."

The velvety huskiness in his voice further weakened her treacherous knees. Mayhap it was as well he still held her firmly with his hands.

"How can you say that? You practically ordered me to encourage those gentlemen. You are not making much sense." Her gray eyes flashed with frozen fire as she stared back at his amused regard. "Don't ever do that again."

He ran the tip of one finger over his mouth, then touched the throbbing satin warmth of hers. "I never make promises I am not certain I can keep." There was a look of bemusement in those eyes, as though surprised by an answer to a question he hadn't asked.

"Please . . . leave me alone. I must finish this painting and you are a distraction." Her voice was ragged in spite of the control she attempted to exert over it. Oh, for the command he seemed to contrive with no difficulty at all! Her shoulders tingled where he had held her so firmly in his grasp.

A thoughtful expression settled on his brow as he slowly stepped away. He appeared to sense how she felt, for he moved toward the door. "I expect to see you at dinner."

"Yes, my lord." She would be there. But she would be cautious, guarded.

The door closed silently behind him. Charity creased her brow in concern, then shrugged before she applied herself to the painting, which had been totally neglected. She would finish this painting, carefully pack the orchid, then once the guests were gone, sneak up to London to deliver it. She would travel as she always did, cadging a lift from one of the people sent on an errand for the estate. No one had ever questioned her in the past; they were happy to give a lift to one of their own, so to speak. Just this one more trip and she would be safe. She ignored the problem of the presentation. It was better not to borrow trouble from tomorrow.

In the shadow of the tall beech tree that shaded the end of the hothouse, a slender figure stood, fists clenched in anger, eyes afire with malice. Her mouth firmed in an unpleasant line as she contemplated what she had just observed take place within the hothouse.

Lady Sylvia slowly relaxed her hands, then looked again at the woman bent over the wooden bench in the hothouse. She glanced at her hands, her ice-blue eyes afire with speculation. Sylvia picked up a fallen branch, then used it like a whip to snap the head from a delicate wand of Queen Anne's lace. She stared at the fallen head of the defenseless flower. With an air of resolve, she broke the branch in half with a decisive, satisfying crack.

Her whisper was barely audible. "We shall see who wins, my dear."

Pausing as she turned to leave, Sylvia took another long look at the woman amid the colorful blooms. The old gardener approached, glanced about in a furtive manner, then entered the hothouse. Sylvia crept closer, curious as to what he might have to say. As she listened, a sly smile spread across her face. First checking around her to see if there was anyone about, she then fled to the house, her lips curving in an unpleasant twist.

12

LORD KENRICK STARED MOODILY out at the curtain of
rain that fell in steady sheets beyond the tall, velvet-
draped window. None of the others had come down to
break their fast as yet this morning. With the gloom of
the day settling within the house, he was just as pleased
his guests take their leisure.

His mother had quite discreetly mentioned the matter
of an heir last night before she retired to her bedroom.
It was strange about that. He had fully intended to seek
the hand of the elegant Lady Sylvia before this house
party began. It made little difference who became his
bride, and he felt she was as suitable as any. There was
no pretense of love between them. She craved his title
and wealth, possibly his physical attentions, nothing
more. Wryly he admitted he wouldn't mind the process
of getting his heir with the cool blond beauty. But . . .
could there be more? Was it possible to find something
deeper? Tolerance was not the best of emotions, but he
hadn't looked for anything like love, whatever it might
be.

He strolled away from the library window to stare
into the flames of the nicely crackling fire in the hearth.
If only he knew what to make of his feelings toward
Charity Lonsbury. He had urged her, taunted her to
find a husband. All the while, he wanted to bar every
other man from her side. The thought of another man,
even his best friend, Charles, kissing those soft, velvety
lips brought his temper to a simmer. She had fought him
with sparks of silver fire in her unusual eyes. He
admitted he hadn't wanted to stop that kiss, nor cease
his hold on that delectable body, slim, yet nicely curved

in such delightful places. She was an innocent, and he had never been one to pursue such, yet she simmered with untapped passion. It was barely leashed; he could sense her tight control over her emotions.

How ironic that a man who ignored young misses making their bows to society should be so affected by Charity. He who had been so scathing in his regard of the "country miss," as he had called her only weeks ago.

Charity had surprised him a great deal. With jaunty courage she had faced the elegant ladies and lords from London, displaying an aplomb that pleased him. Spunk. She had that and more. He recalled her tumble from the tree into his arms while that dratted monkey scampered away. He had been very reluctant to let her slip from his arms at that moment. If Lady Tavington hadn't returned at the time she did, he without a doubt would have kissed those tempting lips so close to his. Little minx. She had gazed up with those limpid gray eyes, looking for all the world as though she was innocent of the longings he could feel. . . . Had she possibly felt them too?

His booted foot reached out to nudge an ember before he looked again to the rain-streaked window. Yes. He was quite certain she had clung to him with an emotion that had nothing to do with a fear of falling to the ground.

Though he had to admit she was not reluctant to seek a husband, at least she was honest enough to acknowledge there was no love for either Charles or Ozzie on her part. By heaven, he couldn't allow her to marry one or the other of them! Didn't he owe his friends that much? Either one deserved better than some tepid union with a woman who merely liked him. David ignored the possibility his altruism might be rooted in jealousy. He wouldn't admit he hated it when Charity bestowed a radiant smile on another man.

As for himself . . . he found he didn't relish the

customary marriage of the *ton*, either. His parents had appeared to have had such an arrangement. Many of the men he knew seemed to rub along tolerably well with their wives. It was deucedly difficult to detect just how warm the marriage was, for they all could be adept at concealinng their depth of feelings. It wasn't good *ton* to be too obviously in each other's pockets.

A scratching at the door brought his head around as his butler, Jameson, opened the heavy oak door.

"Lord Harwood is in the breakfast room wondering where you might be, milord. Will you wish to join him?"

Kenrick pushed aside his mental wanderings and nodded. "I'll join him directly, Jameson."

The butler withdrew and Kenrick strolled from the comfortable silence of the library. He glanced back at the portrait of his great-grandfather as he neared the door, recalling Charity's assessment of him. His lips curved in a reminiscent smile. She had quite liked the old man.

Across the sloping lawns, on the far side of Capability Brown's lake, Charity also gazed out at the steadily falling rain from the cottage window. There would be no ride with Charles and Ozzie this morning.

"No use fretting, dearest child. It will not make the rain go away." Lady Tavington bestowed a sympathetic look on her favorite niece.

"I had thought to ride this morning. Ozzie and Lord Harwood were to come for me." Charity bent over to stroke Chico's head while her aunt sipped her morning chocolate. She wished she dared Mrs. Woods' wrath and invite Roscoe into the cottage. Mrs. Woods firmly held to the belief rabbits belong out of the house.

"And you are very sorry? You wish to spend time with them so much?" Her aunt's tone was not probing, but sharp eyes scrutinized Charity's face with care.

"They are both all that is amiable."

Aunt Tavington made an expressive face at her niece.
"I would wish for more than amiability toward your
future husband. Neither of them has come up to scratch
as yet?"

Charity bristled. "It has been but a matter of days
since we met, Aunt." It was fortunate her aunt could
not be aware of the conversation, if you could call it
that, which had transpired with Lord Kenrick on that
very subject.

"Stuff and nonsense! Your uncle asked for my hand
days after we met. We were wildly happy those early
years." There was a trace of dreamy reflection in her
voice.

"And?" Charity set aside the monkey to sink down
on one of the chairs by the deal table. Perhaps she might
get a glimpse of what she ought to be feeling for one or
the other of the gentlemen.

"And then our affection settled into a steady devotion to each other. I did love him deeply, child. I
would that you care for your husband as well. Do you
carry a *tendre* for Lord Harwood? Or perhaps Sir Oswald?"

Picking at the flounce of her morning dress of a
cheerful daffodil-yellow muslin, Charity chewed at her
lower lip as she thought. "I don't know. They are both
kind, gentle, and quite nice to me. The trouble is, I
rarely see one without the other being around. I doubt if
Lord Harwood, for example, would toss his handkerchief, with Ozzie overhearing every word."

Her aunt nibbled at one of Mrs. Woods' berry
muffins before inquiring, "And what of Kenrick? How
do you feel about him?"

The very mention of Lord Kenrick brought Charity
from her chair to pace restlessly about the small room.
She had tried to subdue the emotion she felt for Lord
Kenrick. She certainly didn't want to put it into words.
Foolishly, she had thought it possible to settle for
another. Now she knew it wasn't. How could she have
been so blind to her feelings?

"I don't know. He infuriates me at times. At other times I find him quite amusing, as when he showed me the portraits of his great-grandparents." She smiled at the memory of his calling his great-grandmother a dragon because she appeared to like a good scold. What did that make him?

Gazing out at the rain, she continued in a faint, wistful voice. "There is a perfect manliness in his appearance. He is so tall and elegant, with a rather nice, rich voice. I quite like his dark, thick hair, and who could not admire those unusual blue eyes of his? He has a charming smile, when he bestows it, which is usually upon Lady Sylvia." Whirling about to return her gaze to her aunt's face, she added, "I must face the unpleasant fact that he undoubtedly intends to offer for Lady Sylvia's hand at the ball tomorrow evening. That leaves me with either Lord Harwood or Sir Oswald. And do you know what, dear Aunt? I believe neither one of them will offer for me. I suspect that each is like a little boy who wants what his friend wants."

"A rather lowering thought, isn't it? I do not share your evaluation, but then, you see more of them than I do." Lady Tavington set aside her cup and rose from the table. "Do I see a figure making his way through the rain?"

Eagerly turning to peer out the bay window, Charity pulled away in disgust. "It's the squire. Pray do not leave me, Aunt. It would not be seemly for me to receive him alone, would it?" She raised a knowing eyebrow, her face impudent.

The wry chuckle from Lady Tavington was ruefully echoed by Charity.

"I perceive you have no fondness for the man. Why does he not settle for the sweet Euphremia? It is plain how obvious her affection is toward him. You may as well let him in, Mrs. Woods. He must know we would be at home in such weather without a carriage of our own." Lady Tavington settled comfortably on the faded damask of the love seat, patting the place at her side. "Sit here and he can have no excuse to bully you. I am aware of his nature, child."

Charity remained standing instead, waiting with resignation for Bigglesby to enter the house and join her and her aunt.

"Dear ladies, a nasty morning, is it not? My man says he feels it will clear before evening. Wouldn't do to miss the dinner at the great house now, would it?"

Looking at his increasing girth, Charity figured it was unlikely the squire would miss a meal no matter what lengths he had to go to accomplish the table.

"Lord Kenrick has graciously offered the use of one of his carriages so we may attend the festivities up at the house. A little rain is not going to prevent us from joining them. Won't you sit down, sir? Charity, join me." Lady Tavington gestured again, and this time Charity obeyed without question.

Aware he couldn't sit down unless she did, she had hoped that by remaining standing, he would limit his visit. However, it was not good manners, and her father would have been appalled at such lack of hospitality. Regardless of what Lord Kenrick thought, her parents had raised her with a good deal of sensitivity as to what was proper. After all, her papa had been reared in the house of an earl.

"What may we do for you this morning, Squire?" Lady Tavington veiled her distaste for this disagreeable man.

His face as usual tinged with red, his eyes revealing annoyance, he ponderously replied, "I had hoped to have a little conversation with Miss Charity, my lady."

"There is naught you need hide from me, sir. Charity and I are very close. Besides, it would not be seemly for me to leave the room, and I feel you are well aware of that." Lady Tavington was all that was polite, but barely.

Flustered, accustomed to making his demands without dressing them up in fine words, the squire hemmed and hawed a few moments before coming to his point. "I am most displeased with the way Miss Charity is behaving. At the picnic she landed in Kenrick's arms, her skirts all a tumble. She allows those bloods from London to teach her to ride. Why, I could have taught her meself!"

Lady Tavington gave him a falsely sweet smile. "But you didn't, did you? And they offered. The mare Lord Kenrick chose for Charity to ride is a very dainty stepper. I am quite pleased with Charity's behavior, sir. I do not see where there is any fault. May I inquire what gives you the notion you have anything to say about Charity in any way?" she said frostily.

"Why, she is my intended! Did she not explain to you?" Bigglesby was very irritated at the thickheadedness of the ladies, both of them. "Enough of these missish airs. I wish to set the date."

Annoyed past beyond belief, Charity snapped, "Then name it with someone else. While I am aware of the honor you do me, I must again decline your gracious offer." Was it possible he was actually that dense? Looking at his bewildered face, she decided it was.

"It seems, sir, my niece does not wish to marry with you. I suggest you look elsewhere for your bride. I will not press Charity to marry." Lady Tavington's voice brooked no argument.

The clatter of horses in the lane brought Charity's eyes to the window. With relief, she noted Charles and Ozzie tie up their mounts and come in past the gate, giving a curious glance at the squire's horse as they came.

Mrs. Woods didn't have to be told to answer the door. Listening as carefully as she did, she knew the squire was wished on his way.

"Lady Tavington, Miss Charity! Surely you are as welcome a sight as a rainbow on this wet day."

"Nicely said, Lord Harwood." Lady Tavington allowed her hand to be bowed over with elegant grace while she shot the squire a dismissing look.

Bigglesby mumbled a farewell, then left the cottage, his irritation still evident on his face.

"I say, I hope we ain't interrupting anything with the squire. Looked dashed annoyed, if you ask me." Sir Oswald gave a thoughtful look at the door, then promptly forgot the squire and turned his attention to Charity.

Mrs. Woods took the many-caped coats and hung them to dry while the gentlemen took places before the neat fire in the parlor hearth. Neither of them had been inside the cottage before, and both were curious. Charity repressed a smile as Sir Oswald's innocent gaze went around the room from item to item.

"Is this one of your paintings, Miss Lonsbury? I had no idea you were so very talented." Lord Harwood admired a watercolor of one of the cattleyas in the hothouse. "It certainly is far above the normal for young ladies. I gather it is of one of your orchids."

Sir Oswald left the warmth of the fire to inspect the painting a bit closer. "Who else grows orchids around here, Charles? I say, it is devilishly well done, Miss Lonsbury."

"We decided to chance the rain to have a little talk about the damage to the hothouse. Have you had any ideas regarding who might have wished you or your plants ill?" Charles had a few thoughts about the squire after observing his face as he left the house.

"I have no notion in the least who would wish me ill, or for that matter, who might wish Lord Kenrick ill. After all, the hothouses belong to him, Lord Harwood." Charity wondered how she was going to manage to keep her work a secret if an investigation was conducted over the hothouse incident. If someone did a bit of discreet inquiring, they would find out about her random trips to London. She must find some way to deflect interest until she had managed to send off the watercolor and the plant to the Horticultural Society in London. Then she vowed she would forget all about such endeavors forever. Only allow her this one more time!

"The squire wouldn't get a bit belligerent, would he? It seemed he was a mite angry when he left here." Lord Harwood raised an inquiring eyebrow at Charity.

"I say, not at all the thing, Charles. Don't make mice feet of the thing. Miss Lonsbury could inspire none but the highest feelings in anyone." Sir Oswald bestowed a fond look on Charity.

Wondering at the depth of his regard for her, Charity returned his look. He was a nice man, so comical at times, so sweet in his efforts to please. If she had had a brother, she would have dearly wished him to be like Sir Oswald.

"I have no doubt Miss Lonsbury is one of the loveliest ladies around, Ozzie. I was referring to a gentleman who might feel a little . . . miffed?" Lord Harwood glanced at Lady Tavington first, then at Charity, seeking a clue to the squire's behavior.

Not wishing to reveal the squire's proposal, nor his utterly obtuse unwillingness to listen to her repeated refusals, Charity shrugged in a helpless manner. "I cannot say as to that, Lord Harwood." She was reluctant to use his Christian name, as Lady Sylvia seemed wont to do with Charles . . . and David.

Apparently deciding to say nothing further in regard to the squire, the men chatted a little longer, then took a most proper leave from the cottage and the charming ladies within.

Trotting along the lane through what now amounted to a mizzle, Charles thoughtfully considered the mystery of the hothouse breakage. As they went over the bridge across the lake that separated the cottage from the great house, he turned to Sir Oswald. "There is something I don't quite understand, Ozzie. Kenrick said he had questioned Miss Lonsbury about the incident, yet he knows nothing more than we do. Miss Lonsbury seems to be utterly in the dark. Yet I suspect it is probably

someone close by, not a stranger. If a strange person
were poking around the place, it would be bound to be
noticed. Right? I'm glad Kenrick has put a guard on
watch down there. I don't like the idea of Miss
Lonsbury going into the hothouse to work without
anyone to watch over her."

"Like her a bit, don't you?"

Lord Harwood nodded, then added, "But I have
watched her when Kenrick is around. I suspect she feels
toward him much stronger than she does for either of
us. Can't keep her eyes off him."

"I saw her in his arms the day of the picnic. She
didn't seem to mind being there overmuch, did she?"

Sighing at his lack of luck with the ladies, Lord
Harwood agreed. "I hope he does not offer for Sylvia."

"I say, do you think it likely? Not that she ain't all
the crack, but I ain't sure they'd suit. He needs someone
more lively." Sir Oswald joined in dismay at the situation.

"You mean like Miss Lonsbury?" Lord Harwood
sighed again and urged his horse forward through the
drizzle.

Sir Oswald nodded without adding a word, and the
two gentlemen continued their ride in depressing silence.
The trees looming up through the mists dripped with
cold moisture, leaves hanging disconsolately as if
knowing they were about to die and fall to the earth.

Lord Harwood wondered why he had such a knack of
developing a *tendre* for women who could not return his
interest. Dashed disheartening, it was.

In the snug warmth of the cottage, Lady Tavington
stared out at the misty rain. "It does seem to be letting
up. I'm certain we will have no problem in going up to
the house for dinner this evening. I confess I am pleased
Lord Harwood and Sir Oswald arrived when they did.
You know, I had not actually believed you when you
told me how thickheaded the squire was. The man is a

nodcock, an utter corkbrain, if he cannot comprehend your refusal."

She took a turn about the room, then watched her niece concentrate on a piece of embroidery. Her needlework was as delicate and beautifully done as her watercolors.

"It would solve at least one of my problems were he to turn to Euphremia. I fear you may have to consider the Little Season for me, Aunt." She repeated her speculations concerning Lord Harwood and Sir Oswald.

"Hmm. They neither strike me as slow off the mark. Perhaps bachelors are like other wild game, they travel in a pack until paired."

"I understand that even then they do not always remain faithful, dear Aunt. Though living in a quiet backwater, I am aware of the life of the *ton*. I am not certain that is the life for me." Charity lowered the embroidery to her lap to send a solemn look toward her aunt.

"After what I have said about a loving marriage, I can see why you might say that, dearest child. Simply because there are marriages among the *ton* that are . . . alliances at best, does not mean *yours* must be such a thing. Follow your heart, do not be swayed from the man you love."

Charity gave her a look of alarm. "Who says I love anyone?" Her expression unknowingly betrayed what was in her heart, satisfying her dear aunt's curiosity.

"Put aside that lovely needlework and have a rest now, so you will be fresh for this evening. You must captivate those gentlemen with that sweet, gentle manner you have."

Charity considered her aunt's words later as she allowed a coverlet to be drawn over her shoulders. Snuggling into her down pillow, she wondered if she truly intended to be an obedient niece. While she desired to accommodate her aunt in her longing to return to her travels, there was a limit to what might be done. She

dozed off to nap with visions of herself on one knee,
begging Lord Harwood to accept her hand. Only Lord
Harwood dissolved into another gentleman, dark-
haired, intense blue eyes, a twisted grin on his well-
modeled lips.

Charity dressed for the evening with an unsettled
feeling. Even as her aunt checked over the aquamarine
silk with dainty bunches of cream and peach flowers
caught around the rolled hem and tucked into the low
décolletage, Charity wondered how she could
participate in this blatant attempt in seduction.

"Lovely, dearest child. You have nothing to fear
from those London ladies. Your mama's pearls give just
the right touch." Lady Tavington fixed the clasp, then
stepped back to admire before leading the way to the
door. "Now, have you given a thought to a suitable
word or phrase for the charades this evening? Lady Ann
thought it might be most amusing to have each of the
younger persons participate."

"I cannot say I have. Perhaps something will come to
me before I must perform." Charity did not look
forward to playing charades. Then the thought of the
elegant Lord Kenrick being compelled to join in the
silliness brought a comforting smile to her mouth.
Mayhap it might not be so bad, after all.

The dinner prepared by Antoine, Kenrick's London
chef, was all she expected and more. It cast the meals
enjoyed at the Spencers' pleasant home into the realm
of the ordinary. She glanced down to where Euphremia
listened to yet another of Bigglesby's interminable
hunting tales. If Euphremia could tolerate such a dead
bore, she certainly deserved to have him. Her high-
pitched replies cut through the dulcet tones of Lady
Ann, who sat closer to Charity. So many variations in
voice. Euphremia was like a rather shrill flute, Lady
Ann had the golden richness of a sweet-sounding
violoncello, while Lady Sylvia had the seductiveness of
her harp. Did that quality lure Lord Kenrick to her side?

Charity ruefully considered she had nothing seductive about herself to lure anyone.

The ladies followed Lady Kenrick to the Gold Saloon, where Charity found herself at the side of Lady Ann.

"I hope the gentlemen will join in the fun, Miss Lonsbury." Lady Ann gave her a sweet look.

Charity warmed to her gentle smile. "Please call me Charity. I have not thought of a single quote or word that lends itself to pantomime. Perhaps the men will be quicker to bring something to mind."

"Turn to Shakespeare, he is always good for a phrase."

Recalling her father's affection for Shakespeare's works, Charity wished she was more familiar with them. She had devoted far too much time to the study of orchids and her watercolors, it seemed.

The gentlemen didn't linger over their port that evening, but soon joined the ladies, turning to Lady Ann to handle the evening's entertainment.

"I suspect I must be first, to set an example, or be the most foolish, I know not which." Her attitude was demure, though her eyes sparkled with laughter.

Lady Ann mimed a quote, then indicated it was to be done in its entirety before she would allow a guess. She motioned first to her head, then her heart, then the bouquet of roses placed on a sofa table nearby.

Charity caught the surreptitious darting glance at Lord Powell before Ann looked around the group.

"I say, dashed hard to get from that. Do it again." Sir Oswald screwed up his face in concentration as he followed her gestures once more.

Seeing no one else was willing to speak up, Charity took a chance. "My love is like a red, red rose."

Lady Ann blushed and nodded. "I did not think you would catch it so quickly. How did you guess?"

Charity could hardly tell her that the glance at Lord Powell had been the clue. "You did point to those roses. I seemed to recall a remark of yours regarding Burns."

"You must be next, you know." Charity found
herself propelled to the front of the loosely assembled
group. Lady Sylvia sat close to Kenrick with Sir Oswald
and Lord Harwood leaning against the mantel.
Euphremia sat stiffly on the same sofa with the squire,
who looked very uncomfortable. No doubt he could not
begin to think of a suitable word, unless he used
"hunt."

Charity thought desperately, her eyes straying to
where Kenrick sat so close to the exquisite Lady Sylvia.
She saw little evidence of a strong attachment on his
part. He appeared to treat the lady much as any other in
the group. Inspiration struck. She mimed that it was to
be a quote from Shakespeare, indicating the latter by
shaking an invisible object quite vigorously.

"Ah, a quote from Shakespeare. Proceed." Lord
Harwood watched the slim woman shimmering in her
aquamarine silk with an intensity that had nothing to do
with the game they played.

Charity first touched her heart, lingering to show it
was more than just herself she meant, then she covered
her eyes before she wound one hand through the air in a
frivolous manner, still covering her eyes with the other
hand as she shook her head. She was fairly sure that no
one would guess her quote, yet she hoped someone
might. She had tried charades before, but usually it had
been confined to a single word, not an entire quote or
line.

Lord Harwood's pleasant voice demanded, "Do it
once more."

Charity went through the actions, looking about with
growing amusement. Perhaps she had been too clever,
or not sufficiently revealing.

The deep voice she admired so much sounded on the
verge of laughter. "If I am not mistaken, you are
quoting from *The Merchant of Venice*, my dear. 'But
love is blind, and lovers cannot see the pretty follies that
themselves commit.' "

Unable to resist Kenrick's appeal, she chuckled as she

nodded. "You are right, my lord. Now you must take my place." As she slipped past him, she wondered if he might take the words of the quote to heart.

Charity did not take his seat next to Lady Sylvia. Instead, she wandered toward the chair where her aunt sat watching the young people, a smile on her lips.

Kenrick wondered how he ever allowed Lady Ann to persuade him to entertain the idea of charades. Charity had placed him out here when he fully intended to watch, not participate. Hastily searching his mind for a quote, any quote he might use, he glared at her in wordless annoyance, noting those soft lips curved in delight. The little minx was tickled to see him in this spot. And then the words came to him, and he gazed back in derision. He also made the motions to indicate he used a quote from the Bard.

First he pointed to his head, then his mouth, then toward Charity's mouth, then he made a mime of arguing. Arms folded, he tilted his head in anticipation. Unaware of his total concentration on Charity and the anger growing in the eyes of Lady Sylvia, he nodded at the others. "Well?"

"Shakespeare, undoubtedly." Lord Harwood hadn't missed the direction of Kenrick's hand. There *was* something going on between Kenrick and Charity, as he had surmised.

The one who finally guessed was Lord Powell. Or at least he was the one who voiced the words. Charity had a knowing look about her, but refused for some reason to speak up.

" 'I understand thy kisses and thou mine, and that's a feeling disputation.' " Geoffrey Powell did not so much as glance at Charity. Rather, his gaze found its way to the rose-cheeked Lady Ann.

When it came to Euphremia to take a turn, she also mimed a quote from Shakespeare. There was much good-natured laughter when the guess was made by the squire.

" 'He doth nothing but talk of his horses.' " He

laughed and complimented Euphremia on her genteel knowledge.

Charity was surprised Bigglesby could participate so well, and hoped he might look upon Euphremia more favorably after this.

Lady Sylvia flashed a smile that was not the kind to calm a woman's peace of mind. After she had done her mime, the following silence was puzzled. It seemed no one could or wished to guess her quote from Shakespeare. When she, triumphant that she had accomplished what others had not, revealed her lines, they made Charity shiver. " 'By heaven. I'll make a ghost of him yet.' "

13

SWIRLING THE CHOCOLATE ABOUT in her cup, Charity considered the wan sunlight that filtered through the beech and oak trees to flicker on to the bay window. The morning was promising. It appeared the rain had departed, leaving ribboned traces of clouds behind as a remnant of the storm.

"Lady Sylvia must have spent hours going through Kenrick's volumes of Shakespeare to find that quote. Do you consider she had any subtle warning to her words? Or am I a silly peagoose with my apprehensions?" Charity peered at her aunt over the rim of her chocolate cup.

"You do not believe someone intends to do you harm, my dear?" Lady Tavington looked askance at her dearest niece. "Though I vow those bricks could have done considerable damage to your tender head. Why? Can it be that there is one who does not wish your orchid to reach London? Banish any notion Lady Sylvia might have to do with that. Look elsewhere. Who might benefit from the loss of your orchid? Another person who raises orchids, perhaps?" Lady Tavington helped herself to another delicate slice of toast and spread orange marmalade thinly over the surface of it, her eyes concerned as she watched her niece.

Charity set her chocolate cup carefully on its saucer, then stared out the window, seeing nothing of the pattern of dancing leaves on the panes of glass. "I know of no one remotely close to Greenoaks who has the facilities to cultivate orchids. There are estates north and west of us where greenhouses and stoves exist. But I hardly think they would be aware of so small a grower as myself. Besides, since I have used Kenrick's initials, how could they trace me?" That thought worried her more than all else.

"You have a point in that, my dear." It was possible someone might be sufficiently curious to figure out the reference, but Lady Tavington suspected it would not cheer her niece to hear such a thought, so she sought to change the subject. "These are unusual dishes. I do not recall seeing them in the past. Not your mama's, I think."

Picking up the plate before her, Charity could feel her face become warm. "It is Queen's Ware, Aunt. I was in London some time ago when I chanced to enter the Wedgwood showroom and saw it. Lovely, is it not? The pattern is called Water Lily. The clerk told me it had been originally designed by Mr. Wedgwood for his sister. I bought a very small set for my breakfast. You know how fond I am of flowers as well as the colors brown and gold."

"I believe I saw this pattern at the great house when I was visiting with Lady Kenrick. Did we not have these at tea the second time we were up there?" Lady Tavington gave her niece a shrewd look.

Flustered and not knowing quite how to avoid the question, Charity blurted out the truth. "When he discovered my direction, the clerk told me he had recently sent a set of this pattern to Greenoaks. Lord Kenrick had come to the showroom to order a set of fine china with his family crest. He saw this and apparently it took his fancy, for he ordered a set for the breakfast room at Greenoaks. It was a mere coincidence, Aunt. We happened to like the same pattern. I am sure there are similar dishes all over England." In truth, the pattern was very popular. Charity knew Lady Spencer desired a set.

"To be sure, dear. Lovely design, with those leaves entwined amid the lilies. And the cup is so ample in size. Quite cheerful to have greet you first thing in the morning." Lady Tavington dropped the subject, seeing how uncomfortable it made her niece. She felt certain the china was purchased more for its connection with Greenoaks and Lord Kenrick than for the association with flowers. "Perhaps you can create your own design for china, a different orchid for each plate. Wouldn't that be exquisite? Botanical designs are all the rage now, or so I am told."

With a faintly suspicious look at her aunt, Charity murmured a vague agreement. "Vastly expensive, I fear."

"If you marry a gentleman such as I propose, you will have no fear on that score, I can assure you. I deem Lord Harwood to be only too pleased to put forth every effort to make you happy in any way he can."

Charity glanced up from the Water Lily plate in alarm. "Oh, dear. Do you really think so?"

"Do you not care for Lord Harwood? I had the notion he has the lead in the marriage stakes." The gentle voice took any sting from the words, yet Charity winced when she heard them. It sounded so conniving, somehow.

"He is a fine man, Aunt. I wish you would not consider it necessary for me to wed. I am quite happy here with my orchids and Roscoe. Unlike you, I have no desire to roam the earth, seeking adventure."

"If you had a husband who enjoyed the same pursuits, you might sail off to South America to hunt for new orchid species. I daresay you might find that exciting."

A bemused expression settled on Charity's face as she allowed her mind to wander. Jungles and mountains such as she had read about in the reports to the Horticultural Society came to her mind. She could see herself intrepidly climbing through steaming wilds, discovering a new species, bestowing her name on it. Her husband would be at her side, facing the wilds fearlessly together. Only the husband did not have light-brown hair. His hair was dark as the wings of the jackdaws that plagued the gardeners. Sighing, she shook herself from the foolish reverie. "Not likely, Aunt. Too silly, by far."

Rising from the table, Lady Tavington swept to the parlor. "Your dress for this evening is ready. I have a necklace and eardrops I wish you to wear with it." She disappeared into her room, to return with a velvet case held tenderly in her hands. "My own papa gave this to me the night I was betrothed. I want you to wear it tonight . . . to please me. It will be yours, you know."

Accepting the case, Charity opened it while butterflies suddenly took wing within her stomach. The ball. She had forgotten about it for a few moments while chatting with her aunt. Now memory returned, all her apprehensions flocking along.

"It is exquisite, dear Aunt." Tears misted Charity's eyes as she viewed what must be very treasured jewels. From the velvet bed a topaz necklace with matching eardrops winked up at her. "I cannot tell you what it means to me to receive these. For they are not only beautiful, but have special memories for you. Thank you so very much." Charity closed the box, then gently hugged her aunt. "They will give an added luster to this beautiful gown." She bestowed a watery smile on her aunt before taking the velvet box to her room.

"Are you going up to the hothouse this afternoon? I have a fancy to wear one of your flowers on my gown this evening."

"What a truly lovely idea!" Impulsively Charity suggested, "Why do I not select an orchid for each of the ladies to wear? Perhaps Parton could assist me to ferret out the colors to be worn? I could have one of the footmen deliver them later, before dinner."

It pleased Charity to think of her orchids adorning the women she had met—except for Lady Sylvia—and there was no way Charity could make an exception of her. Charity couldn't fathom why Lady Sylvia remained suspicious and unfriendly, for it was plain Lord Kenrick desired to marry Sylvia. Why else had he been so willing to have the house party, if not to provide a proper

setting for the announcement of his betrothal? His
mother acted as hostess, but she also appeared to set her
seal upon his choice. Hadn't he implied Lady Sylvia was
his mother's preference?

Mrs. Woods urged a delicious lunch on the ladies,
reminding them the dinner was not to be at country
hours. Lady Tavington announced she would take a nap
while Parton headed for the great house to do her
detective work. Charity conferred with her before
starting on her way to the hothouses.

Up at the great house, Lady Sylvia sat on the window
seat in her room, staring across the gently rolling fields
and wooded hills beyond the neatly terraced gardens
directly outside. As usual, the scent of Red Roses clung
to her gown. She spoke to her abigail as she peered out
with unseeing eyes. "Last night was a disaster in every
respect. I was an idiot to overreact to the foolery
between David and Charity Lonsbury."

A hint of desperation clung to her voice. "No country
miss will steal my intended." She slowly added, mostly
to herself, "There was a look in his eyes I haven't
observed before. This little minx came up with a clever
quote to mime. I intended to use something along the
same line, such as 'Love comforteth like sunshine after
the rain,' or some such thing." She had hunted for lines
dealing with underhanded activities, but not found
them. Could she actually lose him? "It is not to be
contemplated!"

In the Elizabethan brick manor house on the edge of
the village, Euphremia gazed with great surprise at the
carefully boxed orchid of delicate green with rust flecks
on the lower petals that had just been delivered by one
of the under-gardeners from Greenoaks. She half-
turned to her mother to show her the flower. "See,
Mama? How nice that Charity remembered the color of
my gown. The orchid will be just the touch to the pale-

green silk sarcenet. Perhaps the squire might take more notice?''

Euphremia was determined Bigglesby was not going to pursue Charity any longer. In some manner, Euphremia would find a way to stop him. ''Tonight he will see me at my very best, among the gentry where he longs to shine.'' She met her mother's eyes in the mirror. Their faces both revealed the determination that flourished in their bosoms. While she didn't deceive herself she could compete with Charity in looks, Euphremia nevertheless, had much to offer the squire, if the man would but see it. She placed the exquisite orchid on her dressing table with great care. She would wear this flower with pride and hope.

Shadows danced across the shining glass of the hothouse as Parton silently opened the door and joined Charity beside her bench. Parton placed a slip of paper on the bench.

''Lady Kenrick is wearing violet, while Lady Sylvia is to wear pale-sapphire blue and Lady Ann a rose-pink. What will you send to them?'' Parton's rich contralto boomed forth as she gazed about her in awe at the myriad of flowers.

Charity looked around the hothouse. ''I have already sent Miss Euphremia's to her. Lady Kenrick's is an easy choice. That large lavender cattleya with the deep-violet labia is just the thing. For Lady Sylvia, I think this pure white orchid will do.'' The gold-dusted center would perfectly reflect the color of Sylvia's hair. She doubted the purity of the bloom reflected Lady Sylvia's nature, however. Charity fought back the welling ache that settled about her heart as she considered that the delicate white flower would be most appropriate for a betrothal-announcement ball.

''Lady Ann will ahve this white flower with the fuchsia markings. An odd shape, to be sure, with its long spurs, but it goes well with rose-pink. For my dear aunt, I chose this cymbidium in gold with deep-brown flecks. Do you think it will please her, Parton?" She held up the dainty orchids, having cut a branch of three to be pinned to her aunt's gown.

"I am sure it will, Miss Charity. And what shall you wear?"

"I don't know." Charity did no longer wish to attend the ball. If she hadn't promised her aunt to try her best to fix the attentions of one of the gentlemen, she would plead the headache or some such ailment. Indeed, she didn't feel all that well. "Any will do, I suppose. This one?" She touched the branch of a cymbidium that was pale golden with rust in the center of each bloom. At Parton's nod, she clipped it off, then cut a dainty lavender cattleya and added it to the array laid out on the workbench. "This is for you, Parton." She pointed to the lovely lavender cattleya. "I appreciate everything you have done for me, as well as your devotion to my aunt." She smiled shyly at the tall, large-boned woman who so faithfully tended Lady Tavington.

The deep contralto noticeably quavered as Parton murmured her thanks. "I've never had anything so dainty as this, Miss Charity. Usually I get practical things." Obviously overcome by this thoughtfulness of her mistress's niece, she carefully assisted in placing each bloom in a tissue wrapping, then offered to carry the flowers up to the great house rather than call for a footman.

Seeing how determined the woman was to be of service, Charity nodded her agreement. "Thank you, Parton. You are a jewel."

The elated abigail sped to the great house with her precious burden, beaming her pride in bearing such gracious gifts.

Charity checked about her before leaving, the orchids for her aunt and herself, as well as the dainty lavender orchid for the redoubtable Parton, nestled in tissue and ready to go. She was glad she had sent the orchid off to Euphremia immediately. The stove was giving off sufficient heat, the plants had been watered, everything appeared to be in order. She turned to exit the hothouse, content that all was as it should be here, when she saw Lord Kenrick approaching. That fluttery sensation she had noticed before gained ascendancy in her stomach. She met him at the door.

"I caught you before you left for the cottage. My mother is delighted with the lovely orchid you sent up to the house with your abigail. That was very thoughtful of you. I understand Lady Ann and Lady Sylvia also received a gift of flowers. Are those for your aunt and you?" He moved to look at the orchids that peeked from a bed of tissue. "Which one is yours?"

"The large gold ones with the brown flecks are for Aunt. The lighter gold with rust specks is mine and the lavender is for Parton." Her heart must surely be racing much too fast. He always had this effect on her, making her feel nearly faint. For once she could sympathize with those delicate females who went into swoons when sensibilities were overcome.

"Your dress? I hope it is something worthy of such a flower?"

His intimate gaze sent her heart into a frantic dance. His voice was so deep, so rich. Why did he have to be for Lady Sylvia? Charity firmed her resolve to make the best of things. Her aunt was depending on Charity to make a wise decision. Charity wasn't totally convinced her aunt was correct, but it was difficult to dissuade her when everyone else appeared to be on her aunt's side.

"I am to wear a sort of cream color, my lord."

He bent his head to study her face, his regard causing a faint flush to creep over her cheeks. "I feel sure it will be quite lovely. You enjoyed the charades of last evening?" His voice held a curious inflection quite beyond her comprehension.

Her cheeks now positively bloomed with color. "Yes, my lord. It was quite, er, interesting." She couldn't have commented on his choice of quote to save her life.

His chuckle was disconcerting. "I was surprised I recalled that line from *The Merchant of Venice.* I saw a production of it not too long ago, which must account for it. Do you? Understand, that is? I think it was Robert Herrick who wrote, 'What is a kiss? Why this, as some approve: the sure, sweet cement, glue and lime of love.' "

Shaking her head, Charity backed away, butting against the bench in her haste. "You make a kiss sound like something constructed of bricks and mortar. A pity it is not as enduring. I fear a kiss is usually a moment of light dalliance." She decided this was a risky subject at best. Escape was necessary, the sooner the better. "I believe I must return to the cottage, my lord. I think you were the one who said I ought not be alone here. I begin to perceive your meaning."

"I suppose we can postpone our talk until later, if you must go. I shall await the sight of you in your gown and orchid with anticipation." He bowed over her hand, then strode from the hothouse and off toward the bridge.

Charity gave her hand a bemused look before giving herself a scold; then, picking up the flowers with great care, she hurried out the door. She mulled over his words regarding a later talk every step of the path to the cottage. What could he want? Had he a notion of her use of his initials? Could he have found her out? Disaster seemed to loom before her, disgrace right behind it.

Parton was in the parlor as Charity entered the cottage. "They were ever so pleased to get the orchids, Miss Charity," she boomed. "I was quite the honored one to bring each lady her special flower. Even Lady Sylvia exclaimed with much evident delight how nicely the bloom went with her gown. The other women from the surrounding area who are not as favored will be green, I'm sure."

Casting a concerned look at her aunt, Charity replied, "I didn't mean to cause envy, dear Aunt. I daresay it is near impossible to send an orchid to every lady who is to attend if I had the list in hand. Which I do not."

"No one expects you to strip all the blooms from your plants for one evening of entertainment. It is appropriate that the ladies in residence have the orchids." She ignored the small item that Charity and Lady Tavington were not in residence at the great house. They had been asked to stay there, and that was sufficient. "Now, I think you had better take your bath. It will soon be time to dress for the ball. We must arrive in time for dinner, naturally. Are you excited, dear girl? I can well recall how I felt when I was to attend my first ball. I was much younger than you, of course. You should have been having your Season instead of hiding away in the country. Helping your father with his book on Christian names might be an admirable enterprise; still . . . he ought to have considered your future."

Turning away to conceal the smile tugging at her lips, Charity refrained from mentioning the paltry matter of money with which to finance such a thing, *if* she had been able to find a chaperone. "I am certain he meant for the best, dear Aunt. How fortunate I have you to tend to my life now."

This earned a sharp look from her aunt. Satisfied nothing ill was intended by the remark, she urged Charity up to her bedroom, where the copper hip bath awaited, the fragrance of lavender rising with the steam to scent the air. For once the scent of lavender was not appealing.

Lady Tavington was greatly pleased at the appearance of her favorite niece as they left the cottage to enter the carriage so graciously arranged for them by Kenrick. Charity was arrayed in her lovely gown, the design of oak leaves worked in gold thread around the lower edge of the skirt a wonderful success. The topaz necklace and dainty eardrops added the perfect touch.

She watched as Charity toyed with the delicate ivory fan in her lap as they rode along. "Flutters?"

"More than I have ever known in my life, Aunt. I hope I do not disgrace you this evening."

"You have practiced your waltz and other dances, and I am persuaded you know them well. Your manners are very pretty and you look ravishing, dear girl. Now, try to relax and enjoy yourself. After all, Kenrick is giving this ball for you, more or less," she said, blatantly ignoring the intent between Lady Sylvia and Kenrick.

Lady Tavington had said nothing to her niece about her estimations regarding the charades played the previous night. While Charity had been at the hothouse to select the orchids, Lady Tavington had whisked up to the great house to confer with Lady Kenrick about the evening and what it all could mean. Neither lady had drawn any positive conclusions, but much speculation had occurred.

Jameson almost cracked a smile as he ushered Charity and Lady Tavington into the house. He announced them to the assembled group with more than customary relish.

The Earl of Dunstall was standing near the door and hurried to greet Lady Tavington, with Lady Kenrick right behind him, while Lady Sylvia and Lady Ann floated across the Aubusson to thank Charity for the exquisite orchids.

Lady Sylvia expressed her pleasure with scrupulous propriety. "How kind of you to think of us with one of your blooms, Miss Lonsbury." She nodded with exquisite grace, then drifted away again on a subtle note of Red Roses.

Charity was gratified to note each flower suited the dress for which it was chosen. Lady Sylvia had attached her white orchid to the point of her exceedingly deep décolletage, a thing Charity felt improved the dress. Or at least made it more amenable to other women. Lady Ann had pinned her delicate white, fuchsia-flecked orchid with its long spurs on the shoulder of her rose-pink gown, where it nestled amid a row of ruffles.

"La, Charity, I vow I have never had so lovely a flower. I cannot credit you actually grow these. Most remarkable." Lady Ann's gaze strayed to where Lord

Powell lounged against the mantel in conversation with Lord Harwood. "Geoff thought it was prodigiously beautiful."

"I daresay he thought you equally lovely, Lady Ann."

The pink that bloomed on Lady Ann's cheeks was charming. "I will tell you a secret. Geoff is to travel with me to my home to speak to my father. I am thrilled beyond measure. Is he not the handsomest of men?"

"Well-mannered and knowledgeable as well, Lady Ann. I must wish you happy." Charity bestowed a genuine smile of tender regard on Lady Ann. So sweet a woman deserved to be happy. "Your father will accept him, of course?"

"Lord Powell is well-to-pass, I have no fear on that score. That is usually what fathers are concerned about, is it not?" Lady Ann exchanged a knowing look with Charity.

The intriguing topic of betrothals was dropped as Lord Harwood and Sir Oswald joined Lord Powell at their sides. Lady Sylvia and Kenrick were nearby.

Ozzie spoke, his words audible to all in one of those sudden silences that occur at times. "I say, have you heard the latest from Prinny? Seems some devoted souls are to present him with a special orchid named for him. Sort of a thing to cheer him up, don't you know? What intrigues im is the grower of the orchids refuses to use his name, just initials. Funny thing is, initials are the same as yours, Kenrick. Rich, huh? As if you would be growing flowers like some common market gardener. I can tell you Prinny is intrigued with it. You know how he enjoys a good mystery. Determined to get to the bottom of it, he says. I think someone is having him on, a joke, don't you know? Probably picked the initials to conceal some other identity altogether. Good story, what? Wonder if the man will show up to claim the award to be given?"

Charity hoped she wasn't turning as pale as she felt. Ozzie's blundering words, disregarding Charity's connection with orchids, struck hard. What a blessing she wasn't given to swoons. She would now be stretched out on the carpet for certain. She exchanged a darting glance with her aunt and stiffened her spine at the look of reassurance she received in return.

"I think it is an intriguing coincidence. David, are you secretly raising orchids?" Lady Sylvia gave Kenrick a playful tap on his arm, her smile was arch, eyes laughing. Those alluring lashes fluttered down against magnolia-fair skin. "Perhaps Miss Lonsbury can tell us something of it? What about it, Miss Lonsbury? Do *you* know of the orchid to be given to the Prince Regent? Surely you must be aware of such an event? Tell us, please do!" The beguiling smile now had more than a touch of malice behind it.

Charity thought her heart might fail her as she turned away from the cold blue of those knowing eyes. How much did Lady Sylvia suspect, and what could she actually know? Charity prayed she had not turned as pale as she feared. Perhaps the flickering light of the candles might conceal her distress. Surely Sylvia didn't have qualms about bringing Lord Kenrick up to scratch, did she? That thought cheered Charity a bit, and she faced the evening with greater resolution than before.

Jameson announced dinner and Charity escaped on the arm of Sir Oswald. Her sense of unease returned after a calculating look from Lady Sylvia. What was going on in her head now? Lady Sylvia had been near the hothouses only once as far as Charity knew. How could she know anything?

Lord Kenrick had not answered Lady Sylvia, Charity noted. Was he mulling over those damning words? Would he pounce on Charity to accuse her of betraying the trust placed in her that allowed her to use the hothouses? Perhaps that was the little talk he intended to have with her? Charity felt a dampness on her brow and dared not touch it with her gloved hand. She eased onto her chair, taking the flurry of activity as others were seated as an opportunity to fan her heated face.

The dinner was undoubtedly elegant, with many courses and removes. Charity gazed at the lemon ice before her in dismay, hardly knowing how she achieved the dessert course. She hadn't been aware of any of the food on her plates. Grateful for the signal to leave the table with the other women, she joined Euphremia on the way toward the Gold Saloon, where they were to remain until it was time to enter the ballroom.

Lady Kenrick tapped Lady Tavington on her wrist, smiling at her as the two led the way from the dining room. "It was returned from Rundell and Bridge today," she whispered. "The family betrothal ring has been cleaned and is ready to be placed on someone's finger!"

14

IT WAS TRUE! IT was horribly, horribly true! Charity longed to close her eyes and weep in the heartbreak she felt seeping through every bone, every portion of her body. Until the moment she had heard Lady Kenrick whisper to her aunt that the ring was ready to bestow on Lord Kenrick's—David's—choice of bride, she had foolishly hoped for she knew not what to occur. Silly peagoose! Did she actually dream in her inner heart that his lofty lordship might notice her in that special way? They had exchanged kisses, but he undoubtedly kissed a number of ladies and that did not mean he intended to ask them to wed.

And now what of the talk he requested? Did he mean to inform her he knew of her improper behavior? Would he denounce her use of his initials? Would he tell her in scathing accents of his opinion of ladies, of any level, who engaged in trade? How imprudent she had been! Still, what was she to have done? She could paint watercolors that were uncommonly good, but how would that benefit her? Who would buy her paintings? And besides, selling paintings would be no better than orchids, in her estimation. Although she supposed she could sign another name to a painting and go through an agent.

She would not allow anyone to guess how low she felt. Somehow she would muddle through this evening and hope her face did not reveal her inner pain. Her spirits refused to be dampened for long; she had suffered too much adversity in her short life to let a thing like this keep her in the doldrums. Still, nothing close to having the man she loved turn to another woman was likely to come her way again. She sorrowed for the love she could have offered him, knowing it was unwanted.

Strange how she had loved him from afar for so many years, then he had entered her life so precipitately. She had been so hurt, so furious when she overheard is evaluation of her. She had vowed to hate him, to make him eat his words. Yet hate she could not. She had to admit in her heart of hearts he had been right in some ways. It had been impossible to continue her rancor, though she had certainly given it her best try. All he need do was touch her, hold her in his arms, look at her with those intensely blue eyes she loved so dearly, and her animosity went down the creek.

She thought of his description of a kiss from Herrick's words: "The sure, sweet cement, glue and lime of love." His kisses had bound her to him as surely as she was glued, cemented. She was his for the taking, and he didn't want her.

And now she would have to endure the announcement of his betrothal to Lady Sylvia. It was more than she could bear. When the hour came, she would slip away. Perhaps she would seek the comfort of her dear friend Roscoe in the soft darkness of the hothouse. That was one good thing about a pet; it never let you down.

After a brief time, the gentlemen joined the ladies and everyone proceeded to the ballroom. Charity walked near Lady Ann and Euphremia, ignoring the glare from the squire as best she could. It was truly amusing, was it not? Bigglesby desired to wed her, she desired Lord Kenrick, and he Lady Sylvia. Truly a jolly situation. She firmed her lips with as much fortitude as she could muster as she entered the ballroom.

Lady Kenrick and her distinguished son took their places and greeted the local gentry who were slowly beginning to filter into the room. It was a great honor to be invited, for the occurrence of a ball at Greenoaks was exceedingly rare. While the Kenricks, mother and son, conversed with Lady Tavington and the Earl of Dunstall in between arrivals, Charity drifted toward the other end of the room, conscious of the murmurs around her, the scraping of the violin as the orchestra tuned up, preparing to play. Her face appeared exceedingly pale in the enormous mirror down the far end of the ballroom. She ducked her head, pinching her cheeks, first one, then the other. When she looked again, it was to see the squire closing the gap between them at a rapid pace.

In the light of the hundreds of candles, she could observe his ire. Poor man, he must make a terrible card player, with his transparent face.

"Sir. This is a pleasant gathering, is it not?" Charity plunged into dangerous territory. "I trust you have taken my advice and sought to replace me in your interest?"

These were not the words the squire desired to hear from his intended bride. His density was matched only by his tenacity. "I am still annoyed with you, Miss Lonsbury. I know you wish to have your fun, but this is not a subject for levity. I wish to set a date. Rumor has it we would not be the only ones to be doing so this evening." His manner was arch, his tone condescending.

She knew she must have paled again at that reminder. It was even worse than hearing Sir Oswald talking about the presentation of the orchid selected for the Prince Regent. "It was not in jest, Squire Bigglesby. When I said we would not suit, I meant it. I perceive Miss Spencer chatting with Lady Ann. In Miss Spencer is a lady worthy of your attentions, sir. She is an expert horsewoman, accomplished at managing a household, well-trained by her mama in the requirements of being a wife to a man of your position. I have repeatedly requested you look elsewhere. Need I select a suitable lady as well?

At the flush on his rounded cheeks, she knew she had angered him beyond his tolerance. Only the increasing numbers of people flowing into the ballroom prevented him from doing something drastic. Her hand fluttered toward her throat as he bestowed a narrow, hard-eyed look on her.

The small orchestra struck up some lively music and she was spared further conversation with him. Taking advantage of his momentary glance at the source of the music, an ensemble brought down from London, Charity escaped to the other side of the room.

Euphremia had watched the exchange between Bigglesby and Charity. She was certain Charity had no interest in the squire. Charity had paled when he came up to her and spoke. Knowing him so well, Euphremia could not imagine what he could have said to bring that reaction. Charity had given back well, however. The squire had been very angry when he turned to discover his victim had slipped from his grasp. Euphremia nodded in reply to something Lady Ann murmured, then sidled away from that dear lady. She would take every advantage she could. Before the night was out, Bigglesby would find himself betrothed to her, Euphremia Spencer.

Lady Sylvia absently noted the hasty flit performed by Miss Lonsbury, then turned her attention to the object of her own anger. Lord Kenrick still had not made one move toward asking Sylvia to be his bride. She, too, had overheard what was intended to be a private communication between Lady Kenrick and Lady Tavington. The Kenrick betrothal ring was here! Lady Sylvia intended to see it was on her own finger before the evening was concluded. But unless David asked her, it was not going to be! He stood at his mother's side, where Sylvia also ought to have stood if this was truly to be their betrothal ball. *Why* had he waited to ask her? Why had he refused to listen to her remarks about that little country miss, dear Miss Lonsbury, and the orchids?

Panic began to grip Sylvia. Could it be possible David had no intentions of asking her to be his bride? She must consider the unthinkable. Sylvia's annoyance with

Lord Kenrick altered into a cross between fury and fear.

Looking about the now-filled ballroom, Sylvia noted how Euphremia Spencer, that unfortunate-visaged female, clung to the squire's arm. There would be one woman who might also detest the little Lonsbury. The squire had been obvious in his intentions toward Miss Lonsbury, who had been equally obvious in her determination to avoid him. Sylvia mentally filed that knowledge away as Lord Harwood walked toward her. She would suffer him the first dance, as she knew Kenrick must ask Lady Tavington, while the Earl of Dunstall danced with Lady Kenrick.

"You look charming this evening, Lady Sylvia. I see you rated one of Miss Lonsbury's orchids. One can only envy the bloom for its proximity to your beautiful self." He bowed over her hand and Sylvia preened slightly at his fulsome words. With Lord Kenrick virtually ignoring her, it was soothing to hear such kindly praise.

"What a gracious compliment, Lord Harwood. I vow you become more gallant every time we meet."

"I have not forgotten any of those times, Lady Sylvia. Though I fear you have managed to erase them from your mind. You find Kenrick appealing?" There was a flicker of some unnamed emotion in his eyes.

Her brows drew together slightly before she dismissed his words from her mind. It was too ridiculous that Lord Harwood held a *tendre* for her. As an earl he might be a better catch as regards his title, but his wealth could not match Kenrick's, nor could his homes compare, if what she had heard was correct. She needed to marry money, it was imperative! She ought to depress his interest.

"May I have the honor of this dance, my lady?" He extended a hand as he spoke.

Sylvia couldn't refrain from a gratified smile, pleased to have his attention directed toward her and not the Lonsbury chit. "I accept with pleasure, Lord Harwood." She placed her hand in his and they walked toward the groups forming for the quadrille.

"I perceive there are a great many undercurrents this evening. Had you noticed?" He held her hand lightly as he led her to the closest set forming for the dance. As the first of the five figures of the quadrille began, Sylvia glanced uneasily at Lord Harwood.

Ignoring the other three couples in the set, she studied Lord Harwood. He was a handsome man. Why the Lonsbury miss wasn't falling over herself to fix his attentions was hard to figure out. If Sylvia wasn't intent on David, she would definitely turn her interest to Charles. "I cannot say I have noticed anything of the kind, but then I have never been one to search for such things."

When again brought together by the figure of the dance, his warm caressing gaze gave her a start. Coldly, she ignored that gaze and set out to make sure he understood she had a man of greater wealth as a goal. "You are a good friend of David's, are you not? It will be our pleasure to see you here as a guest. Oh," she stammered in seeming confusion, "I ought not to have spoken. Nothing has been made public as yet, you see. But we have our understanding."

The light faded from Lord Harwood's eyes. He flicked his glance to where David was squiring Lady Tavington, noting the gaze that sought someone else, not Sylvia. "I wonder what it encompasses, my lady."

The sudden grim compression of the beautiful mouth didn't escape Charles; nor did the hard flash of blue eyes that sizzled toward, not David, but Charity.

"That is hardly any of your concern, is it, Lord Harwood?" Her words were cold, her manner brittle. Lady Sylvia was revealing a side to her nature heretofore not seen. The magnolia skin had an angry tinge over the cheeks, the ice-blue eyes rivaled the winter sky for chill.

"I'll confess I thought it could be. I understand better now." His warmth disappeared. In a flash of comprehension, Charles realized he had come close to making a serious mistake. The remainder of the dance was completed in silence.

Across the room, Ozzie had sought out Charity before anyone else could reach her side. He was resigned to her polite smile, the knowledge of her friendly indifference to him. Still, friendship was better than nothing at all. "I say, you are the fairest lady present this evening, Miss Lonsbury. It was kind of you to send orchids to the Greenoaks ladies. It appears to be more than simply a festive evening. Seems something special is in the air."

"I am proud to see they all chose to wear them, Sir Oswald." Her eyes twinkled with mirth at his mock frown. "I consider our surroundings, you see. It would never do for the local gentry to hear me address you in such a casual fashion. I must live here after you have gone." She forgave him his blundered words. How could he know they struck a dagger to her heart?

He was separated from her by the figure of the dance for a moment. When they came together again, he held her hand tighter than normal for a partner and quietly spoke. "It wouldn't have to be, you know. Dash it all, I can never be with you but what Charles is around."

Charity looked confused at this abrupt and bewildering conversation. Then she realized Sir Oswald was in a fair way to declaring himself. She could not allow him to be hurt, not when he had shown her such kindness.

She looked over the glittering ballroom, the candles seeming to double in number from the mirrored reflections, the colorful gowns catching light, lively faces smiling with delight in the evening. She must be the only woman here who was in exceedingly low spirits. Lady Sylvia was flirting with Lord Harwood as they performed the last of the five figures of the quadrille. How graceful she was, her skirts so daintily swishing about her feet as she moved through the dance. Charity noted her own heart was steady, unaffected by the sight of the two of them together.

Lord Harwood might be a fine catch, but he was not to Charity's desire. Looking at the more compelling figure of Lord Kenrick, she felt like a pudding that could not rise to its expectations. Those wickedly blue eyes were not fixed in her direction, but rather observing Lady Sylvia as she smiled up at Charles. It was only to be presumed. Kenrick was undoubtedly jealous of Charles' attentions toward the lady Kenrick intended to wed. But, oh, how Charity would adore to have Kenrick gaze at her with those fierce eyes, that possessive look about him.

When Sir Oswald returned her to the spot where her aunt had been sitting, Charity discovered her aunt and the Earl of Dunstall were moving toward the center of the floor to partake in the next dance, a waltz. She had turned away to look for a chair when her hand was gathered in a firm, warm clasp.

"I believe this dance is ours, Charity. I wanted to talk to you, or at least thank you again for the pleasure you have given to the ladies with the flowers."

That rich, deep voice had the power to turn her head to a silly feather and her knees to quivering blancmange. " 'Twas nothing, my lord. You thanked me earlier, you know." She hadn't missed his use of her first name. What could he mean by it?"

"Couldn't you call me David? It sounds much better than my lord. I have a name, as you do. I shall use yours, Charity. Use mine. Let me hear my name from your lips. Now." He swept her into his arms and to the center of the polished floor. Others smiled at the handsome pair so intent on each other. Or at least most of the others. The two of them were far too absorbed in each other to pay attention to anyone else in the room.

Charity was confused at the low urgency of his voice, but she didn't question his demand. "David . . . this is a lovely ball. Everyone seems to be having a lovely time. The decorations are—"

"I know, lovely." He grinned down at her, making it impossible for her not to sparkle back at him before they both chuckled at the absurdity of it all. His eyes glowed with warm admiration. They laughed softly as lovers sometimes do, in complete harmony with each other. They waltzed on, Charity wishing with all her heart the dance would never end. They were as one in spirit, just the manner in which she had longed for earlier. If someone had pointed this all out to Charity, she would have scoffed, but over in the far side of the room Sylvia took note of the intimacy between Charity and David.

It is doubtful that Charity would have been as happy if she could have but seen the face of Lady Sylvia as she waltzed about the room in the arms of one of the local gentry. The poor man was obviously dazzled by the beauty he lightly held. Lady Sylvia, if carefully observed, followed the progress of Lord Kenrick with a frigid blue gaze that would have alarmed, had it been noticed: her delicate mouth firmed, chin tilted up as though in resolve.

Her gaze darted about the room, seeking a form of help. She must get Charity out of the ballroom for an hour or two. David should pay attention to her, Sylvia. Who could she rely upon to assist her in luring the country miss from the room?

Charles and Ozzie were dismissed even as she looked at them. She had been introduced to several others, but they wouldn't do. Geoffrey couldn't see beyond the delicate figure in his arms. Lady Ann had managed to do what Sylvia ought to do . . . bring her man up to scratch. Now nothing could be allowed to interfere with Sylvia's plans.

Desperation drove her to consider further. At the far end of the room, she noted Bigglesby looking like a dog who has had his juicy bone snatched from him. Foolish man. Miss Spencer was the ideal wife for him, if he would only open his eyes to it. She was so besotted with him he could lead any sort of life he pleased, once he wed her. Sylvia searched her mind, her eyes narrowed in speculation. He was just the one to use. He knew the

little Lonsbury; she would listen to him, to a point,
anyway.

Her mind working rapidly, Sylvia continued to
cogitate while she danced with the local gentleman,
dazzling him with her smile while she plotted the
elimination of Miss Lonsbury—temporarily, of course.

David escorted Charity to the area where her aunt had
left her shawl. Turning to smile up at her partner,
Charity was disconcerted by his fixed attention on her
person.

"I like your gown, especially the oak-leaf design
around the skirt. Dare I hope it is in honor of Greenoaks?" He touched a slender petal of her orchid with
one lean, powerful finger while searching her face for a
clue to her feelings.

Charity had the sensation of being totally safe while
she was with him, as though he was in reality her *preux
chevalier*, ready to guard her from harm. She stiffened
those lamentably weak knees and smiled bravely back at
him. "We thought it proper to do credit to the estate. I
have been very happy here these many years. You are
aware I have lived here all my life? First the manse, then
the cottage. I am quite fond of the place." She blushed
at her forwardness. He would think she was pressuring
him to permit her to remain. Perhaps she was.

"I don't recall seeing you when I visited your father."

Charity gurgled a small laugh. "That is because I hid.
I wasn't supposed to be seen, you know. So I concealed
myself behind a shrub, or in the shadow of the stairs. I
saw you, my lord . . . David," she amended at his
reproachful look. "Mama would have given me a scold
if she had known my interest." The blush deepened as
Charity realized how her words might be construed.
Fortunately Lord Harwood came up to claim her for the
next dance, and she managed to escape before she made
a complete cake of herself.

David watched Charity walk onto the dance floor on
the arm of his best friend with a feeling of utter
frustration. He had wanted to declare himself to her

earlier. She had foiled that plan by insisting on
returning to the cottage. All David could think about
was claiming her as his own. He resented the manner in
which Charles looked at Charity, as though she were a
raspberry cream he was intent on consuming. He found
the sight of Charity so close to Charles strangely
irksome. It was an emotion he hadn't experienced
before, one he might admit to being jealousy.

He felt it his duty to dance with Lady Sylvia. Strange
how he had considered asking her to marry him at one
time. Now he couldn't think about her for his
absorption with Charity. Not that Sylvia was not a
lovely woman. She was beautiful in an aloof way, her
clear blue eyes revealing no warmth in their depths, nor
her mouth betraying any tenderness of emotion. They
might have made a go of it, finding a tolerable
marriage. He wanted more now.

Sylvia was only too conscious that David's eyes
strayed toward Charity all too frequently. For a man
who supposedly intended to ask Sylvia to marry him, he
was displaying a regrettable tendency toward another
woman. She would have to seek out the squire, present
her plan to him at the first opportunity. Her desperation
was driving her to do what she would never have
considered in a saner moment.

David didn't hold her as close as he had Charity
Lonsbury, nor did he gaze at her with the fond regard in
his eyes. Lady Sylvia was not pleased one bit. She
attempted to draw out his interest, find out the direction
of his regard. All she got for her pains was a hint David
might not be inclined to wed her. Her scheme must
succeed!

When the dance was over, she curtsied elegantly, then
rustled off to find the squire, leaving an absentminded
marquess behind her. His thoughts were not on the odd
behavior of Lady Sylvia, seeking out Squire Bigglesby, a
man she professed to despise. Instead, he watched
Charity before he invited another lady to a duty dance.

Sylvia shot an angry glance at Charity as she casually

skirted the ballroom. If it hadn't been for Charity, she, Lady Sylvia Wilde, would most likely have the Kenrick betrothal ring on her finger and be preparing to accept the felicitations of the assembled group. Instead, she was required to plot to get that silly miss out of the way for a time. Then Sylvia could claim David's full attention. One could hardly bring a man to the point of offering his hand if he was constantly watching another woman.

Blinded to normally unacceptable behavior, Lady Sylvia was possessed by the demons of malice and wrath. Insensitive to what David's feelings in the matter might be, she concentrated on what she felt had to be done, ignoring the flutterings of her dormant conscience.

"Squire, I wonder if I might have a word with you? It is prodigiously warm in here. Perhaps we might stroll along the terrace just outside the doors?" She had made a pretty curtsy.

His vanity soothed by her speech as well as the magnolia-white hand placed so trustingly on his arm, he nodded in agreement. "Of course, milady. The press of people does tend to generate heat. Just like animals, they are. Giving heat, that is."

He was muddling up his thoughts as usual, but Sylvia paid no attention to his ramblings. She had other things on her mind.

Once the terrace was gained, the music fading into a pleasant backdrop for their exchange of words, she took a claming breath and began.

There was no one present to overhear her softly spoken words. Her intense determination was soon revealed. His reserve was plain to see. Her persuasion prevailed.

At last the bargain was struck. She spoke swiftly, repeating when necessary, in a soft, urgent voice. Finally, set on a course of action, the two returned to the ballroom. Only Euphremia had noted the hour when they left and observed the moment when they returned.

Knowing the squire as she did, Euphremia was quick to mark the expression on his face. What was he up to? She began to weave her way through the throng of people to reach his side.

Near the door to the refreshment room, David, Lord Kenrick, also noted the return of Sylvia and Bigglesby to the ballroom. Curious pair. He considered the odd couple as he searched the room for Charity. It was Charity to whom he had decided he would offer the betrothal ring as well as his heart. He had never proposed before. He hoped he didn't make a hash of it.

Wending his way toward Charity as he sought her hand to go in to supper with him, he forgot the sight of the oddly assorted pair, dismissing from his mind what ought to have struck him as significant.

15

TURNING FROM WHERE SHE stood at her aunt's side, Charity was startled to discover Lord Kenrick approaching with the apparent intent of asking her to go to the refreshment room with him. She gathered her paisley shawl about her, for once unmindful of the faint exotic scent of patchouli that drifted up from it. Nervously licking her lips, she focused her eyes on his elegantly tied cravat with the single diamond winking from the starched folds.

"Charity, I would enjoy your company while we partake of a light supper. I imagine you must be hungry by now, you ate so little at dinner." Lord Kenrick offered her his arm, and Charity placed a trembling hand on the black cloth, feeling the power of the muscles beneath the fabric.

She was amused he had observed her absentminded eating during the elaborate dinner served earlier. With Lady Sylvia attempting to fix his attentions with every glance, every word, it was amazing he had noted anything, let alone what Charity had or had not consumed from her plate.

Unaware of the malevolent stare from Lady Sylvia, nor the disappointment in the eyes of Lord Harwood and Sir Oswald, Charity floated in a glow of happiness toward the room set aside for refreshments. Allowing David to hold her plate and heap it with lobster salad, cut-up bits of roast fowl, Swiss cream, and meringue, and a thin slice of ham, Charity accepted the nicely filled plate, then waited for him to select his own. He claimed a secluded table for two near a window to the terrace. Charity sank down on the dainty gilt-wood chair with a feeling of unreality.

She was scarcely aware of the food she consumed. It had to be utterly delicious, pure ambrosia. Her plate was cleaned of every tidbit as she listened to David chat with an enviably casual air about the ball, the guests, and how lovely her flowers were.

It was then reality began to sneak up on her with the cold, sober truth. Whatever was she thinking of, to be sitting here with the man she deceived? If he but knew her true nature, the business she conducted from his hothouses, he would scorn instead of praise her.

He complimented her on her appearance as though she was worthy of the elegance showered on her by her aunt. Indeed, Charity was so endowed simply to nab a husband! What a lowering thought. But he knew all that, she reminded herself. He was a party to the entire plan. He was trying his best to get her married off to someone—and not necessarily himself. Yet he wouldn't be so attentive if it was merely to fix another man's interest, would he? Or did he think to bestir jealousy in another? Did she want him so desperately she was willing to read desire into his every action? Her mind was in a confused whirl.

He had said nothing about the orchid to be given to the Prince Regent, nor had he commented on the similarity between his initials and the initials used in the Horticultural Society entry. Charity felt the food she had just consumed turn into an unpleasant lump in her stomach. It would be terrible enough for her to be engaged in selling orchids and plants from his hothouses; to have him discover she had engaged in such things was not to be borne. The pang that shot through her when she considered the thrilling sense of rapport was swept aside to be dwelt on at some other time in the distant future.

Her smile was strained as she listened to his flattering words. Her eyes could not meet his as he addressed her with soft phrases, cajoling her, beguiling her. She

longed to be clasped in his strong arms again. The
memory of their kiss beneath the cascades of orchids in
the hothouse would haunt her all her life.

It was possible he merely intended to bring the other
men to scratch. That had to be it. Where had her mind
been? Of course he meant Lady Sylvia for his wife.
What could a reverend's daughter, albeit the granddaughter of an earl, have to offer such a man as the
marquess? Devoted love, answered a wee voice deep
within her heart.

Struggling with her desire and what must be done,
Charity rose from the table and curtsied deeply to the
man she would always love. There was too much that
must remain hidden between them for anything to come
of their attraction to each other. She could feel he was
drawn to her, that much she would admit. Beyond that,
she was adamantly opposed to bringing disgrace upon
his name, as must surely follow exposure of her work in
the hothouses. Secrets that might harm him would keep
them apart. He must never know what she had done!
She hated the idea he would look at her with scorn or
possibly disgust.

"I have enjoyed our little supper, my lord. Thank you
for your most enjoyable company." She ignored his
frown at her formality. "I must return to my aunt.
Please excuse me." She gathered her skirts to one side
and turned to leave him. She stiffened at the touch of
his warm, strong hand clearly felt through the soft
leather of her glove.

"What happened, Charity? I thought things were
progressing nicely." His voice held confusion, which
caused her resolve to falter for a moment.

She could still taste the last thing she had eaten, the
lemon- and sherry-flavored Swiss cream. It seemed to
sour in her mouth as she walked, a stiff figure at his
side. How difficult it had been to swallow that
remaining bite of sherry-soaked sponge cake knowing
that her silly dreams had brought her nothing but grief.
Together, though far apart in thoughts, they crossed the

room to where her aunt stood conversing with the Earl
of Dunstall.

"Aunt, have you enjoyed the lovely refreshments in
the adjoining room? I vow the table is simply groaning
with delicacies of every kind. I hope you intend to
sample some of them." Charity's voice had a
breathless, almost frantic quality to it. She then gave her
aunt a vexed look. "I seem to have torn the hem of my
gown. It should not take a moment to repair it." She
gave a very good imitation of a lighthearted laugh.
Turning to Lord Kenrick, she curtsied once again and
avoided meeting those intense eyes, which she knew
would see through her ruse. "Thank you so much for
the pleasure of your company, my lord. I would not
have wished to show preference to Lord Harwood over
Sir Oswald or the reverse." Gathering her courage into
a neatly stiffened backbone, Charity left the ballroom at
a measured but sure pace that increased with each step,
until she raced.

David stared after her departing figure with obvious
puzzlement on his face. What had happened in the other
room? One moment they had been in total harmony, the
next in complete disarray. He murmured something to
an equally perplexed Lady Tavington. She turned a
mystified gaze to her partner, the Earl of Dunstall, and
walked with him to the supper room in a distracted
state.

The hall was cool compared to the heat of the
ballroom. Charity fled to the ladies' retiring room with
near unseemly haste. Fortunately the footmen in
attendance cared nothing about propriety in her case.
The glimpse of her neatly trim ankles as she sailed
around the stair post might catch their attention, but
they had no concern for ladies' nerves.

The cheval mirror in the retiring room revealed
nothing of her inner turmoil. Remarkable how one's
thoughts could be so cleverly hidden beneath the skin

and bone of the face. She sank down on the charmingly upholstered chaise.

A small two-tiered table sat close to the chaise with an assortment of restoring liquids ladies might enjoy. Charity poured a bit of lemonade into a crystal glass on the tray. Across the room on a chest sat the needle and thread that Charity ought to have been using . . . if she had a torn hem, which she did not. She considered her deception.

She had done the correct thing, however it might appear. The more she could stay away from David, the better for all concerned.

Restored by the lemonade, she rose from the chaise and brushed down her skirt. The door opened behind her and Lady Ann entered the room.

"There is nothing wrong, is there? I was concerned when you disappeared, not to return."

"Merely a thread that would break and needed catching. I sought to relax a few moments from the heat and press of the crowd of people. You are accustomed to all this. I fear it is unusual for me. Would you care for a sip of lemonade? How thoughtful of Lady Kenrick to place a pitcher of it up here for our restoration." Charity attempted a smile and found her face did not crack with the effort.

"Nothing for me, thank you." Lady Ann gazed at Charity with a thoughtful expression on her face. "If I did not think more highly of you, I would say you are here on a retreat."

"Me? How silly. I intend to return in moments. In fact, I was about to leave when you entered. Will you join me?"

"I will come down in a few minutes."

Charity escaped from Lady Ann's probing gaze to the coolness and dim candlelight of the hall. Her skirts softly rustling about her legs, Charity made her way to the ballroom once more. Pausing at the entrance, she searched the room, taking care to note where everyone was. Especially David.

On the far side of the room, Lady Sylvia clung to David, Lord Kenrick, with the possessive hold of a woman who has every right to be by his side. She was sparkling with her cool beauty in the equally cool-blue dress, yet there was something elegantly untouchable about Sylvia that did not appeal to Charity. But then, it didn't have to appeal to her. After this weekend Charity would never see the woman again, if she could help it.

Tears shimmered in her beautiful gray eyes as she sought someone else to join. She was determined to stay as far away from Lord Kenrick as might be possible.

"I feared our princess had fled to her tower." Lord Harwood materialized at her elbow.

Charity turned, managing a smile at his gallantry. "I am here, sir." She placed her hand on his arm and allowed him to draw her into the dance just beginning. It was a waltz. Charity felt her heart falling into small shards as she moved across the floor in his arms. Together they whirled about the room, an incredibly graceful pair. Charity ignored the look of inquiry on his face.

"This is a lovely ball, is it not? But then, I suppose you attend balls such as this frequently during the Season in London. Do you return to your country home when you leave here? What a disgraceful person I am, I have not asked where your home is located. I expect you spend Christmas there, as well, until it is time to return to the gaieties of London. Do you miss them when you are away?"

She was chattering worse than any magpie. She couldn't help herself. Every time they made a circle, Charity could see that exquisite face simpering up into David's. Sylvia could not love him half so much as Charity did.

Harwood's gentle voice interrupted her musing. "My home—would that it really meant something to you—is to the north of London, not far from Oxford. I will spend Christmas with my mother and two sisters and their families. My younger brother will be home from

Eton as well. It is a pleasant time. We have riding and parties. I do not miss the pleasure of London when I am there. We are not all a lot of fribbles, you know."

"I never meant to imply such, my lord." Her indignant words were met by a chuckle. Glancing up at him for the first time, she found his kind eyes smiling at her. "You are bamming me, I suspect."

"I would like to do a great deal more, but I too have suspicions. Your heart is given to another, isn't it?"

Alarmed at his perception, she shook her head. "My heart is quite my own. I consider it impossible to bestow it on another." Fortunately the watlz came to an end and she found they were standing near Euphremia and the squire. Euphremia had a discontented look on her face and Charity felt sorry for her. Apparently Charity was not the only woman for whom the evening was not a joy. She observed Lord Harwood watching Sylvia, standing silhouetted against the terrace windows, charm a local gentleman. Lord Harwood seemed preoccupied; perhaps his heart was involved with Sylvia. Charity could give him her sympathy.

The squire gave Charity a haughty look, which was almost her undoing. If he could but know how ridiculous he appeared when he tried to be elegant. It was not in his makeup.

Lord Harwood graciously offered his arm to Euphremia, having observed that while she was far from beautiful, she was an excellent dancer.

"Squire." Charity nodded her head in dismissal, preparing to slip away from her nemesis.

If he had not been peeved before, this act of condescension would have made him so. The squire narrowed his eyes, nearly losing them in the fat of his face. "I believe this is our dance, Miss Lonsbury." He appeared quite prepared to create a scene should she refuse.

There was nothing she could do but accept her fate. Dipping a graceful curtsy, Charity allowed him to lead her onto the floor, thanking her guardian angel for keeping Lord Kenrick at the opposite end of the room. Her last glimpse of him had revealed him to be in serious conversation with the vicar's wife.

"I suppose you know all about the stranger in the village," the squire said at the first interval they were side by side in the dance.

Charity threw him a startled glance. "Strangers, Squire? I am afraid I know nothing of them."

"Not them, him. Rendon down at the Black Swan said a stranger was staying there. Seems he is some kind of flower grower. Thought you might know of him. Rendon thought . . ."

His words were lost as the figure of the dance separated them. When next they met, Charity most casually inquired, "You mentioned the stranger who grew flowers?"

"Oh, that. Rendon said he mentioned orchids and it made Rendon think of you. Someone you might know? Said the flower man was from over Sussex way. Been here for several days. Perhaps he intends to visit with you? When you are not gadding about with the lords and ladies and have time for the rest of the world, that is." There was definitely malice in his voice.

A chill crept over Charity. She had been thinking another direction when it came to the ruination of the hothouse. Now it appeared it might be from a different source altogether.

"I wonder . . ." Charity felt she would not be easy until she checked her plants. As soon as the house party disbanded, she was prepared to set off on her trip to London bearing the orchid as well as the second painting. She had already approached Josiah, about a ride to the city. He suggested she travel with the carriage taking some of his lordship's things to his home in Grosvenor Square. The event of a stranger in the village changed things considerably.

Ought she reveal the potential for further destruction to Lord Kenrick? After all, it was his property. One look in his direction, the attention he was paying to a lovely lady from a neighboring estate, and she forgot that notion.

"I ought to check on the plants."

Her words brought a sly smile to Bigglesby's face. "Now? Why would you want to do such a thing? Surely the morning would do quite fine." His voice held a fine disdain for her concern with mere flowers when there was more important business at hand . . . the ball.

Realizing she had spoken her thoughts out loud, Charity decided she might as well make use of the squire, since he was bound to make himself a nuisance. "I would not rest thinking there might be a danger to my beloved flowers. While I am aware, sir, you do not approve of my diversion, perhaps you might extend me the courtesy of your company while I walk down to make sure nothing is amiss. I am persuaded all the servants are occupied with the festivities this evening. No one will be watching the hothouses at this hour. If the man from Sussex is the same person who so violently damaged the hothouse before, he could easily enter the estate and do so again. I must confess I have grave concern for the safety of my plants."

"I don't know. Ain't the thing to be wandering off during a ball such as this. Of course, if we was betrothed, it would be different."

His insinuating manner grated on Charity's raw nerves. "I will go by myself if you choose not to attend me. Never let yourself think I will marry you for any reason."

The squire seemed to consider her words final at last, for he nodded. "As you say, miss. And you still desire me to walk with you?"

"I may not wish to marry you, sir, but I doubt you will do me any harm between here and there. It would not look well in the village were word to get out that you had insulted the daughter of the former reverend. Many folk still recall my father with fondness."

The dance concluded. After glancing about to ascertain whether they might slip out undetected,

Charity walked toward the terrace doors with the squire. Lord Kenrick was still occupied and Lord Harwood was talking with Euphremia, thank goodness. Lady Sylvia was not far away, but appeared to be devoting her skills to enchanting the member of the local gentry who stood mesmerized at her side. Aunt Tavington was deep in conversation with the Earl of Dunstall and Lady Kenrick at the other end of the room. It was surely safe to leave now before someone joined her.

She missed the sudden turn Euphremia made, giving her a clear view of their departure. Charity did not know those jealous eyes watched her exit the room, with the squire close behind. Euphremia curtsied to Lord Harwood and, after snatching up her shawl, hastily made her way to the terrace, there to search for Charity and the squire. Seeing their dim shapes in the direction of the hothouses, she followed, keeping well to the shadows.

Near another door to the terrace, Sylvia also turned, noted the absence of the squire, then excused herself to slip from the room.

Charity clutched her shawl about her, thankful she had left it on a chair near the door instead of where her aunt had been sitting. What her aunt might think of her traipsing off to the hothouses at this hour of the night, Charity did not even want to consider.

A wind had risen, leaves fluttered to the ground, blown free from their precarious hold on the branches. As shrubs moved to and fro, Charity imagined she could see all manner of things in their eerie shapes. She shivered, and not simply from the chill in the air. The hoot of an owl made her jump, much to the squire's obvious amusement.

"Nasty night out, it's coming to be. Good weather for a hunt, though, as long as it don't get too cold. Lose all scent when it's too frosty, you know."

Charity thought the hunt an abominable thing, but wisely said nothing of her opinion to the squire. "I'm sure," she mumbled, beginning to believe she was too hasty in her desire to check on the plants. Perhaps she ought to have requested one of the footmen to have a look? Though she had no right to order any of his lordship's servants, it was his property that was in danger, after all. That ought to lend some credence to her request. She shivered again as they neared the stone bridge over which they would pass to get to the hothouses.

The lake was a dark expanse spreading out to the east. The wind tugged at her, tearing the orchids from her shoulder. Charity was sad to see them fly away. She remembered David's touch on them. She would have pressed them in her Bible, a safe place for a treasured memento. It was foolish in the extreme when he was soon to become the husband of another woman, yet she had heard of genteel spinsters who preserved such memories in this manner. And Charity fully expected to become such a spinster.

"You've been putting on airs of late, Miss Lonsbury."

Startled at these harsh words from the squire, Charity tried to make out his expression in the dim light from the stars and the sliver of a moon. "I do not know what you mean, sir. I do not believe in putting on airs, as you call it." The owl chose that moment to call into the night and Charity found her nerves even more on edge. "Come, this is not the time nor the place to be discussing such a thing."

The squire's shoes made crisp clicks as they crossed the stone bridge. Once on the far side, the lights and music of the great house left behind, they proceeded to the hothouses. Charity could see nothing amiss outside the buildings. Roscoe poked a sleepy head from its burrow near the entrance to the hothouse where Charity usually worked. She noted the sight, but said nothing to the squire as she recalled his dislike of the rabbit.

Entering the warm, scented hothouse, Charity put a match to a lamp and held it aloft so that she might look about. "I was foolish to be so concerned. All appears to be in order here. I thank you for coming with me, Squire. Perhaps we could return to the great house now?"

Bigglesby glanced around at the interior as though he had never seen it before.

Charity gave him an impatient look. What was he thinking now? Surely he would want to return to the ballroom, or at least the supper room. "If you have not tried the lobster salad, you must remember to do so. Lord Kenrick has an accomplished chef."

Still he made no move to leave, rather inspecting an unusual white orchid near the end of the hothouse.

Charity walked down to join him, annoyed by his refusal to do as she wished. "Squire?"

Beyond the hothouses, Euphremia shifted so she might see what was going on at the far end of the hothouse. Sliding behind a rhododendron, she brushed off a leaf that clung to her shawl, and persisted in her way along the side of the building until she could find a partial view. She could see part of Charity as well as the squire, who seemed to be examining a flower. As she knew he had no interest in blooms of any kind, she wondered what he was up to now.

Charity checked on the stove and found it to be stoked for the night. Normally she left it to Josiah or one of the men to do the night tending. They had insisted this was no place for her at night, and she was beginning to wish she hadn't come here now. What on earth had gotten into the squire?

"Squire? I am leaving for the great house. Now. Will you come with me? Otherwise I will go alone." If Charity didn't know better, she would believe the squire was stalling. Surely he must have accepted her refusal by now.

"Not yet, Miss Charity." There was an icy quality to his voice that made her draw away from him. She backed against the workbench, taking little comfort in its solidity. He crossed his arms to give her his lecturing look. "You are very wrong to refuse me. I know we could make a handsome pair. Don't think his lordship or one of the other fine bucks from London will ask you to wed. They won't get the chance."

Puzzled and not a little frightened, Charity continued to back away, sliding along the bench, hoping to reach the relative safety of the door. She was almost there when an expression on the squire's face brought her to a halt. She stared at his face, then turned to see what might be behind her that had caught his eyes when she was hit on the head.

Her eyes closed as a shaft of pain seared her skull. As she sank to the slatted wood floor, she breathed in the scent of Red Roses.

16

DAVID GLANCED AROUND THE ballroom, searching for Charity. She had been dancing with Bigglesby earlier, the last time he saw her. Sylvia had been clinging to him like a limpet when he tried to intimate he did not have any serious intentions in her direction. It was a deucedly difficult thing to do. He couldn't recall when he had been placed in quite this position. Usually a lady could tell when he had lost interest. It was perhaps the first time he could recall being grateful that his duties made it necessary he spend some time conversing with a lady like the vicar's wife. A brown sparrow of a woman, with no memorable qualities, she nicely served the purpose to free him from Sylvia—for at least the moment.

But to be fair to Sylvia, inviting her here to his home, with his mother in so obvious attendance, could possibly have led her to believe his intentions were serious. And to be honest, when he issued the invitation, he had been serious. All that changed when he had a clay pot thrown at his head. From that day he had found his interest being gradually fixed on a minx who grew orchids, of all things.

He wondered just how much of a coincidence it was that the initials used by the orchid grower who had won the premier accolade from the Horticultural Society were the same as his. Charity had had a strange expression on her face, and she slipped away from the group very soon after that story was told. Come to think of it, Sylvia had insinuated Charity might have something to do with the Prince Regent's orchid, using initials to conceal identity. It had displeased him to think Charity might have anything to do with so underhanded a scheme. His feelings for Charity were quite strong; he wished no one to think ill of her.

It could be a disaster if Sylvia revealed her suspicions to others less inclined to be forgiving. He couldn't imagine a more forbearing group than Charles and Ozzie, Ann and Geoff. Though the latter hadn't been around either, come to think of it. Ann and Geoff appeared to have spent every available minute by themselves, with only Ann's maid in attendance. It had been difficult to put his mind on other than Charity for the past days.

He must clarify the situation between Sylvia and himself, however. She stood not far away and she turned to face him as she spoke to Charles. She left Charles after a word or two, making her way toward him with regal grace. He observed Sylvia with a feeling of something between pity and relief. She was undeniably lovely, excessively well-bred, but she had a coldness within her he found repelling. He not only wanted more from a marriage, he could have it with Charity. This was not the moment to talk to Sylvia, however. One did not give the congé to a lady of quality in the middle of a crowded ballroom. He had intended to speak with her later and now found himself trapped by her determined approach. He sensed she would not be put off.

Her voice was light, flirtatious. "David, you naughty boy. Everyone seems to have the notion there is to be some sort of announcement this evening. You said you wished to speak with me, and there is no time better than this moment. Your invitation to me, this ball, is there some connection?"

Her arch coyness grated on his nerves. The moment he had small relish for could not be postponed as he had hoped.

"I had thought perhaps we—that is, your mother intimated she would be happy to see me . . ." Sylvia found her words trailing into utter silence as she met David's eyes. The look in them was colder than the ice shipped down from Greenland for Gunthers' famous desserts.

"There can be nothing between us, Sylvia. I tried to tell you before that I fear we would not suit. I have no doubt you will be able to turn to one of your many other gallants. After all, we both knew that neither of us had formed an attachment. My mother insisted I wed, set up a nursery," he said bluntly. "I promised her I would get better acquainted with you since you are the daughter of her dear friend, Countess Wilde. You wished to wed my title, my money, and me, in that order. Don't pretend otherwise."

No trace of emotion showed on Sylvia's exquisite face. "I see." Her normally cool voice was husky; David wondered if there was actually a hint of tears in it. "At first I hoped you might be jesting." Her head tilted in a proud line as she backed away from him. "I hope you will understand if I withdraw. I fear the ball has ceased to entertain me." She waved a vague hand at the swirling figures beneath the glow of the candles. "I do thank you and your mother for your hospitality. Extend my regards in the event I do not have the opportunity to speak with her before I depart. I intend to leave at first light in the morning. That is not too many hours away."

He wanted to tell her that he was sorry, that he admired the courage he suddenly espied. He never suspected she had such depths, if indeed she did. Sylvia had seemed to him to be a superficial person. He suspected her pride would not welcome pity in any form. She threaded her way through the throng of people, a regal figure as she swiftly moved from the ballroom.

Sylvia felt ill. She had lost! David had refused to succumb and she had turned aside Charles, fool that she was. Now she had nothing! There was a bitterness in her mouth as she mounted the stairs to pack. Word would spread quickly. She would be lucky if a local squire would seek her hand.

Dismissing Sylvia from his mind, David continued to
search the still-crowded ballroom for Charity. It seemed
odd that she would disappear right now. He wanted to
talk with her, find out what was going on behind those
lovely gray eyes of hers. Something was amiss.

Bigglesby was engaged in conversation on the far side
and David began to make his way to his side. It was just
possible the squire had managed to keep an eye on
Charity, since he had in the past evinced so much
interest in her. David, his path barred by a number of
guests who insisted in having a word or two with him,
found the going difficult. It was frustrating to stop to
make polite conversation when he wished to be
elsewhere.

At the edge of the throng of people, Euphremia
pinned the squire with a narrow gaze. He had never seen
her like this. Instead of meek and pliable, she was
assertive, commanding.

"Where is Miss Lonsbury, Squire? I vow I saw her
leave with you a short time ago. Went out that door
over there onto the terrace. What happened to her?"
She nodded in the direction of the door while fixing him
with a hard stare from her large hazel eyes.

The squire shifted uncomfortably. He gave the tall,
slender woman who clung to his slide a look of distaste.
Gads, but he detested this woman. "I couldn't rightly
say, Miss Spencer." He sought to free himself from her
vineline clasp. Her next words stayed his leaving.

"You might as well know I saw you out there. You
had a strange expression on your face when you went
out to the terrace. It made me exceedingly curious, so I
decided to follow you. I did, too. Right down to the hothouses, where I saw you hit poor Charity over the head.
Is she still there? What happened? If you think to get
her to wed you after this, you are more of a numskull
than I thought." Her voice was not as sharp or carrying
as usual, but it hit the squire with the devastation of a
cannonball.

Bigglesby suspected it was hopeless. Miss Spencer had

well and truly caught him in a trap from which it could be deucedly difficult to extricate himself. With a forlorn sigh, he nodded. "It wasn't I who hit her on the head, though," he blustered. "It was Lady Sylvia."

"Hah! Expect me to believe that?" Euphremia leveled an appraising look at him. "Or anyone else? Doing it a bit too brown, my good man. Do you know what will happen if Kenrick finds out you were there with her, hit her on the head? I saw you, *saw* the clay pot come up in the air, and she didn't come out when you stole from the building. I peeked in the window before you blew out the lamp and saw her on the floor, tucked back in the corner, all hidden away. If you want my silence in the matter, we will announce our betrothal now, this very night. I will claim we were together all this time; it is Charity's word against ours. After all, a hit in the head might make her muddled, you know. Look about you and note the faces you see. Do you wish to have all these folks, many of them friends and neighbors, know the truth?" Her face and voice were calm, deadly calm as far as the squire was concerned.

Euphremia had never in her life been so articulate. Her powers of persuasion were too much for the befuddled squire. "So be it. It shall be as you wish." Had he faced a firing squad, he could not have been more resigned. Perhaps he could spend most his time with his horses and hounds. Then he remembered Miss Spencer's love for the hunt. There would be no escaping the woman, it seemed.

As Lord Kenrick strode up to them, having at last shaken off the vicar and his prosy wife, the satisfied gleam on Euphremia's face was akin to that of an alligator who has just swallowed its prey . . . whole.

"Miss Spencer, Squire, have you seen Miss Lonsbury? I have been looking for her this age and she seems to have vanished."

Euphremia fluttered her eyelashes and simpered at Lord Kenrick. "My lord, the squire and I have been, er, involved, you might say. You may wish us happy. We are to marry as soon as it can be arranged.'' She tossed an arch look at the squire and patted his arm in a proprietary manner.

Lord Kenrick noted the squire's uncomfortable expression and pegged it to his being leg-shackled to Miss Spencer, a future that might make any man a bit distressed. He turned to the nearest footman and ordered champagne for the delighted Euphremia. The squire looked as though even an excellent hunt would not pull him from the pit of his doldrums. His expression resembled that of the harried fox more than the triumphant hunter.

As a glass of excellent champagne was being poured, Lady Kenrick bustled up with the Earl of Dunstall and Lady Tavington close behind her. "My heavens, what is going on here? A betrothal?'' Her sharp gaze darted around the little group. Seeing the way Euphremia clutched at the squire's sleeve, she jumped to the correct answer immediately. "David, dear, you must make an announcement for our friends. I am quite certain Euphremia will wish to share her joy with the assembled guests.''

Lady Kenrick didn't need to ask if the squire had sought for Euphremia's hand from her father, Baron Spencer. Having heard how her parents had tried quite desperately to get Euphremia wed to anyone, it was unlikely the squire had to do more than look willing to toss the handkerchief in Euphremia's direction for his fate to be sealed.

Impatiently, David nodded in agreement and sought the orchestra leader to make arrangements for the announcement. It was the last thing he desired to spend time doing at the moment. Proprieties must be observed, however. Then he had to locate Baron Spencer and his wife, who looked remarkably like her daughter. The baron was a red-cheeked man with slightly protruding blue eyes and an elegant mustache, a hale, hardy specimen of English gentry. He was only too thrilled to be asked to use this auspicious occasion to announce his daughter's betrothal. It could even save him the cost of a betrothal ball.

Once the announcment was made, David again set out to find Charity, while wondering what might next stand in his path. "Mother, have you or Lady Tavington seen Charity?"

At the use of Charity's first name, Lady Kenrick shot her son an appraising look, then shook her head. "I'm sorry, my dear. It has been some time since we spoke with her. Alice, do you know if she retired?"

Lady Kenrick had been surreptitiously searching the room for her niece for some time, not telling her companions she was concerned at Charity's invisibility. "I'll find the maid. Perhaps she can tell us something. Excuse me." The others watched as Lady Tavington hurried from the ballroom, intent on finding her niece. She had the strangest feeling something was not right.

As David watched Lady Tavington leave, he said in a quiet aside to his mother, "Lady Sylvia said she will be leaving at first light."

Eyes only a little less blue than her son's looked up to search David's face. "You are sure that is what you wish? I confess I have had a doubt or two as to my feelings regarding her."

"We wouldn't suit, Mother. My heart is elsewhere."

A sweet smile of pleasure crept across Lady Kenrick's face. "I'm so pleased, dear boy. I had hopes one way or the other that you might come to know the joy your father and I knew when we were first married." At the flash of skepticism he could not avoid, she nodded, placing her hand on his arm to stress her point. "We were very much attached until he became engrossed with affairs of state. Never neglect what is closest to your heart and you will not lose it. Now I expect you want to find a certain young lady to tell her what you have told me." She made a shooing motion with her fan, smiling fondly at him.

Grinning inwardly as he shook his head in chagrin at his mother's perception, David sought out the butler.

Jameson had no information as to Charity's direction.

"I will check with all the servants, m'lord. Perhaps someone has seen her. Perhaps one of the maids?"

"Lady Tavington is quizzing one now." David turned to find Charles and Ozzie approaching him.

"I say, old man, have you seen Miss Charity? Charles and I have looked everywhere for her this age. Done a flit, it seems. I hope she ain't unwell. Last time I saw her, she looked a bit pale." Ozzie looked about him with an air of abstraction, still searching the now-thinning crowd for the face he desired to see.

David followed Ozzie's gaze about the room. He turned to see Lady Tavington hurry toward him, her furrowed brow causing his heart to sink.

"The upstairs maid has seen nothing of her either. Kenrick, I am very concerned for her. It is not like her in the least to be thoughtless, nor leave her intentions unknown to me. Has no one seen her? What about Euphremia or Squire Bigglesby?"

"They were occupied at the time, I believe." His wry expression told his opinion of their activity.

"I say, let us divide up the area and get up a search party." Ozzie chewed at his lip. "You don't think there could be foul play abroad, do you?"

Seeing Lady Tavington's start of alarm, David shook his head in warning to the irrepressible Ozzie. "I'm sure she is fine. Perhaps she has nodded off in a concealed chair and is quietly sleeping."

Lord Harwood nodded in agreement. "Most likely you have the right of it. I'll check the library. Ozzie, you go up to the second floor, talk with the maids." He paused, searching his friend's face before leaving the room. "David, we know how much she means to you. I mean, old man, it's quite evident she has formed a *tendre* for you, and I suspect it's mutual. Is it not?"

With a rueful nod, David waved his good friends on their way. David knew the servants were likely doing the same business, checking the rooms, talking to those who might have returned to seek their beds, but he didn't object to the direction Charles and Ozzie might search. He had his own ideas about where Charity might have gone.

So, his friends had observed his growing attraction to Charity. Why was it others could see so easily what one thought concealed? David had fought against it, thinking Charity was unsuitable. Now, all he cared for was having her in his arms again, safe, loved.

It was approaching dawn. The faint gray light creeping up in the east could only help in their search. Taking an oil lamp, lighting it, David slipped from the ballroom after telling his mother she would have to handle the departing guests. Touching her lips apprehensively, Lady Kenrick watched him take leave.

The wind was still tossing the trees about as David made his way across the terrace. Branches were strewn hither and yon, littering the path from the terrace, making it difficult to walk. Carefully checking each side of the path, he wondered if Charity was to be found where he desperately hoped she might be, safe and warm. Yet he could not take any chance of missing her. When Ozzie spoke of possible foul play, it had stirred a deep fear within David. Pray God she is safe!

Charity stirred, moaning as the ache in her head intensified at her move. Her mouth was tightly covered by a cloth. Her hands were tied behind her, the cord biting into her wrists as she pulled at them. She ached from the unaccustomed position, shoulders twisted on the wooden slats of the floor, arms straining as they were pulled unnaturally to her back.

What had happened? Slowly the events of the evening returned. The squire had told her about a stranger who was interested in flowers—orchids, to be exact. Where was the squire? Had he too been hit on the head? Straining her neck to peer in the dim light of the hothouse, she could make out no other figure. Had that stranger struck the squire, dragged him from the hothouse? What, now?

She tried to call out, her efforts muffled into an "umph," then a moan. Silence.

She looked down at her gown, hitched up to her knees, the beautiful embroidery covered by a musty, dirty, rough woven sack used for moss and bark. It was damp and chilly on the floor. She couldn't recall ever being so miserable in her life. She had no idea how long she had been lying here.

Where was Lord Kenrick now? The light was growing in the east. She could see pale pink in the clouds, heralding another morn. By now, Lord Kenrick and Lady Sylvia should have announced their betrothal to the assembled guests. An ache struck her heart that had nothing to do with the bump on her head, nor the manner in which she was trussed up like a chicken ready for the spit.

She wished she had told him the truth about herself. As she stared up into the delicate lavenders and whites over her head, she knew she would never rest until she had revealed all of it to him. He might be annoyed, might even tell her to leave the cottage, taking her plants with her, but at least her conscience would be clear. She had hated concealing the truth from him, hated lying of any kind. It was not in her nature to be devious and prevaricating. At least it hadn't been until this business of selling the orchids.

What would he say when he learned the whole of it? He would rebuke her for going into trade, most assuredly! No woman of any position did such a thing. Never mind she wished to eke out the small annuity paid to her each month. He would be like Lady Tavington, believing she ought to have sought help from her uncle. But then, Lady Tavington had a far different view of her brother than Charity did.

She was very weak from the pain in her head, not to mention quite woolly-headed, and as she slipped back into a state of oblivion again, something teased at her memory, an elusive scent, something she should recognize.

*   *   *

As David searched along the path, scrutinizing the shrubbery, one of the footmen hurried up to him bearing some crumpled flowers in his hand.

"M'lord, I found these along the bank of the lake." He pointed to a spot about twenty feet from the bridge.

David looked down at the wilted orchids in his hand. They were the ones worn by Charity last he saw her! "Show me the exact place." He strode after the footman, hoping against hope Charity was not in the murky depths of the windswept waters. His heart grew cold as he thought of his dear Charity in the icy lake.

"Here, m'lord." Pointing to a grassy spot on the bank, they both looked carefully to see whether there was any other evidence Charity might have been here. Slowly making his way to the bridge, David came to the conclusion that no person, or persons, had walked along the bank until the footman espied the orchids. That meant they must have blown there. Directing the young man to continue his search along the lake, praying nothing would be found there, David continued along the path toward the hothouses.

He hadn't ordered anyone else to search this area. He had wanted to do this himself, hoping he might be the one to find Charity. As the minutes dragged by, he was coming to realize she meant more to him than he had ever expected any woman to mean. He tried to proceed with all speed, yet he feared he might miss something in the shadows along the path. So he took care when he desired to rush.

Looking at the hothouse in the misty haze of early morning, he noticed her pet rabbit sitting by the door. What was it she called it? Roscoe, he thought. "Roscoe?" The rabbit turned its head, but didn't leave the door.

David hurried down the path, a surge of hope welling up in his chest. Surely the rabbit sitting by the door like a guard dog might mean Charity was inside? He examined what he could see of the interior as he walked.

There was no sign of anyone within the buildings. Only the orchids sat in their pots, hung from the ridgepole and lined up like soldiers along the shelves.

When he swung open the door, he found the rabbit squeezing in past him, and he smiled down at the little fellow. It seemed it liked to be in here. Possibly it was warmer here than in the burrow it inhabited.

David gazed around the hothouse, looking everywhere he thought Charity might be, not that there was all that much to be seen. The long potting benches were clear. There was nothing on the slatted wood floor, except a cluster of potted palms in the corner. She wasn't there. Turning away, he realized how horribly disappointed he was. He had counted on finding her here.

Just as he was about to open the door a low sound caught his ears. It seemed very much like a moan. Whirling about, he walked down the length of the hothouses, peering around more carefully, examining under the benches. Roscoe crouched by the cluster of potted palms, its little nose quivering with something . . . excitement, if rabbits knew that feeling.

Suddenly David's heart was racing as he espied a broken frond, then the sight of pale-cream satin peeking from beneath a pile of dirty sacks. Somehow he had missed that, probably due to the early-morning gray shadows. Shoving aside one palm, then another, he found what he sought. Charity!

"Dearest girl! Charity, can you hear me?" Another low moan issued from her throat as he tossed the sacks away to find her trussed up, in a heap. He tore the gag from her mouth. Then, carefully rolling her to one side, he fumbled with the cord that bound her slender wrists, cursing most fearfully as he saw how every tug of the cord cut into her delicate flesh.

At last the cord was undone and he was able to gather Charity tenderly in his arms. Fearing to carry her too far just yet, he placed her on the dry wood of the floor near the center of the hothouse. Slipping from his elegant black jacket, he wrapped it around her. He gently rubbed her wrists, seeking to restore feeling to them, trying to soothe the reddened and bruised flesh.

His hand trembled as he caressed her face, then found the knot on her head. Who could have done such a thing? And why? Shards of a clay pot tossed into a corner gave a clue as to what was probably the weapon.

Dark russet eyelashes that had fanned across her pale cheeks now fluttered open. David felt hope leaping within him. He gathered her close in his arms, wanting to cosset her, protect her from further hurt.

"David? Beloved?"

He could barely make out her murmured words, but they were the loveliest he had ever heard. "Charity, dear heart! Easy. You are safe now. Can you talk? Do you know what happened?"

Bemused, Charity stared up at the worried countenance above her. She must be dreaming again. She could see David as plain as day. It was a lovely dream, for he was holding her close in his arms, looking as though he desired never to let her go. She sighed with pleasure, then winced at the throbbing in her head. It seemed she was not asleep, after all. One slender, stiff arm reached out and one small hand awkwardly touched his cheek.

"You are real," she whispered in awe. Never before had one of her dreams come true upon waking.

"I know you must ache in every part of your body. Do you hurt any place else other than your head?'

A becoming color flushed into her cheeks. "No, only my head." She ignored her wrists, unable to grasp that she was held in his arsm, let alone that there was a second source of pain.

"Let me carry you to the house, dearest."

Charity knew she had heard right. He had called her by an endearing term. She shook her head. As much as she longed to settle in a soft, warm bed, there were more important matters at the moment.

"Lady Sylvia? Are you to marry her?" With the

return of Charity's memory came the knowledge Lady Sylvia had been involved in the injury to her head. She now recalled the scent of Red Roses very well.

"No. I found my heart had been captured by a little lady whose diversion is growing orchids." His voice was low, thrilling Charity with its rich emotion. She decided to leave the subject of Sylvia in the past.

She shook her head in protest. "You mustn't say such a thing. You don't know the truth."

"You didn't grow these flowers?" He was almost dizzy with relief she was safe in his arms, apparently returning his esteem. He couldn't understand the confused knit of her brow.

Even though she knew in her heart that she wanted him more than anything in the world, she also knew her integrity would suffer if she didn't reveal the whole of it to him. "There are a few things I must say." She unconsciously snuggled up against his chest, preparing to unburden herself. Looking up at him with complete faith and trust that he might see the situation as she did, she began.

Relating as quickly as she could the history of raising the orchids, how she came to correspond with the others who sought to buy plants, thinking Lord Kenrick had assumed the management of them. She explained how the annuity would never stretch quite far enough to cover their needs, that a few sovereigns made all the difference in their life.

At last, her budget emptied of all, she shyly peeped at him through the fringe of her lashes, as alluring as any woman could ever hope to be.

Charity concluded, "I know that what I did was probably wrong in the eyes of most of the world. I mean, a lady doesn't sell plants or blooms. That is going into trade, I suppose. But I meant no harm by it. If you hadn't arrived when you did, no one would have been the wiser. I never intended to appear to accept the award. I got carried away by the thought of one of my orchids given to the Prince Regent."

He gave her a mock frown. "You were using my initials. I'll admit to a few suspicions concerning that item. I think something ought to be done about that."

Her heart contracted in anxious concern. "I am sorry, my lord."

"You are, you know. Mine, that is," he added, seeing her confusion. "And I am persuaded I have just the solution to the dilemma of the initials. Who could question it if we presented the orchid together? I promised Lady Tavington I would assist in finding you a husband, but I found that none of the others would do for you. Do you think you could accept me as a substitute? Then our initials would be the same. I believe I could grow to enjoy the raising of orchids . . . as a diversion."

He touched her lips lightly, worried he might hurt her. His good intentions flew away when Charity pressed against him, fervently returning his kiss with a hungry ardor he found increasingly arousing. He kissed her until they were both breathless, releasing her only when the need for air became acute.

"I believe that settled all points." Those intensely blue eyes were filled with love, cherishing her as she had longed.

"Thank heavens. Now I can set out for Egypt with a clear conscience. Well done, Kenrick." The bracing voice of Lady Tavington startled the pair apart.

David made no move to rise, knowing he would have to wait a time before doing so with propriety.

The Earl of Dunstall smiled at the couple snuggled together on the slatted wood floor. "I trust, my dear, that the propensity for strange places to make love does not run in the family. I fear I've grown to enjoy my comforts. When we are in Egypt together . . ." They left the hothouse, talking of their plans for the future, content to allow Lord Kenrick to take care of Charity, which he proceeded to do, again, in a most satisfactory manner.